A novel

The Fox Trot

Raea Gragg

for
Mrs. Jane Jones
and
Mrs. Beverly Lathrope,
teachers who believed in me

Thank you

This book was a team effort. I would like to thank all my friends and family who helped me pull off one of the hardest challenges I have ever faced: writing a book. Without all of your enthusiastic support and creative input, I'm afraid I never would have had the courage to allow this story to escape from my mind and become real ink on paper.

First, I would like to recognize all of my wise Beta Readers: Grandma Patti Gragg, Aunty Jennifer Overaa, Carey Starn, Annika Overaa, and My Stella (Burford). My little brother Carson was the first and most enthusiastic reader. So excited, in fact, that he begged me to hurry up and write the next chapter so he could read it. I would also like to acknowledge my little sister Mup, for her constructive criticism and my big brother Jared for pointing out my lapses in logic. Thank you Isabel Powell for being my cheerleader. Cover photo creds go to Renee Sweeney. Thank you to my editor Kathy Kaiser for polishing the story.

And finally, thank you Mom and Dad. Dad, your botanical knowledge, while sometimes excessive, has rubbed off on me in more ways than you know. Thank you for that. But I really need to express my deep gratitude to Mom, my faithful editor and adviser during this whole project. You transformed my dyslexic gibberish into a novel.

I love you all,
Raea

Prologue

"Tabitha, grab my hand," said the middle-aged man with the perfect suit and tie and the perfect, surgically enhanced face.

"No!" cried the three-year-old girl with the crisp, clean blue dress and matching strapped blue shoes.

"Dear, we're about to cross the street."

"No!"

"Don't make me pick you up."

"No, Daddy!" she shrieked.

Just then, an old man drew near to them on the sidewalk, and both daughter and father turned to stare. He had to have been in his nineties. He hadn't had the surgery that would make a person look younger or smarter. Nor did he have the star tattoo on the back of his neck, the universal symbol of a surgically implanted Internet connection. At age ten, all human minds around the globe were implanted with the tool of connectivity and endless data.

The little girl had a mind free of the world's thoughts; she dwelled only on her own.

"Daddy. Who is that?"

"I don't know, Tabitha. Take my hand. You know it's against the law to stare."

But the girl refused to take her father's hand and stared at the old man anyway. He was strange. He had on jeans, dirty and well worn, and a sweater. There was no suit or tie. But that wasn't all. He had little hair and lots of wrinkles. She had never before seen wrinkles. But what really sparked the child's curiosity was what the old man carried. There, in his two ancient hands, was a small uprooted plant decorated with purple buds of soon-to-be flowers. And most bizarre of all were his hands, covered in scars, rough and calloused from digging in the dirt and combating the elements.

Her father lifted her up. Her small head craned to look back at the old man.

"Tabitha, Mother is going to hear about this disobedience."

But the child was silent. She was in a different world, and in that world was the old man. He turned to look at her. His eyes were a striking blue, and they seemed to see her for who she was meant to be, not for who she was genetically engineered to be. He plucked a flower, the only one from the cluster that was open. As her father looked straight ahead, she reached out and took it from the man's old, scarred hands. Then the light changed, the symbol to walk flashed, and she watched the old man disappear from her view. She studied the tiny flower and wondered about his story.

1

It's been delayed. The flight. Now I have to sit right here and wait for it. For eight more hours. But I just got this new, insanely cool laptop, a gift from the best dad in the world. To be honest, however, after what just happened to me, nothing seems real anymore, not even this computer and these words I'm typing right now. I don't know what's going to happen to me. I'm scared. My life seems on pause. Like what's happening in this airport: nobody is going anywhere; we're just stuck in this point in time, suspended for the next eight hours. I'm going to write in a way that I've never written before, and you're going to read every single word. Got it? I feel as though I can't board that plane until I tell you exactly what's happened over the past year. So listen up, because I'm going to walk you through it.

It all started at the end of summer. Like every year, I went back to the lamest town anywhere. Picture an old, rundown place with tumbleweeds rolling by. Well, OK, it was a swamp, so there were no tumbleweeds there, but it was the kind of place that would benefit from the excitement of a tumbleweed. It was the slowest place on earth, and the people cared only about themselves. It was called Duncan and it was in the outback swamps of Louisiana, that boot-shaped state in the armpit of America—the pelican state.

Well...where did it all begin? The day, the very day I got dumped into the dump.

I was riding my bike to the Stop-N-Shop, a small store with the worst paint job you have ever seen. Trust me, that place was abysmal. It was nothing but a small shack sinking deeper and deeper into the swamp every year; well, I guess it did belong to the earth in the first place, so I guess it was only right that the earth was slowly taking it back. The store always had the best snacks though, and for only 50 cents each. The best were Madam Marian's famous fresh-baked moon pies. Those always sold out really quickly. The Stop-N-Shop was where every single kid in my school went for essentials, mostly soda and chips from one of the three humming glass-front refrigerators in the place. Where the electricity came from was a mystery.

I rolled up from the narrow dirt trail that continued on to the high school. After arriving in Duncan that morning, I had decided that my bike would be the thing to get my mind off leaving New York, so I took it for a spin at midday. When I arrived at the Stop-N-Shop, it had not changed. It never changed. OK, one thing had changed: the store had sunk a few more inches into the mud, and the greenery around it had engulfed even more of the building, trying to strangle it.

I threw my bike to the side and strolled in. As I opened the door, the bell jingled. I left the door open and jogged over to one of the three refrigerators. Opening it, I looked inside for my favorite, Dr Pepper. I popped the lid and took a long swig. It felt good and cold—unlike the weather in Louisiana. Louisiana was full of thick humidity, and the air was teeming with flying invertebrates.

I walked up to the counter. There, I fished coins out of my pocket. I slapped them down on the counter and tried not to make eye contact with Madam Marian. She was a mountain of a woman, in terms of both her substantial mass and the way she sat there, unruffled and unmoving. Only her eyeballs were moving, which you noticed because the whites of her eyes contrasted with the deep black of her skin.

There she was as usual, slumped on a stool, reading the same paper she was always reading. The paper was spread out on the counter and she was mumbling. She was always doing that, mumbling things to herself. No one could understand why she sat in the heat every day in a little doomed shack where hordes of high schoolers painted the walls with graffiti. Some said that she didn't give a damn, but others said that because she was always reading, she didn't notice when you did any of that stuff. As far as I was concerned, Madam Marian was a painting on a wall. She was abused in a way that a really bad painting might be, silently taking insult after insult.

As long as you paid your 50 cents, she would not even lift a finger, and everyone always paid their 50 cents. But last year this one kid didn't. He just took a whole six-pack of RC Cola and walked out. The kid's name was Mark Wright. He got run over by a car that day. That ass. He was always doing stuff, such as farting in your face in the locker room and just being a jerk. Some kids said he deserved having to spend three months in the hospital, and after that, six more in a wheelchair. Others said because he didn't pay, Madam Marian cursed him. I thought it was a whole bunch of bull, but from then on, everyone was extra careful about paying the 50 cents. Today, as I laid out my dough on the counter, I saw that my quarter and three dimes made more than 50 cents. I clunked the coins into the jar next to the label that said Madam Marian's Stop-N-Shop. "Keep the change."

And I turned to walk out, taking another swig of the Dr Pepper. Man, it felt good, nice and cold. The door swung shut in a gust of wind. The small bell fell off the door and dropped to the concrete floor, making a racket, and then rolled to a stop at my feet. That was when the impossible happened: Madam Marian talked for the first time ever.

"Jaden! My boy, Jaden!"

I turned around to face her. She had dropped the paper and was leaning way over the counter, her enormous bosom pressing against the glass. She was hysterical: laughing and shouting at me as though the greatest thing had just happened. I slowly took a step back. I wanted to get the heck out, to be anywhere but there. Also, in the back of my mind, I was thinking about how I didn't want to be run over or something worse.

"What in the name of the Lord almighty are you thinking, boy! You paid 5 cents extra, boy! You know what that means, dontcha!"

"No, ma'am, I don't."

I was shaking slightly, as she was yelling up a storm. Then, like a madwoman, she lunged across the counter and grabbed me. I screamed in surprise. I mean, I like to think I'm a strong guy—180 pounds of muscle from varsity lacrosse—but somehow the woman had me in her grip like a Burmese python.

"Jaden, my boy."

She was shaking me. My hair flopped into my eyes. To tell you the truth, I was scared.

"Jaden, my boy!" She was yelling at the top of her lungs, as though she wanted the whole damn swamp to listen in.

"My boy! You just a-given to Madam Marian, ain't you, boy? You the giver! Ain't you!"

"I don't know what you're talking about. Please let me go!" Now I was yelling, too.

"Giver Jaden! Boy, never in a thousand years did any of you chillen give me nuttin', boy, you a-gonna get extra, too. I shall give you giver a gift. A gift of knowledge." She leaned in so close I could smell her vile breath and feel her dreadlocks brushing my face.

Suddenly, she stopped yelling and began to whisper. And let me tell you, as if her yelling hadn't freaked me out enough, her whispering was even worse. It scared me more than anything else; what she said made my blood run cold.

"Someone dear to you, boy, will die within the year."

Then the madwoman let go. I fell to my knees, staring in terror at Madam Marian laughing, her massive bulk shaking as she did. I got to my feet and ran to the door. I pushed but it did not budge. It was a locked escape route. But just then it opened from the outside, and a friend from the team, a huge junior named Luke Twain, appeared. I bolted past him, all sweaty and terrified, running as though my butt were in flames.

"Hey, Jaden, why the hurry?"

"Gotta—have to—*go*!" I shouted that last word and looked back. Madam Marian was writing a big number on the chalkboard outside the store. Then she retreated back to her chair and ever so calmly started reading the paper again. It was as though time had frozen and I was the only one who seemed to move through it.

I got the heck out of there. I grabbed my bike, hopped on, and raced down the dirt path toward school. I rode as fast as I could, spraying mud everywhere, especially, I knew, on my butt. The swamp faced me on either side. I was late, as usual. I was always late. I tossed the bike to the side and sprinted up the grass to the auditorium. Swarms of people were milling around. It was sign-up day for sophomore year. I stopped, remembering that I was covered in mud.

"Man, look at you bro, looks like a gator wanted to do the tango with ya."

I turned and saw my friend, my best friend since kindergarten: Scott Clark, tall, dark, and skinny, with a blondish Afro. You might think he's weird, but he's funny as heck and is always there to convince you to get off your butt and party. I wouldn't be half the guy I am if it weren't for him.

"Hey, Scott."

"Dude, hey, how's it been, man? Your summer? You gonna make me deaf again talking about your grand adventures in New York?"

"Yeah, man."

We waded into the crowd and got in line to figure out our classes. Then all of a sudden, the girls' lacrosse team showed up.

"Jaden, heads up. Three o'clock hot."

I turned and saw the flock of girls in a V formation. Scott was right: all I could think was *hot.* Approaching us was the hottest girl in our grade, Brook Jackson. She was heating up the auditorium as though it were an oven. Every guy turned. Every girl stepped aside to get out of her way. Guys and girls looked her up and down, the boys assessing her with greed, the girls with jealousy. Her long hair, crispy blonde, almost pure white, flowed down her back like a waterfall; she wore a tight pink tank top and the shortest jean shorts I'd ever seen. Her legs reached out, tan and golden, striding right over to me.. Following her was Ally Martinez. She had wispy brown hair down to her shoulders. Her outfit was nearly identical to Brook's. Her skin was equally tanned from the summer. On the other side was Jordan Killian, a tall black girl with a hundred tiny braids glowing with some kind of hair product. There they were: the three queens of the school, leading the flock of the other lacrosse girls.

"Look at you!" cried Brook in her high-pitched, flirtatious voice. "You're all covered in mud. What were you doing? Wrestling alligators in the swamp? That's dangerous, Jaden!"

Scott looked like an idiot as he gaped and stared at her.

"Actually—"

She grabbed my shoulder, leaned close, and whispered in my ear: "Hey, what happened last year was a whole year ago. Forget it. Now come on, silly, sit with us at the rules meeting."

"We will. We would be happy to. Right, Jaden?" Scott bleated.

"All right then," she said.

She smiled, pinched my cheek, and walked off, but not before Ally could quip, "Jaden, you look like Indiana Jones." She kind of sighed as she said it.

Then some girl whispered, "He's so hot!"

The last thing I caught was Brook snapping at the girl, "He's mine. Keep your claws off him, Sarah."

"Man, why don't *I* look like a male super model? Dude, do you realize all the lovely ladies are fighting over you?" Scott griped.

2

After I got my photo snapped for the yearbook and the packet of junk for my mom to sign, I finally got my list of classes: English, geometry, woodshop, biology, PE, history, and creative writing. The last class, creative writing, was Mom's doing. She made me take it. Then we had to sit down in the auditorium and listen to the same old list of rules: no smoking, bullying, firearms, or leaving campus at lunch—the same first-day speech that we had heard the preceding year.

Our principal, Mr. Alamo, a dark man with gray hair, gave the speech and told us the general history about the greatness from which the high school was created. Our high school was the stupidest school ever. Trust me. With its own student body of stupid people, too. Hampton High: best drama channel in town. I mean, like, it was your classic high school. You had your geeks, freaks, idiots, jocks and wannabe jocks, special ed, Barbie beauties, and last, but not least, the invisibles. The kids you never realized were even there.

I mean, you can figure out what each of those groups looks like, so I'm not going to get into that. But I will tell you where I fit into this wonderful family of Hampton High: I was a jock, one of the best—no lie and no joke. So I had a prestigious social position. I'd dated some of the Barbie beauties. Sorry, I'm not going to get into that right now. Maybe later.

But Scott, well, he was my friend, so most kids didn't care where he fit in. But he was half geek, half class clown, if you get where I'm coming from. The Barbie beauties? Well, you guessed it: those were Brook, Ally, and Jordan and their clan of wannabes. I have to say, I'm almost embarrassed to admit that I was one of the kings of the class. You've already met the queen. As I was sitting there in the auditorium next to the queen, she was all over me, trying to get her iPhone to work so that she could show me photos of herself in her bikini.

"I swear! This town sucks!" Brook was holding her iPhone up in the air and waving it around, trying to get service. Most everyone else was sitting on their hot metal seats and thinking of thousands of things they would rather have been doing on their last day of summer than sit there and listen to Mr. Alamo.

"When you need to leave school premises, you must sign out with your first *and* last name at the attendance office and provide written notification from your parents..."

Scott mocked Mr. Alamo, silently mouthing everything he said. I laughed. Then I nudged him and pointed to Tommy. This geek actually picked his nose in front of everyone. Scott loved that and immediately began to imitate Tommy. Then Miss Carlson, my unfortunate-looking English teacher with an unfortunately large derriere, came over and gave me the deadliest look. So I knew, even before stepping into her classroom, that she was going to give me a B– at best, both semesters. Some teachers are just like that, especially the driest sacks of flour on the planet like her.

We sat there quietly until she walked off. Then I looked up, and in her place near the wall was a girl. I was paralyzed like some dim-witted deer on a swamp road caught in your headlights. I stared. There, standing in the corner, was the most beautiful girl I had ever seen.

She was average height, around five feet five inches, and slender. She had on two well-worn pieces of clothing: a T-shirt, faded orange, with Joe's Tacos written across it, and a pair of torn and muddy skinny jeans. Plus flip-flops.

Her face, it was so pretty. It captivated me. It was sort of square and sort of heart-shaped at the same time. She had full red lips, and you could tell she was not wearing any makeup at all. It was amazing. Her nose was small and adorable. She was too far away for me to tell what color her eyes were, but her eyebrows were thick and arched perfectly over her eyes. Her hair—now that was the scene-stealer, for it was a river down her back. I mean, it flowed, thick and shining, cascading in waves, not curls. It was a deep glossy brown, almost black.

She seemed to stand there like a skittish deer on the side of the road trying to find the best way to slip back into the forest. She looked super uncomfortable, as if she wanted no one to notice her, so she stood off by herself in the corner. She must have been the only one in the whole place listening to what Mr. Alamo had to say. And then, at the last moment, my eye was drawn to her hands. Even from across the room, I could see that her delicate hands were covered in cuts and scrapes. Some were healed, but some were still fresh and red.

"Who is that?" I whispered out loud.

"What are you talking about?" That was Brook. I turned to look at her like a kid caught stealing cookies off the counter. She looked at me, confused as heck, and scanned the auditorium, craning her neck. She did not see the girl, and when I turned to look at Scott, he was drawing all over the new backpack of the poor kid in front of us.

"Hey, Jaden, you seem strange. What's up?" Brook eyed me.

"Brook, do you see that girl over there by the wall?" I pointed to the corner.

"Umm, who, baby?" She followed my finger.

"There. Over there by the wall." This was getting frustrating.

"Oh, I see her. What about her?" She seemed irritated that I was talking about some other girl and not her.

"Have you seen her before? Do you know her name?" I looked at the girl in the shadows.

Brook shook her head and went back to trying to pull up her bikini photos again.

"Who is she?" I pressed.

"I don't know. Never seen her before in my life." Then with a burst of joy she exclaimed, "Oh yeah, here we go, look at this! My two-piece. I had it shipped from New York. I know just how much you like New York."

And as soon as I looked at the photo of Brook Jackson in her bikini, the girl with the bloody hands slipped out of my mind, the same way she had slipped out of the auditorium.

3

All I can really remember about the rest of that day was that I got home late after a long afternoon at the beach with Brook, Scott, and some other guys and girls. It was Brook's idea, of course. After showing me her bikini photo, she just had to show it to me in person. So by the time I got home, it was late; I was always late. When I ran up the brick steps to the small, two-story, wood-paneled house, there on the porch was my mom.

"Jaden, how was back-to-school day? What classes did you get? Was your picture good? Where were you? It's late!"

Typical. Very typical. That was my mom—never letting you out of her sight until she'd hammered every question into you.

"It was fine, Mom. Everything is fine."

"Well, that's good to hear! Let's have dinner."

We walked inside and I stood there, staring at our unchanged house. I mean, it was as though it were frozen in time, a time that was good. There were old pictures of when Mom and Dad were still married: photos of the two of them laughing, photos of their wedding, and photos of me as a baby. Looking at the walls, you'd think that everything in our life was picture perfect, and neither my mom nor I had a worry in the world. Those photos always made me wish I had someone else with me in this SOS situation—a brother or sister to go down with me. But no, it was just me.

At dinner, everything was normal: we didn't say a word. It was funny that way. My mom was used to living alone in the summers, so I guess she got used to the peace and quiet, and sometimes she would just run silent for hours. It kind of made me depressed. You knew something dreadful was on her mind when she ran silent, and most of the time I could guess what it was. She was thinking about Dad.

She met him after college in New York. Tall, handsome, rich, and a lawyer. They got married and seven months later had me. So on account of me, and my unplanned conception, they moved back here to this small home that had been in her family ever since they moved to the United States five generations ago. My dad, however, hated it from the start. So when I was five, he moved back to New York, where he grew further and further away from Mom, and she grew ever more quiet.

That's my history in a nutshell. I would bore you with details, but to be honest, I become more like my dad every year I spend stuck in this god-awful place. I can't stand it here.

4

After dinner, I climbed up to my room. It was late, very late, and oily black outside. There was the normal ruckus of our satellite TV attempting to get on air. That was one of the many problems with Duncan: Our town had almost no cell service. Our cable service worked only randomly. There was practically zero connection to the world outside of that swamp. Many houses had only electricity and old-school phone lines—that was it. Most of us had super slow dial-up by modem, not fast enough to support even the slowest video game. One rain storm would threaten our whole electronic infrastructure.

But Duncan's working people—the ones up to their knees in shrimp—didn't give a damn, as long as the tide rolled in and shrimp came up in their nets. My mom loved our isolation. She said it provided next to no distraction from her books and her garden. But like all the other kids from Hampton High, and most of all me, having an iPhone that sputtered to a stop as soon as you crossed county lines was a personalized hell.

I stepped into my perfect square of a room and turned on the light. I began to unpack. It nearly killed me every time: I didn't know why I even bothered to take my nice clothes down there to the mud hole. Those things were irrelevant. There was no place for that stuff there.

My room seemed to represent my childhood growing up in Duncan, with its pictures of me doing everything a kid does down there: fishing, building mud castles, and catching fireflies. There were several photos of Scott and me in which Scott's hair chronicled our childhood: buzz cut, Afro, dreadlocks, and then buzz cut again. Scott's dad was white and his mom was black, and he had the coolest hair.

The bedroom was filled with the stuff that makes you grin when you're by yourself and cringe when you're with friends. I gazed at my trophies from Little League and lacrosse. And I glanced at my treasures from the bayou: antlers, feathers, and snakeskin. All up on my shelf. Also on my shelf were stacks of notebooks with stories I have written, or, I should say, stories I have written and never completed. Besides looking at my stuff, I used my room mostly for my favorite thing, sleeping. But tonight, I wasn't tired. When the light finally went off downstairs, I opened my window. The cool night air felt good, much nicer than the heat of the day.

I climbed out onto the old hickory tree and shimmied my way down. I had forgotten my flashlight, but I knew the way like the back of my hand. I slunk silently through my mom's beloved garden.

I followed the well-worn path, guided by fireflies and a nearly full moon. Why was I going out into the forest-slash-swamp behind our backyard in the middle of the night? I had no idea. My body guided me there, as if on autopilot.

My feet knew exactly where to take me: my sanctuary, an old tree house Scott and I had built a few years earlier, before middle school. It was an old thing, but it was my hideaway. It was sort of like you might picture a tree house, but it was surprisingly sturdy and had a good tin roof. Perched above the swamp, it had a hammock and the walls were covered with shelves and windows. And the posters—just about every square inch of the place had posters. Everything in there had something to do with New York. When I climbed in, I unrolled my latest poster, lit the candle on the shelf, and looked for a good place to hang it. It was the Empire State Building. Every summer, I went to see the Empire State Building. It was one of my favorite skyscrapers. As I looked at the walls, I realized that there was not one inch left; they all had something else from New York on them, so I pinned the poster to the ceiling. I climbed into the hammock, looked at the poster, and desperately tried not to think of my days in the Big Apple.

Let me tell you about New York. I practically live for New York. I'm a born city boy: the crowds, the energy, and the sights. I love it. I barely managed to survive each grueling school year in Duncan, so those short months with my dad in the most fantastic place on earth were heaven.

I just couldn't wait to go back. It surprised me that I had been stuck in Duncan for only a single day, and I already ached for the sounds of bus hinges, the shouts of people in Grand Central Station, and even the lame tourists, walking around like blind bats, trying to find someone to point them in the right direction. I even missed the bird-brained pigeons and especially the girls in my apartment building, Amelia and Sophia, the

Sorensen sisters. I missed their big smiles, their high-heeled shoes clicking on the marble, and the way they giggled encouragingly at everything I said. Well, that was what I was thinking about when I yawned and closed my eyes—the smells and sounds of the city. I thought about those while blocking out the sounds of frogs and crickets. That is, until her face popped into my mind again. My two last thoughts before I nodded off were, *Who is she? And what's up with the bloody hands?*

5

It wasn't until the sun hit my face through one of the many windows that I suddenly realized it was a school day. After a cursed-filled dash to the house and a quick change, I hopped onto my bike and blazed to school, taking every shortcut I knew. I was zipping down the old dirt road when I remembered at the last second what had happened the day before.

Then I swerved past the giant gate to Madam Marian's Stop-N-Shop. I just barely turned my head to sneak a peek through the open door, expecting her to be putting down the newspaper to look up at me: her only customer who paid more than the obligatory 50 cents and now regretted it. But as I gazed into the store, I saw that she wasn't there. Then I saw her: she was standing outside her shop, writing a number on the old chalkboard.

As I sped by, I saw the number. It was 273.

By the time I got to Hampton High, the first bell had already rung, and most kids were settled into their classes. I pulled out the card with my class schedule. English. *OK*, I thought, *I can do this.* I sprinted up the stairs, three steps at a time. Then I ran into the building, counting the numbers on the doors as I passed them. After what felt like a millennium, I found my room and strutted in, right in the middle of Miss Carlson's speech. She turned to look at me. Some kids looked relieved for a break in the monotony of their first day; others seemed amused. The one person in the room who was not at all amused was Miss Carlson. Boy, you should have seen her face! Red like a tomato and hot like a pepper. I could almost picture steam coming out of her ears. Almost.

"Jaden Miller, how delighted we are to see you." Her voice was metallic and malicious. *Oh man, here it comes.*

"I was giving the class a speech on the importance of promptness, how tardiness shows a profound disrespect for the sanctity of higher education."

Oh man, she's mad.

"I was just about to discuss the consequences for being late." She was taking her time with this nugget of information. Like a fish in a barrel, I had nowhere to swim. She marched to the whiteboard and began to scrape the pen across its surface. The pen shrieked as she wrote in a neat longhand.

"Two options, Mr. Miller. The first option is...." She pointed to the words with the pen as she paused in her writing. "Detention after school with me."

I groaned and the class held its collective breath, wondering what this awful woman would say next.

"Or..." She held up the pen with a flourish, as though it were a magic wand or some kind of medieval instrument in some hideous Shakespearean drama. You know what I'm talking about; she was an English teacher. She turned back to the board. "You can compose for me a perfectly written short story." She paused to write it all down. "And it must be more than twenty pages long, single-spaced."

I looked at her with my mouth gaping open. *Isn't that a novel?* I wondered.

"So Mr. Miller, what shall it be?"

"Detention," I said, for there was no way I was going to write a mind-numbing, incredibly long short story.

She smiled at me and I detected an ounce of disappointment in her smirk. I took the only seat available and then groaned again because it was next to Billy Beckham, this red-haired kid covered in freckles. Billy Beckham's dad was one of the hillbillies of the swamp; maybe that was why his kid was named Billy. When I sat down next to him. he started to fart, the evil kind of fart. You know, the kind you can't hear but you smell. Five minutes in, and I was already feeling seasick. So were the kids in a two-seat radius around Billy and me. To make myself feel better while Miss Carlson rambled on about the syllabus for the year and her absurd laws, I got out my new notebook and began to scribble and draw my very sad drawings of stick figures and machine guns sniping each other. I got the idea from the English textbook next to me, which was so covered in drawings that it was hard to read the text. Shakespeare, in various poses, stared down at me from posters tacked to the walls of the classroom.

I slogged through the rest of the day, attending my other classes and their boring lectures. Each teacher talked about more rules, the gist of which was, Break my rules and risk death by principal's office. The bad news was that I had no classes with Scott or any other friends, except English and PE.

6

Everything fell into the most boring routine you can imagine, except for the numbers. Every morning since the freaky day at the store, Madam Marian had been writing down numbers on her chalkboard. I saw her do it every morning as I rode by her shop. Each day, the number was one lower—a countdown to something. All the kids at school were talking about it; it was a big mystery. But then some math geek figured out that the numbers counted down to the last day of school. What a hero. The mystery was solved, talk stopped, and life resumed its pace. Its stupid, boring pace.

It wasn't until the dissection of *Macbeth* that my life went from boring to hell bound. It was only a week into school when Miss Carlson told us we were going to perform *Macbeth*, and we were going to rehearse this irksome play every day. Ugh. Each of us had to pick a role, and guess who got Lady Macbeth? Surprise, surprise: Brook Jackson. She, of course, was thrilled by the prospect of performing onstage in the drama room with all of our parents there to watch. As though it were a big deal. The whole real, Shakespeare deal. Just swell for me, because I'm some guy named Macduff.

One of our many grueling homework assignments was to practice with a buddy-bud. So at lunch that day, we got the whole thing slammed down our throats like nasty medicine that doesn't come in pill form and tastes like caterpillar. Oh yeah, by the way, don't ever eat bugs of any sort out of your backyard. I did it on a dare one time. Didn't end well, I'll tell you that much. I'm really bad at dares, as you're about to see. Well anyway, lunch went like this:

"Hey, Scott, you know the *Macbeth* thing?"

We had both gotten our trays of cafeteria slop and sat down outside at our usual table filled with the popular kids: a pack from lacrosse and basketball and even some lame football guys. Football had lost its attraction as soon as the school made it a no-cut sport. So you didn't have to be buff to play football. Those guys thought football was church and the ball was their god. They annoyed me, the football guys. It was funny, too, that as soon as football lost its appeal, cheerleading became the sport of wannabe girls. So the popular girls, including Brook, Ally, and Jordan, found a new and improved sport: lacrosse. They got to practice on the same field as the team. Honestly, they just ran around in those little skirts, showing off their cute asses. Shaking their lacrosse sticks as if they were pom-poms. Get the picture? Not that anybody—any guy—was complaining.

Scott looked up at me as though I had just ruined his can of soda.

"Dude, did you have to mention the stupid play? I was trying to forget all about that. I'm trying not to have some sort of stroke or anxiety attack," he grumbled and went back to sipping his RC Cola.

"Sorry bro, but do we ever, like, I mean ever, actually do what we're actually supposed to do?"

He just gave me one of his crazy Scott smiles. We could be talking in Chinese pig Latin, and somehow we would still understand exactly what the other was hinting at.

Too bad it wasn't Chinese pig Latin, because someone else barged in on our conversation. Brook suddenly looked up from her pile of what looked like raisin bran oatmeal from the cafeteria and hopped and skipped her way over to us.

"Hey, Scott," she purred.

Scott looked as though he would faint. He dropped his RC Cola, letting it spill all over the ground, probably soaking into someone's backpack and ruining both their homework and their phone. But Scott was too busy staring at Brook's impressive cleavage to pick it up. Brook had a special power over guys, and she knew it, too. She then turned to me and put on her best show.

"Hey, Jaden." She leaned way over and patted my shaggy brown hair and twirled it in her pedicured fingers.

"Hey, I heard you guys were talking about meeting up today after school to rehearse *Macbeth.*"

A stampede of excuses ran through my brain. I was ready to deflect her invitation, which I knew was coming right up.

"So I'll bet you two will need me around to keep you guys focused."

She leaned way over the table, and when she did that, Scott gulped down the soda that he had been holding in his mouth. I watched his Adam's apple move up and down, and before I could open my mouth to let out a tidal wave of excuses, Scott blurted out, "Brook, Jaden and I would love it if you came over. How about tonight, my house at 8:00? Sound good to you?"

"Lovely. See you then." Satisfied, she took one look at both of us, twirled around, and pranced off to join the lacrosse girls, no doubt to tell them the good news. I just glared at my friend, but he was still mesmerized.

7

Spending the evening at Scott's, waiting the whole time for Brook to make her appearance, was miserable. We sat in his hot living room, our feet up and our shirts off, sweltering in the heat. Scott's house was a dump. He had only his dad. His mom had died in Hurricane Rita, and his dad was a piece of excrement. You can look that word up. Anyway, Scott's dad was a fat drunk. To give you an idea of his derangement, he cut the tail off of Scott's dog. The yapping dog wouldn't shut up, so he cut off his tail, cooked it in a big pot on the stove, and then put it into his dog bowl. The dumb thing ate it. And it seemed as though ever since then, the dog was trying to get revenge on every male human being who walked in the door. He was a black Pomeranian–pit bull mix and he was mad. My theory was rabies. His name was Tazz, but we—me and Scott and all of Duncan—called him the Tasmanian devil. Anyway, Scott and I sat there, getting more and more uncomfortable by the minute and waving our *Macbeth* books to fan away the heat and gnats. It was in moments such as this that Scott and I cooked up ideas that were frowned upon by the mature.

We sat there fanning ourselves, talking about the usual: girls we wanted to see in their prom dresses, cars we wanted to own one day, and lacrosse—how we would get recruited to an Ivy League school and then play professionally.

Then Scott began to play around with his trumpet. That trumpet—I swear, he'll marry it someday. It's the same story as the football for the football guys: it's their god. Scott's shiny trumpet is his god, for real.

Scott tried to whistle through his trumpet when I mentioned the smokin' legs of Ashley Collins, a blonde senior. Then out of nowhere, I asked Scott something I immediately regretted.

"Scott?"

"Hmm?" He blew into his trumpet again, making it soar way high, and started to play a happy classical piece I didn't care about.

"Hey, have you seen this girl who has really dark hair that's all wavy and long?" I was looking out the window and my face was getting hotter than it should, even given the hellish room temperature.

He stopped playing and rubbed a smudge off his golden instrument. "Who?"

"You know the girl...umm, with old clothes and she's, like, really pretty. Actually, she's gorgeous." I winced as I said it. I bent down to pick a chip bag off the ground. I was nervous.

"Who?" He turned to look at me.

"You know, that girl who's like a shadow? Like invisible? With the scarred-up hands?" I popped the chip bag open.

"Dude, have you lost your mind? I have no clue who you're talking about." He went back to playing the trumpet, lost in the jazz melody that so captivated him. The guy has serious skill, too, if I haven't already mentioned that. I dropped the subject of the girl, even though her image from that first day of school had popped into my mind and decided to stay put. It was really bugging me. Scott did not know who she was, and it seemed as though no one did. *Who the hell is she?*

And just then, she walked in. Brook.

"I'm crashing the party, boys." She sashayed into Scott's living room as if it were her runway and she were a Victoria's Secret model. Why did this girl have to look so good! She was wearing a short dress and high heels, but she blushed when she saw me without a shirt. I lunged for my shirt, but she snatched it with those delicate talons of hers and threw it into the bathroom.

"We don't want to ruin the heat in here, do we?"

I just groaned. She then walked off into the kitchen and brought out another bag of potato chips and a bottle of Scott's dad's vodka. *Oh no!* Three shot cups were stacked in her other hand. She smiled deviously. She sat down right next to Scott, who dropped the trumpet, which clanked onto the hardwood floor. She put the shot glasses on the coffee table, pushed our *Macbeth* books out of the way, and filled up the glasses. I stared at her and when she looked up at me, she seemed shocked.

"Why the look, Jaden?" she asked in feigned innocence.

"That belongs to Scott's dad!" I growled. I was mad but I had no idea where the anger was coming from. "He'll *kill* us."

Scott got pale when I said that–as though his brain had finally registered the danger we were flirting with.

"Relax, Jaden, we won't get caught. Trust me," said Brook mockingly.

All I could think was, *I don't trust you,* but then she then slid a glass over to me. I didn't even look down at it. She turned to Scott, rubbing her hand along his jeans. I rolled my eyes. Her spells would not enchant or entrap me this time. I was immune to her. Just then, a big smile spread across her face.

"Hey, you know what we should do? We should play Truth or Dare!"

One of my secrets was that I couldn't turn down a game of Truth or Dare. It was a lame, self-esteem thing I had.

"You or me first?"

She just smiled, crossed her legs, and leaned across the table toward me.

"Truth or a dare?" I sputtered.

She fluttered those long eyelashes and said, "Truth."

I leaned back, thinking, and then put my hands on the table that separated us and posed the question like a liturgical chant: "Have you ever killed someone?"

I don't know why I asked that; it just sorta popped out. I guess I wasted my chance, as I could have asked her any juicy truth question. But the moment I asked it, just for a split second, I saw it: she blinked twice.

She laughed her cute falsetto laugh and looked at me, shaking her head as though I had said something absurd. But I could tell she was bothered. Scott, too, looked confused, leaning forward on the edge of his seat, waiting for Brook to answer.

"Jaden, where did that come from?" she asked and laughed again.

I didn't know, so I said nothing.

"No. Of course not." She shook her head, still smiling, sort of. "My turn now." She picked up the shot glass and drank it all in one practiced motion. When Scott saw her do it, he grabbed his own glass and tossed the foul liquid down his throat. Immediately, he picked up his trumpet and began to play.

"Truth or dare, Jaden?"

"Dare."

She smiled and pushed my shot glass into my hand. I looked at it. *Oh man, I walked into that one.*

"Drink up, baby."

Ugh. I downed it, glaring at her, and I sent a silent apology to my dad.

I don't remember everything that happened after that, just snippets of the night. What a night. What a night. I remember strutting around like a madman, sloshing the vodka in my glass, Scott was improvising the best music I had ever heard, swinging that trumpet all the way up to heaven. Brook was having a blast, flipping her long, whitish hair as she danced all around to the music. I remember dancing on the couch, the coffee table, and, at one point, the kitchen table. In fact, Brook and I were on the kitchen table when we heard it: the old Ford truck, gasping and sputtering as it pulled up in the driveway. A small figure appeared at the sliding glass window, yapping at us, and then a broad-shouldered figure loomed at the window of the front door.

I scrambled down from the table and turned to Scott. "Dude."

"Indeed," he said and smiled warily. We waited for the storm.

The storm came too soon, while Brook was still dancing barefoot on the table. His guttural voice pounded into the living room; he must have heard the music and seen the empty bottle of alcohol. Then he saw us. He ripped the back door screen off the track with those old Army muscles. He was like a hurricane.

"Scott!" he bellowed.

The sound echoed over the backyard, a grass lot.

"*Scott!*" he yelled again, the sound coming from the guts of a beast. Finally, Brook stopped dancing. I slowly grabbed Scott's arm and backed him out the door into his yard. We had to get out of there right that instant. Then all of a sudden, Tazz, the devil dog, dashed out of the house.

"*Everyone run!*" I screamed in a drunken panic. The dog was at my heels. And then the dog was ripping my jeans to shreds, so I kicked him off and kept running. Brook was right behind me. I ran into the bayou and kept going until the duckweed was around my knees. That was when I saw it. Scott's old motorboat, which he had worked on lovingly for years. *That engine had better start.*

I pushed it over to Brook, and before it even touched shore, she was in. Somehow she got the hiccups right then and was hiccupping like mad. I laughed but then Brook and I heard a scream: Scott's drunken dad was taking swings at his head with a baseball bat! Scott, however, was quicker and nimbler than his dad and kept ducking. The Tasmanian devil, meanwhile, was tearing away at anything within reach. I ran to Scott and kicked the dog off him. A scary game of tag ensued. After several long minutes, we made it past Scott's crazy father to the boat. The dog was faster than the dad, and when it lunged at us, I hit the thing with a paddle right smack across the face. Then we pushed off and Brook was hiccupping and sobbing. I paddled madly as Scott tried to choke the motor into action. And then after what felt like the longest thirty seconds of my life, the old piece of junk coughed to life. And we were off: into the bayou at full speed and stupid-drunk.

After a while, we all calmed down, and I remember clearly what happened next because it involved a daring feat on my part. Daring and dorky. I don't know whether it was on account of intoxication or boredom, floating along in that boat in the dark bayou with nothing better to do after our thrilling escape, but I did it.

"Truth *hiccup* or *hiccup* dare."

I looked over at Brook. She had a finger dipped into the black water, kind of twirling it around, the way she had done earlier that day with my hair. That day? I was so confused by everything, I couldn't even remember what day it was. *Hmm. Oh well.* I decided to play along.

"Dare."

She gave me a mischievous smile, as though she had the greatest dare in the entire world.

I just stared at her as she hiccupped and laughed to herself. She was sitting on the floor of the boat and looking back at me. I smiled. "Give me something good."

"*Hiccup hiccup hiccup* Oh, Jaden, *hiccup* it's really good."

Scott picked up his trumpet and let it rip. There, squatting like primitive people in our small floating world, he started playing every jazz song that he could come up with. I felt so good, so drunk, that I even began to sing.

"Sittinnn' down yonder on the bayouuu!"

"Sing it, man!" he yelled.

"We just hang and close our eyes!" I sounded like a dying cat.

Brook started to hum to our beat.

"Oh yaaa, we's a-sittin' 'n' singin' and we's a-knowww / That we's a-waitin' for the stars in the skyyy."

And then I shouted in my dying cat voice, "Dare!"

"I dare you to go inside old man Barley's shed."

As soon as she uttered the words, Scott stopped playing, and we both just stared at Brook. She was still pitifully humming and hiccupping as she sat cross-legged on the bottom of the boat, and somehow she looked as hot as ever. Even though we were drunk as skunks, the words "old man Barley's shed" rang in my ears like a rattle from a rattlesnake, and it scared me just as much.

"Old man Barley's shed! Brook! You can't be serious!" That was Scott.

"Sure. OK, Jaden, don't go inside. That's *too* crazy. Just go up and touch it, and *poof*! *Hiccup.* You'll be back in the boat, and it will be as though *hiccup* nothing had ever happened."

I could not back down now. I had self-esteem issues. I could never, ever pass up a dare. I had to prove myself.

"Sure, I'll do it."

Scott scrambled across the boat, nearly tipping the craft over. He hissed in my ear: "Jaden! Are you nuts? This is old man Barley's shed we're talking about!"

"Yeah, I know," I whispered.

"Dude, you do not have to do this. Brook won't care. She won't even remember any of this in the morning!"

That made me feel even more determined. If my best friend, who was up and off his ass in a second when it came to stranger danger, couldn't handle this, then I could not pass it up. This was my chance to best him.

"It's not as bad as the..." I paused as I searched my brain for a retort. "It's not as bad as the Duncan Shipyard." I felt the power of the name slip off the tip of my tongue.

And when I said that, I killed whatever bit of sanity had been hanging out in our boat.

Brook's eyes opened wide.

"You did not just say that," said Scott.

"But he did," Brook said.

Even in the dim light, I could see their horrified expressions. I felt the goose bumps rise on my arms. I had spoken the unspeakable. I had said the name of the place that both repelled and fascinated me. No one that I knew of had ever had the courage to visit the Duncan Shipyard. Would I? Could I? Ever? The codes of the youth in Duncan were severe. The small mud hole had its share of deathly secrets and superstitions, but the Duncan Shipyard legend was the deadliest of them all. You were never, under any circumstances, to say the name out loud.

The boat fell into an unearthly silence. As a matter of fact, the whole bayou shut up as well. I had just broken the code of Duncan, the one code that should never be broken. To do so was as drastic as cutting a hole in the circle of life. How much more drastic and dangerous it would be to visit the Duncan Shipyard! I kept my mouth shut about that half-wish.

Everyone looked down at the water, which was black and murky and creepy. The cypress trees' long moss hung down like drapery.

"Let's get out of here." That was Scott, and his voice was no louder than a mouse squeak. He made his way back to his seat.

"Not until I touch old man Barley's shed," I said. I was an idiot. A lunkheaded, drunk idiot with self-esteem issues.

After I yelled at Brook, who tried with no success to persuade me not to do it—after she had goaded me into it, I wrestled the motor from Scott, and off we went to old man Barley's shed. I didn't tell a soul that night in the swamp, but I was downright terrified.

So who was this old man Barley? And what was up with his shed? Well, he was this old grandpa hillbilly, just like Billy Beckham's dad. But this guy was older. He lived alone deep in the swamp in this old shed, and trust me, it was all very strange. He was a wild man. Cobwebs were said to live in his beard, and his best friend was his shotgun, which was always strapped across his fat, shirtless belly. He lived off possums and frog legs and who knows what else. He guarded his shed with his life, and he would blow your head off if you were within earshot of him—but it was a known fact that he was nearly deaf. A few legendary kids had done it—they'd touched his shed and gotten away with their lives—but this had been long before our time. Many kids had been injured trying. One had been shot in the shoulder. But if you were a guy who could say he had touched the shed, you won the badge of total badass. Like someone who went to the moon or survived the plunge over Niagara Falls. So on we sped to old man Barley's shed.

We cut the engine as soon as the gloomy yellow candlelight could be seen glowing in the distance. We inched forward, with Scott again at the helm. With his mad skills, he maneuvered the personalized piece-of-junk boat over to the shadows behind the dock. I could see old man Barley sitting there, holding his gun and chewing contentedly on his tobacco. And then it was showtime. I was half terrified, half curious. I took one last look back at Scott and Brook. Scott gave me that stare, our silent Chinese pig Latin for *Dude, don't do this. Please, let's get out of here.*

Still drunk as a skunk, I slipped out of the aluminum boat and into the swamp, wearing only my torn jeans. And then I was swimming through the thick muck and between the lily pads. I felt the soft, silky mud and the warmth of the leaf litter. The gooey texture of the mud squishing between my fingers and toes as I edged closer to my target was bad enough, but then I had the brilliant realization that gators were likely lurking all around me. But instead of freaking out, I focused my mind (as best as I could, given my inebriation). I swam under the dock, through the reeds. Climbing out from under the dock with its pillars of crooked tree limbs, I pulled myself into the shadows.

I heard old man Barley mumbling to himself and I shuddered. The act I was about to commit ran through my head like a short horror film. I looked back at the boat. Brook was all pale and then she just slumped to the bottom of the boat. I heard a loud clap as her head hit the aluminum floor. *Oh no!*

"Who's there!" shouted old man Barley, rising on his stubby legs.

I did something that could have gotten us all killed. Madman that I am, I began to sing: "*Whooouuuooo, who, who, who.*"

Old man Barley sat back down, muttering.

I sang the song of the mourning dove. My mom had taught me how to do it when I was little; it's kind of our secret.

I breathed a quiet sigh. *Thank god.* I crept over to where the floorboards were broken. Then I somehow— don't ask me how—squeezed my way through the small opening without so much as a creak from the old wood. Once above the dock, I saw the dirty, disheveled old guy just sitting there, mumbling through his bushy beard, his tired eyes darting over the water.

I moved slowly to the back of the shed, where I was in view of the boat, and I laid my hands on the rough, mossy surface of the small building. I heard a mad whisper from the water. And click, flash! Scott had taken my picture.

"OK, you did it. So let's go!"

And then old man Barley turned into a bloodhound. He was up on his feet, hollering into the darkness.

"Show your damned face so I can blow it to dust! Coward, come forth!"

Well, at least, that part is true. But for some reason, I couldn't leave the place without going inside. That had been the original dare: Go inside the shed. But then old man Barley came around the corner, and then with nowhere to go, I just stepped back, pressing myself against the wall in the shadows, and prayed that my head wouldn't be blown to smithereens. He walked right up to me. I could smell him: he smelled like hot BO.

I closed my eyes, as if by some miracle that would prevent him from seeing me. Miracles of miracles, it worked, but only because he was looking out over the bayou, not at his own wall. He then crawled under the dock onto the mud bank below it, still mumbling. I admit it, I did it—the impossible and the suicidal. I stole into the shed.

The walls of the shed looked like those of my tree house: covered in stuff. Clearly, he lived here. My eyes scanned the room; then they fell on one thing and stayed on it. My eyes were glued to it. Dazedly, I walked over to it. There, on a wooden stool, covered with cobwebs, bloodstains, and who knows what else, was the strangest thing: a dried-up yellow rose. I picked it up, carefully avoiding the thorns, and looked at it. I mean, think of what a Bigfoot's cave must be like, and then think of seeing a rose among the bones. That's how weird it was to me. Sweat poured down my face because this rose terrified me: it was so out of place. I was about to put it down when I saw the letter. I picked it up and read it:

Dear Jed,

Thank you so much for the pruning shears. I can't tell you how much they mean to me. They are the best gift I have ever received.

- Eyes of the Bayou

What? Who is Eyes of the Bayou? I could tell that it was a girl's handwriting, all loopy and tidy. I tried to run out of the place as though it were filled with the deadliest disease. But I fell against a shelf, and glass shattered all around me. Horrifying contents spilled all over me. Dead snakes and dead fish, which had been saved in the glass jars. Old man Barley had heard that for sure, and now he was on the deck, running to the door.

I ran to the door and swung it open, hitting the old man in the face and sending him flying. He lay sprawled across the uneven deck. I jumped into the water and ducked as he fired away from where he lay. I swam so hard and fast that I slammed into the boat. Together, Scott and I managed to haul my mud-streaked self into the boat. I fell on top of Brook, who was passed out. Scott pulled the trigger on the motor. Nothing. He did it again. A rumble of metal and combustion, but still nothing. Then he tried again, and it sputtered to life. None too soon, because old man Barley's aim was getting better and better as the seconds were consumed. With the motor now purring, we hauled ass, leaving a stream of disturbed water in our wake, an inky trail leading away from the little shack in the swamp.

8

I was in such a daze that I don't remember much of what happened next. In fact, the only thing I do remember was waking up the next day feeling foggy. Oh yeah, and I woke up in a tree.

My tired eyes squinted in the bright sun. Strangely, the first thing that came to mind was, *Oh no, I'm going to be late to English...again.*

I forced myself to wake up, and I slapped my cheeks to speed up the process. I groaned and heard, to my utter surprise, a similar groan from below me. Sitting up, I rubbed my eyes open and looked around. I discovered I was about eight feet up in a leaning tree, which was blanketed in moss. I was over a patch of dry land. To make myself feel a little less anxious, I nervously began to sing the song of the mourning dove.

And then out of nowhere came a red fox. I shut up. I was not scared or surprised. It was as if this were a very normal thing to do, to wake up in a tree and then see a red fox trot by. His head was down and he passed right below me, never seeing me at all. I could see in great detail every hair on his back, the curve of his ears, and the fluff of his tail. It made me smile. That little guy was kind of cute. When he was about fifteen feet away, I called out to him.

"Hello?"

He immediately stopped and raised his big ears to the right, as though that were where the sound had come from. After a few seconds, he trotted off and disappeared into the swamp. After a few minutes of trying to register what I had just seen, I slid down the tree and that immediately put me in a bad mood because I realized I had a hangover. My first one. A bad one. I legs wobbled and I thought I might barf. As I turned, I saw that lying there asleep—the side of his face in the mud and his butt in the boat—was Scott. I walked over to him, picked up a stick, and poked his cheek with it.

"Scott, I just saw a fox! We're in the swamp. Wake up."

"Who?" he grumbled.

"A fox. It just trotted off."

"Fox trot?" The guy was asleep, mumbling to me as he was wandering through dreamland. I poked him again, harder this time.

"The girl." He pointed like an idiot.

"There, now I see her, the girl. She's strange... Her hands...." I waited, almost sure Scott was speaking of her, the girl. The mystery girl.

"Blood,"

My mind was reeling. He was dreaming of Bloody Hands. That must mean he had seen her before.

"Who is she, Scott? What's her name?"

But the guy raised his invisible trumpet to his lips and began to play a silent riff.

When I slapped the moron awake. his eyes flew open and he fell out of the boat and into the mud. He looked around him as though it were the moon he was stranded on.

"What the hell?"

"I know. We're in the bayou. I just woke up in a tree, dude, and I saw a fox!"

"No way! A fox? Do they even live here?"

"I guess so, man," I said, shrugging.

"A fox. Sneaky and foxy, looking around, always sneaking around," he mumbled. His eyebrows knitted. He seemed to be trying to pull information about a fox from his hungover spaghetti brain.

"Yeah." I was thinking about the fox also, trying to remember what foxes do.

We were silent as we worked to straighten out the boat and our heads as well. Then I stated the obvious: "We are so doomed."

"How so?" He looked down at Brook, asleep in the bottom of the boat in about two inches of dirty water. Luckily, she slept face up, so she wasn't in danger of drowning in that little bit of filthy fluid.

"English, man. Who knows how late it is!"

"Jaden, it's Saturday, you idiot!"

While I was recovering from the shock, I remembered everything, or at least something, of the night before.

We hopped into the boat, and I almost fell on top of Brook. I shook her shoulder to make sure that she wasn't dead; she moaned. I didn't know what it was about her, but she really seemed to be getting on my nerves lately. We shoved off and after a long hour of circling, trying to find our way back to civilization, we set off in the right direction.

"Hey!" I called to Scott, who was camped out in the back of the boat, attending to the motor. "That was some deep trouble we got our selves into last night."

"No kidding," he mumbled, staring at a blue heron as it spread its wings and took flight. His hand gripped the outboard motor and steered us toward home.

"What kind of punishment do you think is waiting for us?"

He didn't even look at me. He was looking at his trumpet, which was on the floor.

"I can't even picture it, man, but one thing's for sure..." He reached for the gleaming instrument.

"What?"

"We's on the highway to hell!" And then he picked up that trumpet and started blasting out that very old AC/DC song. I couldn't help but smile. That's my man Scott!

9

Yep, hell bound we were. We got to my house by way of the swampy route to my backyard. I was pretty fed up with the bayou by then. We all were. Brook finally woke up but didn't speak. She just clutched her knees to her chest while she curled into a ball on the bottom of the vessel, looking green from seasickness, hangover, fear, or all of the above.

As soon as we pulled up, my mom came running out of her garden. If Scott's dad is a hurricane, then my mom is a tsunami.

"Jaden Miller! What on earth do you think you're doing?" She was standing at the edge of the swamp, her hands in tight balls on her hips. Loose strands of her hair had escaped from underneath her bandana and sun hat. She was lit up in the yellow morning light.

I waved pitifully at the storm I faced and took it head on. "Hi, Mom." We must have been a sight to see: two bare-chested, mud-smeared boys in a beat-up aluminum boat—which, judging from its remaining flecks of paint, was once blue—appearing from nowhere out of the swamp.

"Get your butt up here this instant, young man!"

Ever so slowly, I crawled out of the boat, and Scott helped me drag Brook out as well.

When she saw our mute and crumpled cargo, my mom went silent. I took that as a bad sign. Then she exploded: "*What* is going on?"

"Mom! Mom, let me explain. We were at Scott's house. Brook came over and then she got into his dad's liquor. We all drank some and I'm sorry. I really am. But then Scott's dad went berserk on us, and we ran off into the swamp." I felt beads of nervous sweat appear on my brow. And at that instant I suddenly realized how bad I smelled.

She stared at me. She appeared to be having trouble breathing. "You're in big trouble, young man," was all she managed to say. She inhaled a gulp of morning air.

And then the entire Duncan police department came around the side of the house and approached us. "Son, you're in trouble, indeed," said Sergeant Cultan.

10

Well, you might be able to imagine how the trip to the Duncan Police Department went, and after several hours of lectures about our immature and regrettable actions, three things happened. One, the best: Brook came back to the world and spilled my heroic deed to the entire universe; thank god she forgot much of everything else. She denied that she ever forced alcohol into the evening agenda. The second thing that happened was I was put under house arrest for the next month. No doubt I would have been put in an electronic anklet if the Duncan police department had funding for such measures. As it was, I was let loose on my mom's promise to keep me grounded. And last but not least, Scott's dad was finally put behind bars. That pile of worthlessness. It was decided that Scott would live with his grandma, his mother's mother, who would keep him locked up, too. Brook was released to her father, and I'm not sure what happened to her when she got home.

But the ultimate catastrophe from all this was that I had to call my dad and tell him what had happened. That nearly broke my heart. I put it off as long as possible, but finally, finally I had to. I had to spill the beans. How I hated spilling those beans.

A few days after the incident, I was upstairs in my bedroom and looked out my window. Even though the weather was threatening, Mom was hunched over her camellias, trimming dead bits away from the glossy petals. My mom was obsessed with flowers, and she was constantly struggling to keep them alive. Especially roses; she kept trying to get them to grow in our swampy conditions. They, like many of her flowers, usually succumbed to black spot or powdery mildew, the bane of gardeners around there.

After a while, I went downstairs and reached for the old telephone—the only kind that worked in Duncan. After a moment's hesitation, I finally punched in my dad's cell and listened to the gloomy weather outside. Claps of outraged thunder punished the skies. My dad's phone rang once and then paused. I waited, my fingers curling around the cord, getting more and more edgy. It did not help to hear sheets of rain begin to batter the windows. If I closed my eyes, I could imagine that the thunderclaps were the claps of hands there to discipline me.

And then I heard his voice on the other end of the line.

"Jaden, I thought you were ignoring me!" I could close my eyes and see him, stationed at his favorite coffee shop, drinking a latte. Or maybe he was in his office, letting an attorney wait outside his door until he hung up from his important call. Yes, I could hear the hinges of his leather chair as he spun around to look out at the skyline of the city. As he said my name, I could almost see the crinkles around his eyes as he smiled.

"Hey, Dad." I took a deep breath to steady my nerves.

"How's my man? How's Mom? Is she OK?" His voice sounded tired and a little happy for the unexpected break from paperwork.

"Great," I muttered. "How's Pip?" Pip was my fat orange cat, who spent most of his time on the kitchen windowsill. I'd had him since I was, like, six.

"Pip's lazy as usual. Hey, how's life down in the mud hole?" Dad and I shared a not completely secret disdain of Duncan and its swamps and its armies of mosquitoes.

"Awful, as usual." I looked at my mom, now on the porch, reclining in her favorite chair, sipping coffee and engrossed in one of her many novels, which lined the shelves of our house. My mom had a theory about life: A person can overcome all obstacles as long as he or she has a coffee machine and a good book. I agree with the coffee part, but the book part, well...maybe a good video game instead.

"I suspected as much." He laughed. His laughter reminded me of the jokes we shared during our summers. I would say something sarcastic about an abstract painting at the Metropolitan Museum of Art. Then he would say something like, *It was the best the artist could come up with once his comely nude model went home to Brooklyn for the evening.*

"Yeah," I said and sighed.

"Same old, same old?"

"Yeah." I leaned against the wall.

"Well, you'll be happy to know I just bought us season tickets to the Yankees for next summer. I got great seats." He sounded pretty pleased with himself.

An electric current of guilt pulsed through me. *Tell him. Tell him now.* I decided to cut to the chase. "Hey, Dad, listen, me and Scott—you know, that kid I hang with here?"

"Sure." His voice was suddenly quiet.

I paused, readying myself to drop the bomb. "Well, the two of us and this girl, we got into a situation the other day." There was a long pause as I let him digest the information.

"What did you do?" His voice was displeased.

"We got drunk and spent the night out in the swamp in Scott's boat."

"Jaden, you're fifteen, going on sixteen. I would be more worried if you called saying you just got an A on your math exam. So there's a girl, huh? Same one that we had long conversations about?"

"Yep, that one." I was so relieved I could feel invisible hands rip off the chains from my back. I had expected to hear something stern. And I had expected to receive long-distance punishment.

"Well, look who's a chip off the old block." He chuckled. I was relieved that Dad didn't give a darn about the incident on the bayou, but to be honest, something in his voice scared me a little. The fact that he was happy about my recklessness was out of character. He was being too nice; it was weird.

"Hey, Jaden, are you going to ask her to homecoming or what?"

Wow, talk about a lack of fatherly concern. But I could surf his wave. "Umm, more like she's going to ask me."

"Really, so it's that kind of relationship?" He really sounded interested. He sounded so excited that it killed me to burst his bubble.

"Yeah, actually I hate her. I can't stand her. She's fake and arrogant and thinks the world revolves around her. She bugs me. So does my English teacher, Miss

Carlson. I don't know what her problem is, but she's a total snot. We're doing this irritating play, *Macbeth*, next week."

Dad coughed a very deep cough. Then he cleared his throat and changed the subject. "Halloween's coming right up. What do you plan to do?" His voice was rough around the edges.

"Scare kids."

"And what about homecoming? If you're not going to ask this girl and if you tell her no, what are you going to do then?" I heard him pause and I could see him glancing at his watch, his mind wandering to his next task.

I paused, too, thinking about it for the first time. The girls at school were buzzing about it like mad, talking about dresses and that sort of stuff. I had been so preoccupied with other things I hadn't even realized homecoming was just around the corner.

"Oh man, I don't know."

"Ask a girl you like, Jaden."

I could tell my dad was winking. "At the moment, I don't like anyone." And briefly I flashed back to the gorgeous girl I had seen on back-to-school day. I shook my head and sighed. I imagined her face appearing in the raindrops that formed on the window, and I lifted my finger to trace the image.

"You do like someone. I know it. I can read your mind, Jaden," my dad teased. "I saw Amelia and Sophia today. They asked about you. Those Sorensen sisters sure are foxy."

"Foxy? Really, Dad? Did you just say 'foxy'?"

"Hey, listen, I don't feel up to snuff right now. I'll give you a buzz later."

"OK." Something in his voice did not sound right, and mild panic set in. "You OK, Dad?" I said it way more seriously than I had intended. It was his turn to pause.

"I'm fine, Jaden. Good luck with your dream girl." Then he hung up. I hung up, too, and then I punched the wall hard, so hard I left a dent. I pulled away, scared of my own outburst. *He's fine; he said so himself. Madam Marian's prediction was just a bunch of stupid hoodoo voodoo.* But the part of my brain where the doubt comes from was being more persuasive than the other parts.

11

The day of the play, which I had dreaded from the beginning, had almost arrived. Hey, you might be wondering about my other classes by now. Trust me, English, to my utter disgust, was where all the action was, and the other classes weren't worth my time, except of course P.E. and maybe Creative Writing. But stick with me, because something was about to happen that would shake my world—again.

On Monday of the following week, I woke up in the tree house again. I had wandered out there in the rain. I was feeling, well, to be honest, I was feeling lost. But I always felt safer in the tree house, looking at my New York stuff. Usually, the posters could get my mind off the fact that I was stuck in a swamp, separated from my city life by thirteen hundred miles.

A mourning dove. That was what I had heard. It was singing low notes right outside my window. I was pulled out of my dreams and tumbled from my hammock to the floor. The loud thud of my own body woke me up. I had scared myself awake. I took a glance at my watch, saw the time, and almost had a heart attack.

I'm going to be late for English again! The only time I had been late was the very first day of school, the previous month. I grabbed my raincoat off the ground, swung it over my shoulder, jumped down the stairs, and sprinted to the house. I ran in, grabbed my backpack, and shoved three granola bars and a carton of chocolate milk inside it. I popped a granola bar in my mouth as I ran to the porch. I jumped on my bike and maneuvered past potholes and puddles before I put my raincoat on all the way.

While the sky dumped rain on my head, I raced bumpily along the trail. It was awful: my hands were practically frozen off. It was Antarctica cold for a change. And gray, everything was gray: the clouds, the rain, the ground, and my mood. Once again, I had to ride past the Stop-N-Shop. I didn't even glance up to look at the chalkboard, knowing two things: one, the chalk would have washed anything away, and two, the number was 218. In 218 days, I would say good-bye to Scott, spend one last night in Duncan, and then board the plane that would finally swoop me out of that mud hole and take me where I belonged.

I hated everything in Duncan: the swamp, the bugs, the animals, and the people—just everything. It was a dreadful place, sinking into the bayou. The rain pounded down on my back and head. Rivulets of water ran down my face. I could barely see a thing! Not to mention that I was going to be tardy.

Fifteen minutes later, I tossed my bike into the bushes and sprinted through the vacant parking lot and up the steps. I swung the door wide open. The one good thing, thank god, was that the hallway was dry and vacant of people. I raced through the halls, my footsteps echoing all over the place, keeping beat with the thunderclaps and pelting downpour on the windows. When I finally stepped into the classroom, I got Miss Carlson's full attention.

"Welcome to class, Jaden Miller. What shall it be?" She smiled at me: it was a thin, dry smile, covering her fangs.

I grunted while walking to my seat. "Detention," I growled. The class snickered.

"In the library. I have a meeting after school."

That Miss Lady, she doesn't even have the time to dole out her own punishments. Miss Carlson returned to her work bringing the projector to life. *It's not what she said, it was the way she said it, like, I could go to essay hell or something. I hate her!*

I walked down my aisle past the other kids. There was the sleeper, the gamer, the off-in-space guy, the girl braiding her hair, the doodler, the nail polisher, the snacker, the eraser flicker, and last but not least, the upright napper: the kid with eyes half closed who had one arm fully extended out over the desk and the other bent to prop up his chin. I nodded at Billy, swung my ass into the seat, and pulled out a soggy notebook and a wet pen. I hung my dripping rain jacket on the back of my chair.

I looked up at the clock and noticed that underneath the clock, in the corner desk one row away from me was a silent occupant. But before I could get a good look, Scott came in the door, looking even more panicked and wet than I did. Muffled giggles spread through the class.

Scott took off his hoodie and made it to his seat. As soon as the lights flickered off, Miss Carlson rose like a zombie from the dead. The projector started to blast whatever it was that she wanted to show us, and she walked over to Scott's desk. I looked at my friend, he caught my gaze, and I gave him a shrug. He laughed.

"Something funny, Scott?" asked Miss Carlson.

"Umm, no," came his mellow-toned answer.

"Choose," she demanded.

"Detention," he hissed, sinking a little deeper into his seat and playing with his number two pencil.

"Library." She said the word as though it needed to be slowly harpooned to a miserable death.

He started to draw on his binder paper, also wet as mush. Well, at least I'd have someone to talk to while I sat in the library and waited for an hour to eat itself alive.

"We shall watch *Macbeth*, celebrating the fact that tomorrow, we get to perform our play before a live audience," Miss Carlson said grandly.

Great, I thought; I hadn't practiced at all. I was doomed. Most everyone in the class seemed to be on the same page as me. That was good; at least I wouldn't be the only kid onstage who, once the red curtains parted, revealed to the audience what an idiot he was.

The film appeared on the screen, and all the students with a B– or lower checked out. I tore a piece of paper out of my notebook and scribbled on it.

Pass this to Billy

Dude, who is the person sitting opposite me in the next row?

Jaden

Kind of sad, really. Hampton High must have been the last school on earth where you still passed notes *on paper*. Thunder boomed over our heads, and a few girls shrieked. With the lights turned off, the storm was actually kind of fun. Girls, man, they get so scared so fast. I handed the note to Billy, and the imbecile passed it on to the next kid without taking his eyes off some manga book. I moaned, slumped lower, and gripped the edges of my desk in frustration. But the kid with the note passed it right back to Billy, and Billy saw that the note was addressed to him. He read it and turned to look at me. I glanced up at Miss Carlson to see if she noticed, but she was staring at *Macbeth*, or maybe, like the rest of us, was staring straight past *Macbeth* and thinking about something else.

He craned his head to the left to the figure in the corner desk, and his eyes widened in surprise. He was genuinely puzzled, as if he had had no idea she was there or as if he had no idea who she was.

"That girl? I've never seen her before. Sorry," he whispered to me. I could smell his foul fish breath. The guy shrugged and plunged his fat nose right back into his manga book. Sometimes—well, most of the time—losers are actually decent guys, more decent than the dudes on the lacrosse team. But I think I'm pretty decent. I'm a good guy, right?

I turned again to look at the girl. It was indeed a girl, so that meant she could be any of the invisible girls. There were plenty of them at our school, hard to say how many, exactly. So I tried again. I sent a note to Keisha, across from me.

Pass this to Keisha

Hey Keisha, it's Jaden. Do you happen to know the new girl's name?

I got the same response. She had no idea. Defeated, I allowed myself a glance at the desk next to me. I was itching to find out who she was.

But then I happened to look at the screen and saw Lady Macbeth hold up her hands, dripping with the king's blood. She started rambling on in that pompous Shakespearean language that takes too much concentration to understand. Then she was washing her hands, vigorously, trying to free her hands of the bloody deed in a pail of water.

Out of the corner of my eye, I took a look at the girl, wondering, *Can it be? Is it possible? Is it* her? The girl, an arm's reach away, took a hand from under her desk and brushed aside a lock of hair. In the dim light, I could see a purple silhouette but no details. Then she clasped her hands together and held them close to her chest, her thick hair making a veil over her shadow.

I turned back to the screen, my mind reeling: *It's her! It's Bloody Hands!*

As soon as the film was done, the lights flickered back on. The bell rang and I tossed all my soaking stuff into my backpack, squinting from the blinding fluorescent lights that now assaulted my eyes. The seat next to me was empty, and the girl with the bloody hands was gone all over again. As though she were never even there.

The school day went by in a haze because my mind was traveling every which direction.

Brook seemed to pick up on this at lunch because she said, "Hey, Jaden, you look pale. Are you all right? You should go to the nurse, baby." She reached out to feel my forehead as if I were dying or something. I pushed her hand away and when I did that, I could see a flare of annoyance in her eyes. As though she realized that she could not control my thoughts, that her powers of beauty did not faze me.

"I'm fine!" I barked.

"No, you're not fine. Tell me what's on your mind; what's troubling you?" She fluttered her long eyelashes. Her crystal-blue eyes were boring into me. For a second, I pictured her as Medusa, turning her victims to stone.

"I'm fine," I said again. I couldn't keep the impatience out of my voice.

She turned away, flipping her blonde hair in my face. I pictured it as snapping vipers, just out of my reach.

12

After school, I sat in the deserted library with Scott, and both of us thumbed through *Macbeth*. I looked up at the clock. We still had a half hour to go, so finally I got out a piece of binder paper and began to write, because I couldn't stand the boredom. The librarian was like a hawk when it came to any noise uttered on the planet. She could probably hear a whisper in Siberia. The grandma had superhero powers or something. That reminded me:

Hey, Scott, how's life with Granny?

Ever since his dad had finally been put behind bars, Scott had been living with his grandma. She was the sweetest-slash-craziest person in the world. You might think of a grandma as someone who bakes cookies and knits sweaters; Scott's grandma, however, rode a motorcycle. She was the coolest person on earth. Even if it was a rainy day and your pet goldfish just died, she could make you laugh hysterically. OK, before I sugarcoat her, she did possess an evil twin. On her bad days. That's what I mean by crazy.

He got a piece of paper and wrote back:

        Sweet. But the damn dog is going
to ruin any chances of another party.

I responded:

Dude, I'm not up for any more parties anytime soon.

He just looked up at me and smiled that Scott smile. I smiled, too. Luckily, Scott possessed more of his grandma's traits than his dad's. Maybe too much of the crazy side of her, though.

`Homecoming is soon. Gonna ask Brook?`

He slid the paper over to me. The librarian's eyebrows shot up, but she didn't act. I turned a page in my *Macbeth* book. Then I wrote fiercely across the lined paper and shoved it back in his direction:

No way, man! Not her. I can't stand her.

`Why? She's so hot!`

She annoys me, Scott.

I paused. I couldn't explain myself. What was it about her that I couldn't stand? Then somehow I managed to write it down:

She's so fake. Besides, I have my sights set on someone else, someone who's a thousand times prettier than Brook Jackson.

When he received that, he just looked up at me in disbelief. His eyes bulged and his mouth turned into a perfect circle as he mouthed, *Who?*

Then I watched as he madly scribbled on the paper. He couldn't push it over to me fast enough.

"Gentlemen!" The librarian was standing over us. "Are you doing your homework or passing notes?" The librarian's heels clicked rapidly as she circled around us. I could smell the lemon conditioner she used on her graying hair.

We shook our heads, slouched down in our wooden seats, and dove into *Macbeth* once more. But after five minutes, Scott kicked my foot and gestured toward the slip of paper on the table between us. I snatched it and surreptitiously slid it across the surface toward me. I stuck it into my open book and read it:

Dude, who is prettier than Brook Jackson? And why haven't I ever seen her? Who?

The script was barely legible because of the force and speed with which the words had been scratched onto the paper.

Then I wrote slowly in perfect script:

The girl who is invisible to everyone. The girl with the bloody hands.

But before I could hand it to him, the librarian was right there next to us again, and she snatched the paper from me.

"Jaden Miller, I expected as much!" She held the creased binder paper tightly in her grip. Then she read it aloud: "The girl who is invisible to everyone. The girl with the bloody hands." She paused for the longest time after that, her small brown eyes staring at the words. I looked at Scott, who cocked his head to the side. silent Chinese pig Latin for *You have an invisible girlfriend?*

"What is this?" the librarian demanded, holding up the paper with an outstretched arm, as though it were a dead fish that reeked.

I looked up at her wrinkled face and smiled. "A mystery."

"It's no mystery, gentlemen: the students who study get good grades," she snapped. "Kindly apply yourself to your homework." She stalked off, her spine rigid.

Shrugging, I turned to Scott, who got his iPhone out. So did I. With luck, there would be cell service. The rain hadn't stopped; it was pummeling the roof. Sure enough, two bars, miracle of miracles. I will never understand this town's flickering connection to the real world. So our thread of conversation continued via text:

Who r u talking about? This girl with the bloody hands?

She's new to our English class. Sits right next to me.

What? You've lost it, man. Lost it.

"No, trust me," I whispered. "She's real. I know she is. And I've seen her before. Plus when I mentioned her at your house the other day, you said the same thing. But that next morning, when we were out in the swamp, before you woke up, you were dreaming about her. Honest, you mentioned a girl with bloody hands," I whispered.

"Jaden, I was dreaming about the fox, not some mystery girl walking around campus with bleeding hands. Dude. Seriously? I would have noticed." Then he added, "Hey, man, sorry to burst your bubble, but I know everyone in Duncan, especially all the hot girls. No one has bloody hands."

I could see that he knew I was upset. I hated being proved wrong, so I further stated my case: "OK, they're not always bloody, but her hands have recent scabs on them whenever I see her, and some of the wounds are fresh. And no one knows her name, so what else should I call her?"

"Dude, you've lost it."

"Scott, what if I can prove that she's real?"

"Be my guest and I'll stop calling you insane." He smirked from across the table.

"Fine. I will," I said confidently.

He seemed to take that in for a moment at least, and then he replied, this time via text:

Hey, I no it must be hard for u to leave NY, but dude, get your head on straight. With privilege comes responsibilities. U r the captain of the lacrosse team. U look like an escapee male model, not to mention your family is the only sane one in Duncan. Your life isn't like my life. Mom's dead. Dad's in jail. Granny's a lunatic! U have to get it together.

I ferociously keyed him back:

Sane? U couldn't be more wrong. Nothing about my life is sane. Mom and Dad hate each other. Mom is so depressed, she just digs in her garden all day, planting tulips that die every time. And Dad, who is, like, a multimillionaire, who's the best dad ever, at the same time probably doesn't really give a damn about me because his only language is money. Here, Jaden, want a Lamborghini? Here, Jaden, want a CIA-designed computer?

When he received that, we were both fired up. But instead of responding, he just dropped his phone into his backpack. I did the same, stashing mine in my jacket pocket. I looked at the clock. Fifteen minutes to go. We just glared at each other the whole time, but at the end of the 15 minutes, he got out his phone and texted me:

Sorry, man, no one's sane in Duncan. Both our lives suck, so what do u say we go to stop n shop as soon as we're set free?

Our hour of imprisonment was at an end. Finally, I was able to speak out loud. "Oh no, I don't go there anymore." The tension between us had evaporated.

"Really? What? Why?" asked Scott. "Did Madam Marian ask you to homecoming?" he said and laughed. We walked out the double doors of the library, the librarian glaring at us the whole time.

"More or less." That got his attention.

"More or less? Did she say something to you?" His eyebrows shot up.

"Yeah, actually she did," I said calmly, as if it were perfectly usual to have a chat with Madam Marian.

"No way, dude! What did she say?"

"Umm, weird stuff. Weird stuff." I realized that I didn't want to tell Scott the details.

"Dude! You have to tell me."

We reached our bikes. I grabbed the handlebars of my bike and pushed the bike to level ground. I can't wait for my license. As I looked at Scott, I remembered all over again exactly what had happened on that day, that very weird day. I remembered Madam Marian's words, which I had conveniently repressed until that moment: "Someone dear to you, boy, will die within the year."

Beads of sweat dripped down my face, and my mind raced as I ran down the list of the names of those dearest to me. I remembered my Dad's coughing spell on the phone the other day and shivered. *What if it's him?* I looked at my very best friend, Scott. *What if it's him?* "Yeah. No. Not today, not tomorrow, definitely not ever. But a word to the wise, Scott." I swung my leg over my bike and sat on the wet seat.

He looked truly disappointed, like Brook when she doesn't get her way.

"Don't ever give Madam Marian an extra five cents."

I began to pedal toward the most deserted town in the world.

I heard Scott call from the parking lot, "Not fair, man, not fair!"

"Swell!" I shouted back. "See ya onstage, Scott."

13

I biked through town, pondering how it would be a great place for a big Hollywood production company to film a story about a zombie apocalypse. Like I said before, tumbleweeds should have been—if it weren't a swamp—rolling across the roads. Sort of reminded me of the town in *To Kill a Mockingbird*, the book we read last year. The setting was a town named Maycomb, a godforsaken place with only one decent restaurant.

Well, downtown Duncan had only one decent restaurant, too. Naturally, it was a shrimp place. Next to that were a broken-down tavern/pizza place, a grocery store, a gas station, and a motel. The motel was pretty much always vacant, which I guess was good because if we got those zombies to show up, they could stay there. That summed up downtown. If you wanted something the town didn't offer—excitement, for instance—you had to make the three-hour drive to New Orleans.

There were a just a few residential neighborhoods. Most areas, including mine, were relatively normal. Some were dumpy. Then there were the swamps, if you could even call them a neighborhood. They were made up of shacks hanging over the water, which were built with pieces of things that had washed up on shore: sheet metal, branches, and parts of boats. Sadly, that was how our high school students could be categorized as well: normal, dumpy, and swampy. Yep, it was no mystery why I hated the place.

Yeah, well, I finally got home. I took the long way, not wanting to go past the Stop-N-Shop again. I said hi to my mom, who was in the garden. Then I ran into the kitchen, ate some cold lasagna, and gulped down a quart of milk.

That was when I heard my mom calling me, all excited.

"Jaden! Come look at this!" So, carrying a handful of chips, I walked out the back door. Mom was standing near her lily pond, holding a hose and pointing to the roof. She had her big sun hat on, even though it had been raining all day. A slight drizzle still filled the sky. Then the fat clouds broke apart and let some blue sky shine through.

"Look, it's a mourning dove." Her gloved hand pointed to the roof.

I walked over. Sure enough, in one of the hanging flowerpots was a dove, the same dove as from this morning.

"Oh yeah," I said and smiled. I popped a chip into my mouth. "That's the little guy who woke me up this morning." I didn't know whether to be grateful or pissed.

Mom turned to look at me and smiled. People say we look alike, my mom and me, but all we share are our huge smiles.

"What should we name her?" she said.

"Her?"

"Yeah," she said smiling hugely again. I loved it when she smiled like that, and all it took was a bird in a flowerpot. Trust me, she was the most earth-enthusiastic person ever.

"How do you know it's a girl, Mom?" I asked. I tossed more chips into my mouth.

"Look at her eyes. She's a little lady for sure." She went to go turn off the hose.

"Ha! Let's name her Ricardo."

She sprayed me with the last water in the hose when I said that. "Ricardo! Have some respect!" she said, but she was laughing, "No, let's give her a proper name. How about...Flower!"

I just rolled my eyes and shook the water from my hair. "Why?" I said. "It's just a dumb bird, Mom. Let's name the thing Ricardo."

She ran to the faucet and sprayed me again, making my chips soggy. She stood there grinning like a naughty kid, her hand gripping the faucet, ready to attack again.

"It's not just some dumb bird, it's a mourning dove! Now look, she loves those purple geraniums up there, so Flower it shall be."

We left Flower to her own bird fun, and I inspected the garden. It was gorgeous as usual, and my mom quizzed me, pointing to the various plants.

"Camellia, bougainvillea, Amaryllis belladonna, ginger, bird-of-paradise...." I knew the names of the plants in Mom's garden better than the names we studied in history or geography class, that much was sure. We walked into the Japanese section, the desert section, and the African section, and I was rattling off the names. For me, botanical names just stick.

We finally reached the bayou, looming somberly beyond the riot of color we had just walked through. I turned to my mom, who was kneeling by the dandelions, the weed that pops up in yards. She gave me some dandelion leaves. I had run out of potato chips, so I ate them. We sat down on the grass, which was beaded with rain, and looked out into the swamp.

"You still hate it here?" she asked, her mouth full of dandelion greens.

"Yes."

"Really? Still?" She sounded sad.

"New York is where I belong." I said it with ease; I'd had a lot of practice.

She sighed and handed me a fuzzy white dandelion puffball, the mature form of the yellow dandelion. The white fuzz, which is sort of a parachute, is attached to the dandelion seeds. The wind picks up the fuzz and can carry the seeds a long way.

"I don't like to disperse weed seeds, but I want you to make a wish," instructed my mom. The way she said it made me feel guilty.

I took the puffball from her and just held it, looking at the amazing circular pattern. All plants have a pattern, a beautiful pattern, if you just look.

She abruptly changed the subject: "Any girls that I should know about?"

"Mom!"

"Well, I can't help but wonder about it."

It's this kind of conversation that I, and every other teen in America, steer clear of with parents. It was my turn to change the subject. "Mom, do you remember when I was seven, and a dove was eating seeds in the garden?" This was a good Mom-topic.

"Oh, Jaden! Of course I do!" she said brightly.

See, I was right about the topic. "We were in the backyard and you were gardening, and then a dove swooped down and started to eat the seeds you were planting!" I said.

She laughed and nodded.

"But instead of getting mad, the way you do with gophers and squirrels, you sang to it. So later that evening, I asked you about the song. You showed me how to mimic the dove's song, and you told me it was a mourning dove. I had thought the birds were morning doves—early-in-the-day doves. When you told me that they were actually mourning doves, you explained to me what *mourning* is: a longing for someone or something that has been lost. We made jokes from then on about the doves." I was looking out over the bayou, memories spilling from my mouth.

Mom sighed. She remembered. She started the song and I joined in: "*Whooouuuooo, who, who, who.*"

Mom said, "What I remember most was that you asked me who the dove was singing to. Who was the who it was singing 'who' to?"

I laughed and then we heard Flower sing back to us.

"I'm still trying to figure out who the who is."

"So," she said, nudging me with her elbow, "Who is the who?"

"Mom!" I growled. We had fallen back into the no-talk zone.

"Sorry." She was still smiling.

I picked up the dandelion puffball and looked at it, thinking, *What should my wish be?* Then I thought, *Duh! Who is the who?* And then I blew those tiny white parachutes into the darkening bayou as the evening light danced off the brackish water.

14

The play.

Most of us had our lines written on our hands in Sharpie. It was the most embarrassing thing ever, especially staring down at our parents, who seemed to mirror our discomfort. I mean, it's cute seeing five-year-olds onstage, but fifteen- and sixteen-year-olds? Seriously? We were an embarrassment to the human race, or should I say, to Miss Carlson, who looked as though she wanted to die. But hey, it was her fault for even thinking it was going to work. We had signed up for English class, not drama class, lady.

But you know who turned out to be a good actor?

Brook.

So good, in fact, she enchanted me.

I remember standing behind the curtains, waiting for the next scene. Even though I was backstage with a bunch of panic-stricken teens, I felt as though I were completely alone, looking out my little window on to the stage. It was like standing on a curb back in New York, and suddenly you stop, not sure why. There are countless people streaming by. For once, you take a moment to think of yourself, about how alone you really are. It might be that no one would know or care if you decided to go another direction or even disappear. There you stand, one among thousands, and you realize the world is immense—endless, maybe. And your moment and your ambitious plan suddenly seem kind of small and insignificant.

Sorry, excuse my rambling.

So playing out in front of me was the scene in which Lady Macbeth is center stage in her dream state. Where the doctor and some other guy (honestly, I forget this name) are standing. There was Brook, earnestly and loudly delivering her lines. The audience was stunned, transfixed. Somehow, she managed to make us all forget our awkwardness and empathetic shame.

Brook strode confidently around the stage, real tears sliding down her painted cheeks. She was in pain; we could feel it. She was wearing some dress, long and white, and she looked like a ghost. The audience, sitting in the shadows, was absolutely still. At stage left was a suddenly radiant Miss Carlson.

I was glad that at least something was going well. Brook knelt down, leaned over, and pounded the floor with balled fists. My mind tried to pinpoint what scene it was and ultimately failed. The two other kids onstage gawked at Brook. Then one snapped out of his daze and said," How does your patient, doctor?" And the other guy mumbled, "Not so sick, my lord, as she is troubled with thick fantasies that keep her from rest." Miss Carlson slapped her forehead and furiously scribbled some remark on her clipboard.

Great, we're getting graded, I thought. But then my eyes returned to Brook, and something in me, deep in me, realized that there is more to Brook than we had known.

She threw her head back, screaming bloody murder. Thrusting her hands up above her arching back, she muttered something about her hands that I couldn't make out. She clasped her hands to her chest, weeping. She collapsed on the floor. But still she was trying with desperation to clean her hands, as if something were stuck on them.

My mind searched for the scene, but of course I didn't know it. She scrubbed, hit, washed, and rubbed her hands, but with each attempt, she cried in pitiful defeat. Whatever it was on her hands, only she could see it. Brook was possessed by the character. *Damn, she is a good actor.* The thought made me feel sick inside; I felt guilty for being a jerk.

I was that thickheaded teenage guy. An asshole, maybe. I wasn't the good guy I had thought I was. When I looked at Brook, I winced. My boredom and hostility must have been behind her suffering. I had broken her heart.

"What, will these hands ne'er be clean?" Brook screeched, rising from the floor.

And then Brook plummeted into the darkest depths of despair. I thought back for just a second on what she had told me before...when we had played Truth or Dare...her awkward pause when I had asked her if she had ever killed someone. The world is so messed up when you look at it closely. Sometimes things seem perfect, everything fitting together so nicely and neatly, like one of those perfectly geometric spirals of the dandelion, waiting for the wind. But if you look at the world closely, you see that we don't fit into a nice, orderly pattern at all...not at all.

"Here's the smell of the blood still: all the perfumes of Arabia will not sweeten this little hand. Oh, oh, oh!" I hadn't heard her a moment before, but I could definitely hear her now.

She sank back to the floor, once more weeping real tears. Suddenly, I remembered what scene it was: the one in which Lady Macbeth has posttraumatic stress disorder because she talked her husband into killing the king. She sees her hands stained with the guilt of her deed. The blood isn't real; the guilt is. *Why did she want to kill the king?* I couldn't remember that part.

I looked past Brook for an instant, and there she was: Bloody Hands. I froze, a deer in the headlights. I stared at her, unable to turn away.

She was directly across from me on the opposite side of the stage, both of us concealed from the rest of the world by the red velvet curtains. She was watching Brook, tears dripping down her own face. She was silent but so gorgeous that I gasped. I doubted that any other human could be so breathtaking. My knees buckled a bit and I swayed and then staggered, but I regained my composure before I made a scene.

She clasped her hands together gently. Wrapped around a pinky finger was a dingy-looking bandage. Bloody Hands then unpeeled her eyes from the stage and our eyes locked. Her solemn look told me she had known I was there long before I had noticed her. My heart was a bird fluttering, trying to get away; I thought it might burst from my rib cage.

She looked at me and her expression froze; my direct gaze seemed to discomfit her. But it seemed as though she could not unlock her eyes from mine. She, too, was a deer in the headlights. Bloody Hands somehow seemed to have been waiting for this forever:

waiting for someone to look her in the eye. But then her long, wavy, and glistening hair fell across part of her face, and she was lost to me again. She stepped back into the shadows and vanished from my sight but not from my mind.

"Hello," I said really quietly, the way I had with the fox. *What is your story?*

15

The girl with the bloody hands didn't come to class for three painfully slow weeks after that. All I know is that when she finally came back to class, it was a Thursday. That Saturday was homecoming and I hadn't asked anyone yet.

I walked into English and went through my usual routine: glare at Miss Carlson behind her back, and if other kids were watching, mock her in some manner, and then saunter to my seat. I had gotten so used to the disappointment of finding Bloody Hands' desk empty that I had stopped looking for her. So I sat down at my desk, and Miss Carlson took her position at the whiteboard, scribbling gibberish all over it. I can't tell you what it was, because my habit was to forget it as soon as I passed the test with a C.

It's funny. If only a teacher could see me as more than that C student in the back of her class, gazing out at the world on the other side of the windows. If only she could recognize my type of intelligence, the kind that doesn't count for much in class, but might, someday, out there. If only she could see. So there I was, staring out that window, when I heard a pencil fall under my shoe. Automatically, I bent down to reach for it. It was a battered and chewed yellow pencil.

My hand collided with the owner of the pencil, reaching her delicate fingers toward it like the wings of a great white egret stretched out in flight. Though graceful, I saw many small scabs and one tiny fresh red cut. Shocked, I looked up, slowly, and there she was. She looked up at me, too. Our faces were so close I could smell her. She smelled like roses, not some suffocating perfume but real roses. She probably could smell me, too, and with any luck my breath still smelled like toothpaste. As I looked at her, her face so close to mine, I could swear my heart escaped from its rib cage prison.

Slowly, I put her pencil in her hand. Her eyes moved down to the pencil and her hand gracefully closed around the battered thing.

Then I smiled at her as she started to turn back to the world in front of us. She saw me smile and paused. It was not my usual cocky smile, my, *Hey, I know I'm so cool. Look at me, everyone* smile. The smile I gave her was a quiet one, the kind that my mom and I had shared the night before. The looking-at-a-dove-in-a-flowerpot kind, the real kind.

She looked at me through purple-blue eyes, and then I saw the spark, if only for a second. It lit up her face like fireflies dancing over the bayou at dusk.

But then she turned back to the class, and that dark curtain of hair fell over part of her face, a wall between us. I managed to peel my awestruck eyes from her and look at the whiteboard again. The lesson would soon vanish from my mind.

As soon as class ended, she was gone. I got up, threw my backpack over one shoulder, and twirled and danced my way in and out of people in my row. I ran into Scott at the door.

"Hey, Jaden, I was thinking—"

"Not now, Scott!" I yelled. People glanced my way as I ran after the girl. I saw her head down the hall and disappear around a corner. She was going in the opposite direction of my next class.

I chased after her, determined not to let her out of my sight, not to lose her again. And then as I rounded the corner, I was overwhelmed by the crowds of people swarming out of the music room all at once, most carrying instrument cases. I got swallowed up by the crowd, and I saw the faces blur and the voices converge until all I heard was fragments of conversations.

"He did not!... / ...and then we kissed... / I have to go talk to Ms. Cunningham..." Everything was out of focus except one thing: her. As I battled my way upstream, I felt panic rise. I was losing sight of her. I looked frantically in every direction, and then finally I saw her. The waterfall that was her hair: she was ahead of me, making her way upstream in a river of teenagers. I pushed and jostled my way through the crowd.

"Wait!" I screamed, and my voice broke and bounced off the walls and was drowned in the voices around me.

And then she vanished, the crowds thinned, the bell rang, and I was left standing there in the nearly empty corridor. I had lost her again.

16

At lunch, I ate my peanut butter and jelly sandwich in contemplative silence. Scott turned to me. "Jaden, what's up? You seem off."

He had his elbow propped up on the table as he tossed grapes into his mouth. He squinted his amber-brown eyes, his mind seemingly hard at work. Whether it was his next song or that girl at the other end of the table, I didn't know.

"How so?" I mumbled. I was a thousand miles away.

"Well, in English, and just all day, really, you've been weird. What's up, man?" He leaned over and snatched my apple, taking a big bite. "What's on your mind, bro?" He seemed concerned. Well, as concerned as a guy friend ever gets.

"Why do you care?" My skin felt cold and I shivered.

He raised his hands. "No reason, dude. Chill, OK? It was just a question."

I forced myself to come back down to earth and looked at him. Then I looked around at the other kids, as equally wrapped up in their own lives as I was. At the next table, I saw Luke Twain, the enormous lacrosse player, give a bouquet of red roses to Ally.

"Will you go to homecoming with me?" Luke asked.

Ally squealed with joy. She reached for the roses, and Jordan and Brook also squealed and hugged her.

"I *told* you he was going to ask!" said Jordan.

"Oh! Oh! Ally!" sang Brook.

There was a moment of silence, and then Ally jumped up from her seat. shouting, "Oh, Luke, I would love to!" He smiled a winning smile, as though he had just scored a goal.

Brook turned to me, expertly flipping her hair out of her face, and tilted her head like a question mark. I felt as though I had just been stung by a bee.

"Well?" she said. "Don't you have something to ask me, Jaden?" she said with such sweet innocence it made me feel that I was the bad guy—almost.

"No," I said coolly. I shivered involuntarily as goose bumps raised the hair on my arms.

I saw it in her eyes: the hurt, the pain. That did make me feel that I was a bad guy. She turned away. Ally smiled blissfully. I felt horrible. Scott saw everything. He grabbed the shoulder of my shirt, pulled me away from the table, and maneuvered us through the crowd.

"Excuse me, Brook," he said as he ushered me out the double doors. She didn't look up: she kept her head down and shoulders slumped. The vertebrae of her spine showed under her thin shirt as she tried to hide her hurt.

He pushed me into the hallway; it was cold and vacant.

"Dude, what was that? Brook Jackson just asked you to homecoming! Have you lost your mind!"

His screaming caught me off guard. It surged through me like a jolt of electricity and echoed off the metallic lockers.

"Yes. I have lost my mind," I said. I had no energy to hide my feelings from him or anyone.

Shaking his head, he leaned in and put both hands on my shoulders. He was five inches shorter than I was, so he had to tilt his head up to meet my gaze.

"Where did Jaden Miller go? Dude! Wake up!" This was my best friend. Maybe I *was* seriously messed up.

I hung my head in defeat as a cocktail of mixed emotions and confusion swirled through me.

"I feel kind of sick, Scott. Sorry. I think I need to go home." My excuse was pitiful, but it was the only one I had. Somehow, it worked.

Scott looked relieved as he slapped my back. He knew I was in there. Somewhere. "Oh, good. I thought you were possessed or something," he said and laughed. "I'll tell Brook you were about to barf on her shirt." He laughed again.

"Don't."

He just turned and winked, throwing his index finger at me. "Feel better, man."

And so I started my way to the nurse's office, practicing my fake cough.

17

By the time I got to the nurse's office, I did not want to go in there. So instead, I just walked by and out the front doors and got on my bike.

Skipping school was something I had never done. *I must really be messed up.*

I just pedaled and kept pedaling. I rode past downtown and I automatically thought to go home, but no, I couldn't go there. So I just kept riding, I just kept on eating up the road with my turning wheels. I followed the main road to where it ended at the docks. When I got near the docks, I dismounted, pushed my bike to the side of the trail, and looked out over the harbor.

The tide was out. When it's low tide at the shipyard, the water retreats more than 100 feet out, leaving a stretch of mud and tethered boats huddled together, waiting. The boats were shrimping boats, the main source of income for most of Duncan. The boats themselves looked miserable, as if they were trying to keep warm. The lack of water exposed their gross underbellies, rusty and barnacled. The image was a fitting symbol of the town of Duncan's despair.

I walked to the end of the pier to where the water starts and turned around to look back at the haphazard boats and shore beyond. The shore was heavy with Spanish moss–covered trees and muddy banks. A small, dilapidated shack stood on the shore. The sight could depress anyone. It wasn't long ago that the place had been in even worse shambles.

People remember only Katrina. I watched it on CNN from the comfort of our New York penthouse, and thankfully, it mostly missed our little hellhole. But not a month later, and while I was in Duncan for the first month of second grade, Hurricane Rita swung through Duncan, obliterating the docks and leveling much of the already miserable town. Then in fifth grade, as if to finish off anything that had been left, Hurricane Ike blew through. The town just couldn't catch a break— and I had to live there.

I crouched to study the names scratched into the weathered boards of the pier. Someone had collected the names of those from Duncan who had died in the storms whipped up by the Gulf of Mexico and carved their names into the wooden boards of the pier. I recognized almost none of the names, except the few who were family members of my friends, such as Scott. He once showed me his mom's name, etched in deeply.

Right then, I heard a scratching noise below me on the dock. I walked over to the edge, and there in an old red canoe was a boy of about eleven. I could see only the tops of his dark curls, not his face. He must have been from another parish, because I had never seen him before. He was scraping a pocketknife over a pillar.

"Hey!" I shouted.

He was so surprised that he dropped his pocketknife into the gray water. He reached after it, and then I felt kind of bad. So in a softer voice, I asked, "What are you doing?"

He looked up at me, eyes wild.

"Nothing." He said it so fast that I knew he was lying.

"Oh yeah?" I said, smiling hugely at the kid.

He seemed to register the swift change in my mood, like a girl on her period. "Yeah, nothing," he said with such practiced force that I smiled again. He leaned way over the boat, holding on to the pillar. He swayed a bit as the water rose and fell under him.

"Let's see." I began to lean over the pier, reaching and extending my arm to feel what he had carved.

"No!" He swatted at my hand and looked up at me.

"Why not?" I asked as though I were hurt. It was a performance worthy of a Shakespearean actor; if only Miss Carlson could have seen me then, maybe I wouldn't have gotten the C–

"Because," he said, looking down at the water. "It's a secret."

I had guessed that much. Still smiling hugely, I said, "I'll tell *you* a secret." My stomach began to hurt from lying on the uneven boards.

Again he looked up, his gentle deep brown eyes taking in my own big blue ones.

"I am the king of keeping a secret." I whispered and winked at him, charming him with my act. "Trust the Fox Boy." I came up with that on the spot; somehow I felt it fit.

He smiled and then pointed to the carving. Really quietly, he said what had been eating him alive from the inside. "I wanted to put my brother's name on the pier."

"What?" I was taken aback; that was the last thing I had expected to hear.

"He died last week. Car accident." His voice was folded over into a million little pieces, and as he unfolded them, he choked and tripped on every neatly folded scar.

I paused for a second, digesting what the kid had said.

"You're not from Duncan, are you?" My stomach really started to ache.

He shook his head. A bigger wave lifted his boat up, and he had to catch the pillar to steady himself. I continued, "First of all, the carved names are on top of the pier, not underneath it."

"I was afraid I'd get in trouble if I carved it on top."

"Secondly, this is the pier for the victims of Rita and the other hurricanes." Simple and plain, that was how I said it. Like a fact. Like a bowl of oatmeal.

He looked up, astonished. "Rita?" He paused, thinking. "But I thought it was the pier for the lost."

"No. It's the pier for the victims of hurricanes. But it's a secret now, ain't it, kid."

He thrust his hand back into the water, looking for the knife. Finally, I got up and jumped into the water. It was only three feet deep, and I found it easily and gave it to him.

"Thanks," he said so quietly I almost didn't catch it. "Fox Boy," he added. I smiled again and took his knife from him. I held it up to the old, weathered wood.

"How old was he? What was his name?" I readied the knife in my sturdy fingers, waiting to hear his voice behind me.

"Seventeen. Ollie." When the kid said that, I had to hold back a tear. (This is embarrassing. But I promised to tell you exactly what happened. Possibly, you think I'm a wuss.)

I stepped back to look at what I had carved. The kid ignored me until I blurted, "Kid?" I turned to him. He was sitting in the canoe, his feet drawn up, and he was looking away from me, off to the sea.

"Yeah?" his voice was shaky, his eyes fixed on the Gulf of Mexico.

"Do the Fox Boy a favor, will you? He has to watch over the secrets. He is their keeper and he needs you to do something for him." I wondered why I stood there, thigh deep in the ocean, bargaining with a kid I had never seen before in my life but yet...yet I felt a tug, a tug of some other nature.

"What?" he said, hope rising in his sad tone. Turning, he lifted his eyes from the distant horizon to meet mine.

"That canoe—it belongs to this harbor, right?"

He nodded, his curls moving up and down.

"Leave it here and put it under those bushes. That way, I can use it to look over the secrets. Do you get it?"

He nodded. I pulled myself out of the mud and the cold water and heaved myself up onto the dock. Looking down at the kid again, I saw that he was looking at his dead brother's name. I called down to him: "Kid?"

I heard the small voice. "Yeah....Fox Boy?"

"It's OK to cry. You're sitting in the ocean; it's all saltwater. A tear will not bring another Katrina."

He looked up at me.

I winked, gave him that big smile of mine, and saw his small smile in return.. He did not raise his hand to wipe away the tears flowing down his cheeks.

"It's our secret!" I cried. And then I walked down to the end of the pier, feeling the etched names of the dead beneath my Converses. Getting back on the bike, I pedaled home without a trace of my normal bursting ferocity.

18

I actually did get sick, probably from my ocean plunge, and I did not show my face at school the remainder of that week. If you think getting sick had something to do with my cowardice in dealing with Brook, then you're wrong–well, half wrong.

Scott came by every day to drop a pile of work into my lap and to catch me up on things. He always had a mouthful. What I remember most, though, was when Scott said, "Jaden you have really changed!" His face was serious and his eyes were wide.

"How so?" Honestly, I wanted to know what he meant. We were both sitting on my couch, clicking through channels, which were all just flickering, buzzing static.

"Like your mind is preoccupied with New York—or something. But, you know, even more than before. A lot more. Your preoccupation." He glared at the dysfunctional TV.

I just went quiet, wondering. It wasn't New York that had taken over my thoughts. But I just said, "Yeah, dreaming about pigeon poop in New York." I laughed, feeling the cool sweetness of a good lie roll off my tongue.

He laughed.

19

Then it came. Homecoming. Like a crashing storm on our roof, it was unwelcome.

I managed to find my suit and tie from the year before. I went downstairs and walked toward the door, with my mom snapping away on the camera, taking a shot of me as I breathed each breath. After many—too many—Mom-is-misty-eyed-because-her-baby-is-growing-up-too-fast kind of moments, she was finally done.

"Have a wonderful time, honey."

I was already out the door. The suit was tight in the shoulders. I had grown some.

"Jaden?"

I turned and there she was in the doorway, still in her work clothes.

"Yeah, Mom?" I asked, annoyed. I didn't have time to waste.

She looked around, trying to collect her thoughts about something that obviously bothered her. But then she just shook her head, seeming to dismiss whatever it was.

"Have fun tonight." She smiled pleasantly and waved.

I wondered only briefly what was on her mind. Things that go unsaid often catch my attention the most. But I had to go, so I tucked the thought away.

"Thanks," I managed to grumble, and I ran to the car waiting in the driveway, an old, beat-up sedan, filled with four guys from lacrosse. I had tried to convince Granny to let Scott to come with me, but he was still grounded and would not let him out of the house.

It's a good thing I have a lenient mom and older junior and senior friends with cars. That's what happens when you're good-looking and popular. Guys like me are lucky.

I jumped into the back seat and gave a wave to my mom. Then we sped away. One of the older guys, a big dude, named Joe, handed me a beer.

"Drink up, Miller. Tonight we're going to party!" he shouted. He was so tall his head hit the ceiling as we bumped along the deteriorating road.

I took it, of course. I thought about my visit to the police station and about those horror films they had showed us the previous year in health class. All about driving under the influence. But I wasn't driving, Bryce was, and we could count on him to be designated driver. I could feel the dare in Joe's voice. I popped the lid and chugged it.

To be honest with you, homecoming was more than awesome: it was wild! It got out of control fast. It was as though we were a mob, swelling with power and size and strength. The poor teachers and chaperoning parents were ineffective. All they could do was block the exits. The DJ took every one in the auditorium on a ride. The time passed so fast, I seemed to take in things only off and on throughout the night, like a strobe light. I might have been drunk again, or maybe it was just the music and the pack of girls shimmying up against me.

At the stroke of midnight, the lights flickered on and the mood was killed. It felt as though only seconds had passed since we first took the dance floor. We were quickly ushered out of the auditorium.

Then came the after-party. We stepped into the cool air; around us was a blanket of darkness. All of us, guys and girls, felt invincible. Our lives would go on forever. Nothing could touch us. We were the royalty of the earth. We would not walk or run: we would dance upon it.

Off we went, dancing through the night. Soon we were stationed on the football field, way back in the corner, so as not to be heard or seen. One of the basketball guys had brought an elaborate speaker system with him and set it up on the turf. He plugged in his phone and blasted his playlist. We danced around that thing for hours. We revolved around the music as if we were planets moving around the sun, the sweet music propelling us along.

"Brook!" I yelled and lunged for her in the swaying bodies around us. She was dancing in a pack of basketball guys. My jealousy got the better of me. I could not stop thinking, *She's my girl! Get your hands off her!* And so I somehow pulled her out from the swarm, but I missed and my hand fell on a guy's leg. He grabbed it and shouted furiously at me for breaking some sort of bro code.

"Hands to yourself, Miller!" Oh man. He recognized me. He then tossed me back, and I landed on my butt on the grass.

A girl smiled and stuck her phone in my face. "Cheese!"

I made my best I-hope-you-die-and-go-to-hell face, and then I was back on my feet. I lunged into the wolf pack. Somehow, in my delirious state, I was in an *Animal Planet* episode. The only reliable channels in Duncan are the news, ,some sort of cooking channel—which I try to avoid, and Discovery Channel. In this particular episode, a large pack of timber wolves were circling and trying to take down a graceful, panic-stricken elk. So for some reason my brain thought of the boys as wolves and Brook as the elk. They were circling her, getting ready for the kill.

I wove my way through the masses and made it to the epicenter of kids. There, with every momentarily emboldened guy rubbing up against her, was Brook. She was enjoying being the center of the universe. *Who knows, maybe she is.* I grabbed for her hand, crying out through the shouting voices and blaring hard rock music.

"Brook!" She kept her head down and her arms in the air, dancing. She had not heard me. I tried again.

"Brook!" That was when I saw a guy, Tyson, reach down Brook's backside, his hands sliding to her ass. I'm sure at that moment my eyes would have been a thousand miles wide and twenty million miles deep. Deep with outrage.

I freaked. I lunged, grabbing her small shoulders. I lost my footing. We crashed down onto the muddy, grassy field.

"Jaden!" was her first word to me. She rolled in the mud, a circle of spectators trapping us as I struggled to get up on my hands and knees. We both fumbled there on the ground, recovering, trying to find our sanity and our feet. She looked at her fluffy pink dress, covered in mud and grass. Little bits of earth were in her golden curls.

"Jaden!" she shrieked in such red-hot anger that the people around us could hear it over the blaring music. The wall of spectators grew bigger.

I just stared back at her sheepishly, mouthing, *Sorry.* She screamed at me again and then I saw hands. Male hands. Reaching for her to pull her up and away from me. I lunged, grabbed her shoulders, and I yelled so loudly I knew she could hear me.

"The wolves!" I gasped, the air sucking me dry.

Someone turned off the music.

She just stared at me, no doubt thinking I was insane. "What are you doing, Jaden?" she cried. Flicking my grip from her, she shook her head again and more seriously this time said, "What are you doing, Jaden?" Then the hungry timber wolves picked her up, and she disappeared somewhere into the pack.

I plunged my forehead into the grass and mumbled under my breath, "The wolves."

But it was already too late.

The other guys picked me up and tossed me off the makeshift dance floor. One gave me a good smack in the jaw. Good enough to make my face bleed all over the place. I just fell back to the ground, and I think I fell asleep, falling out of the rotation of the planets, a slave to gravity.

20

When I woke up, I was lying peacefully on the field in the dark. It was warm and the crickets were chirping up a storm. Their song seemed to be in combat with the ringing in my ears. I moved my eyes around in their tired sockets and surveyed a field with crushed grass, mud, and party leftovers: cans, ribbons, bags, bottles, and just plain old trash. It must have been early in the morning, maybe 2 or 3 a.m. A nearly full moon hung over the black silhouettes of trees. The sky was a deep purple-black, and the sparkling stars looked like a spectacular Christmas light show. A swarm of fireflies flickered their yellow bulbs off and on, off and on, as they floated over the open field. It seemed as though fireflies and stars were fighting for space in the night sky. I smiled. Lying there on the field, I was surprisingly content.

Then she was there. Her face was there. An angel's face. Fireflies landing in her hair, she looked as though she were a part of the heavens. Her arching eyebrows knitted in a look of concern. She looked into my eyes and seemed confused by the fact that they were wide open. As though she expected me to be asleep or dead. Her tender hand reached to my face. I stayed still as her hand felt my forehead—for a fever, I guess. Her hand was warm and soft, like the touch of a feather.

I reached out and grabbed her hand, trying to be gentle. I held it up to the moonlight, examining the front and back, and then I turned to her exquisite face staring right back at me. She looked a little scared, so I let go of her hand. Her face was lit up by the moonlight, and tiny strands of her hair shone in the light.

"Who are you?" It came out sounding weak and lame but took every ounce of courage I had.

She put her finger to her lips and said, *Shh!* So I closed my eyes and fell back into my mind.

The second time I woke up, it was nearly sunrise. I peeled myself off the soft earth, stood up, and stretched. My limbs screamed at me to lie back down. But knowing that my mom was probably freaking out about the lateness of the hour, I forced myself to stay upright.

I stood there gazing over the field. Pink rays began to paint the horizon. There was no sign of fireflies, stars, or the girl. I reached for my jaw, which was throbbing. My nose hurt, too. Man, I was sore: my face was sore and my mind was sore. I had drunk only one beer, and that had been in the car on the way to the dance, so I couldn't be hung over. *So why was last night such a blur? Did someone spike the punch at the dance? Anyway, I'm 99 percent certain Bloody Hands was right here, next to me.*

I was pretty sure that her presence had not been a dream. But all I knew for sure was that my face had to be covered in bruises where that asshole had hit me. My knuckles were sore and I noticed that my hands were covered in dried blood. *I hope I punched the snot out of that kid.*

21

I spent the rest of that weekend hanging out with Scott and his grandma. We went on a fishing trip, and it offered some diversion from my obsession with Bloody Hands. But even as I sat in the boat, my mind drifted away like my fishing float. When I got a bite, it took a lot of effort to reel it in.

By Monday, I was so overwhelmed with the thought of makeup work from the week before that I glared gloomily at Miss Carlson when she handed me a packet of papers. She handled it as though it were a precious newborn, and I handled it as though it were a bag of dog poop.

"Feeling better?" she asked in her metallic voice. But we both knew she did not care at all if I had a life-threatening disease or if my cat had died. She did not want to hear whatever excuse I had, real or not.

So I just mumbled, "Yeah."

I turned and walked back to my desk. I slapped the dog poop on my desk and lowered myself into my chair, slipping off my backpack. I got out a pencil and began to tap it furiously on the desk. Then Miss Carlson hauled her fat ass out of her chair and began to address the class. Today's lesson was something about Charles Dickens.

However, I spotted something much better than that illustrious author. I saw that *she* was sitting in her seat beside me. I pretended to be looking up at the board while my peripheral vision was locked on her. She was wearing the same clothes. She was a gorgeous angel, dressed as a dumpster diver. No matter what Bloody Hands wore, she would still be gorgeous. As Miss Carlson nattered on happily about *Great Expectations*, I decided to try something new.

I tore a piece of binder paper from my notebook and quickly wrote down what had been itching at the back of my mind. I looked at my illegible handwriting. *Drat!* I stuffed the paper into my pack and tried again, more slowly. This time, I made it neat.

Hey, my name is Jaden. What's your name? Who are you? Why do you always seem to disappear?

I paused, my mind running wild. But instead of writing something moronic, I forced myself to put the pencil down, fold the paper in half, and wait. I waited until Miss Carlson had to reach up on tiptoes to scribble something high on the whiteboard. And then I lunged to the side and placed the note on Bloody Hands' desk.

I quickly retreated. She looked so surprised, you would have thought my hand were made of octopus tentacles. She gave me a quick sideways glance. I read in her eyes that she was more surprised than anything else, shocked really. And then very tentatively, I mean agonizingly slowly, she reached a hand out to the folded paper sitting on her desk. Using her index finger, slowly, turtle-slowly, she moved it over to her other hand at the edge of her desk.

That was when I realized that I was staring at her as if under a spell, and I forced my eyes away from her. Finally, after glaring at the jiggling backside of Miss Carlson for two agonizing minutes, I turned to Bloody Hands.

She was reading it carefully. I watched those purple-blue eyes scan the note maybe five different times. A century had gone by; I now had gray hair. She placed it back on the desk very carefully, as though at any moment it would explode and burn her hands. Very slowly, she looked up at me, and it took my breath away.

Then the world collapsed as I heard a metallic voice pluck me out of the crowd.

"Jaden, in what year was Charles Dickens born?"

My bubble of solitude in the back of the class had been popped. I swear, of all moments to call on me...

"What was the question?"

Miss Carlson smiled. She took joy in tormenting her stupid jock students. "You heard me, Jaden." She said it coolly and leaned against the board. I cursed mentally. This woman could and would take up this entire precious hour—my only chance to be in the same room with Bloody Hands. Put Miss Carlson in the ring with a bull, and the bull would run away with his tail between his legs.

"1000 BCE," I said and smiled. I was no scared bull.

Miss Carlson just smiled with a tightly closed mouth, concealing the fangs, but I could feel her venom.

"Jaden. Oh, Jaden. I'm afraid that's not the correct answer." She paused, taking her time. "I'm afraid that you need to see me after school. You will spend two hours researching the life of Charles Dickens." The class fidgeted in their seats. A few students smirked and then it seemed as though everyone was smirking. Well, everyone except Scott. He was staring at Brook's tank top. I cursed silently and Miss Carlson went back to her lesson.

I turned to look at Bloody Hands. The note was gone and she was sitting there, calm as ever.

Frustrated, I tore out another piece of binder paper and wrote the other thing I really wanted to know, the thing that had been bugging me since the beginning of time, even, I would say, since 1000 BCE:

Why are your hands always cut and scabbed?

And then I handed the note to her and waited, itching like mad in my seat, staring at her until she opened it and read it.

But this time her eyebrows knitted in confusion. Feeling like an idiot, I realized she could not read the damn thing. I ripped out another sheet of paper and began to rewrite it, this time with painstaking handwriting. But then the bell rang. And when I raised my head, she had vanished. Again.

22

Scott, could you pass me that can over there?" Scott handed me the Dr Pepper. I was about to pop it open when the kid in line next to me muttered something to his friend. The friend looked up at me.

"Eww it's Jaden," squealed a girl I didn't know as she got in line behind me.

"Scott, what the hell is going on?"

He swallowed and looked at me, confused. Then, like a sluggish computer, it registered. "Oh yeah, apparently Brook and a few dudes are spreading a rumor that you attacked her on the football field at homecoming. Don't worry, man, this stuff will die down if you give it a few days."

We went to find a place to sit and I swear, every eye glanced my way. Then a junior from the lacrosse team crumpled the wrapper from his sandwich and threw it at the back of my head as we walked across the room.

"Ignore them, Jaden, they're just a bunch of idiots."

We walked up to our usual table and Jordan, who was stabbing a slab of mystery meat, looked up at me, "Sorry Jaden, that seat's taken. We don't dine with molesters." As I turned to leave, I caught Brook's eyes. She was slowly sucking chocolate milk from a straw. She looked self-satisfied, like a cat licking her paws after killing a mouse.

"It will blow over soon," said Scott as we headed outside. *More like weeks.* Brook would be slow to give up on a juicy topic. She had jawed about the incident regarding old man Barley's shed for almost a month, using the story as propaganda to reinforce her status as a cool chick—the coolest. But this incident was even better: Brook Jackson, the coolest chick, had been attacked by Jaden Miller, the superstar athlete. Her popularity would soar to new heights..

All I could think was, *Let her have her fifteen minutes—or maybe fifteen weeks—of fame.* Trust me, it meant little or nothing. Besides, I had my mind wrapped around someone else, who, to be honest, I was falling for.

But in those weeks after my first attempt to communicate with her, she did not show up to class. And the more I realized how little I knew about her, the more I wanted to know.

As a matter of fact, I was so preoccupied with homework, lacrosse, and the new mystery girl, I completely spaced on calling my dad. Weeks passed between calls.

I was out in the backyard, doing something resembling nothing: trying to fling my pencil into Flower's birdbath. I had finally hit my target, and at the same time I heard our old-fashioned telephone ring like mad back in the house. I heard my mom shout from a plot of periwinkles, "Jaden! Honey, that's probably your father. Can you go pick it up?"

"'Kay!" I shouted back at her, and then I collected my stuff, trotted into the kitchen, and picked up the phone.

"'Ello?"

"Jaden! My boy, how's it going! How was homecoming! Your mother told me you broke your curfew, and she pushed the end date of your house arrest even further down the line!"

"First, Mom totally forgot about my house arrest. Second, I kind of fell asleep on the football field at the homecoming after-party. She was pissed about that, and now my curfew is 9 p.m." It bugs me how Mom and Dad refer to each other as "your mother" or "your father." It's just a reminder that I'm the only thing holding them together.

"Wow!" He sounded happy. He was probably leaning over his desk, holding the phone and pressing it to his ear. "That sounds like a chip off the old block! So who was it? Did you use birth control?"

"What! No! Nothing like that! Dad, that's an invasion of privacy, please!" I was sickened to be having this conversation with my dad.

All he did was laugh hysterically over the line. "Well, it's good to hear you're still a virgin."

There was a long pause, and I was getting ready to say good-bye, but then he said something I didn't quite hear. "What was that, Dad?" I looked out the window.

"Jaden, seriously, I'm worried about you. Your mother said that she's heard rumors that you assaulted that girl Brook Jackson. She said that you're doing poorly in all your classes. And you've been acting oddly and somewhat detached. What's going on, son?" His voice spilled from the phone, and his honesty stabbed me right where it hurt.

I froze.

"Jaden?"

Then I snapped back. "Dad, it's not true! I barely laid a finger on Brook Jackson. I was trying to save her from a pack of drunken guys. And I haven't been acting strangely at all!" I was shouting. Anger boiled in my lungs and spurted like hot lava from my tongue and into the phone.

"I figured that it was something like that, Jaden. I know you would never hurt someone. And I don't actually care what the people of Duncan might think about you. But you *have* been acting strangely."

"You're in New York!" I was really yelling now.

"Cool it, son. I'm just concerned, is all." He said it really quietly, trying to calm me down. It backfired, however.

"Dad, just butt out of my life, OK? I don't need you or Mom, and I don't need the kids at Hampton High...." I paused, thinking of the one thing that I needed. "I need answers."

"What? What are you talking about, Jaden?"

I slammed the phone down on the receiver and sprinted outside to the tree house. I wanted to be alone to cool off. But as I passed my mom, crouching in her flower beds, she called to me: "Jaden, what did he say? Is it snowing in New York?"

Snowing? In October? "Leave me alone, Mom!" I yelled. Wow, now that I think about it, you must think I'm bipolar.

She yelled something back to me, but I couldn't hear it because I was slamming the hatch door of the tree house. I walked to the hammock and sat down, running my hands through my shaggy hair. Looking at my skyline posters, my miniature replicas of Lady Liberty and the Empire State Building, and my many other lamebrain, touristy New York things somehow made me feel slightly better.

I was grateful that my mom did not come pester me; she knew when to let me be by myself. I tossed an old snow globe of the Empire State Building up into the air as I lay there, thinking. I watched a snow flurry envelop the famous edifice and then fall to the ground.

I need answers. First of all, what does Dad mean that I'm acting strangely? I'm not, for crying out loud! It's just that, thanks to Brook, the whole town thinks I'm twisted. And the most beautiful girl on the planet doesn't seem to exist. Who is Bloody Hands? What is her name? Where does she go? Is she hiding? What is she hiding from? Why are her hands always so damn bloody?

And Madam Marian, you crazy freak, who is going to die? Who?

Man, the list was long and unanswerable. After maybe two hours, I heard a knock on the hatch door.

"Done with the testosterone tantrum? Because dinner's on the table."

"Coming," was all I managed. I climbed back down and headed to the kitchen, where Mom and I ate in complete zombie silence. Eventually, I couldn't stand the silence any longer, so I said, "Mom. How's Flower?"

She seemed lost in thought. "Who?"

Stuffing my mouth with rice, I said, "You know, Flower, the mourning dove, in the flowerpot?"

And then a light bulb flickered on. "Oh, Flower! She's fine. Sings to me all morning long."

Flower was my peace offering and she accepted it. She began telling me about her plans for the garden. I was all ears and no mouth.

23

I was so lost in my search for answers that I did not realize that it was Halloween.

Scott came to my house after dinner. I was up in my room knocking out geometry. Sort of.

"Hey, Mrs. Miller, is Jaden in his room?"

"Well, hi, Scott. Nice costume! Yeah, up in his room."

And then I couldn't miss my mom shouting, "Jaden! Scott's here. He's brought you a costume to wear!"

I put down my pencil and looked up from the textbook. I had just been adding a new doodle to its pages: Army guys shooting each other. The word "costume" had me thinking, *Huh? A*nd then Scott the mighty stepped in.

"Hey, man, how does this look?" He said it with such joy. I couldn't see his face because he was wearing some swamp man outfit. He was covered head to toe in leaves and fake moss. He looked like a bush.

"It's a ghillie suit. I made it myself."

"Wow, Scott. I see that the bayou is your friend." My eyebrows were hitting the ceiling, for it was an impressive costume.

"Yeah, you can laugh all you want, but first, here you go." He tossed me a brown shopping bag. I caught it midflight, looked inside, and pulled out...a pink dress, full of ruffles.

"Seriously, man?"

"You like? Found it at the thrift store. It should be just your size," Scott said and chuckled through his pile of bayou.

"I'm not getting in that thing. Hell, no. What are the costumes for anyway? Is this some bloody trick?"

"Dude, hello, have you not registered the pumpkins, scarecrows, and cobwebs? Cinderella, it's Halloween night." He smiled. I couldn't see it but I could picture it perfectly.

"What?"

"Yeah, Jaden, it's trick-or-treating time."

"Scott, we are both fifteen years old and in our sophomore year of high school. I'm not—no matter how you might try to drag me out there—going trick or treating."

"Cinderella, don't be blonde. Look at the rest of your costume." He motioned to the bag at my feet.

So then I pulled the pink pile of dress all the way out, and there at the bottom of the bag was a plastic, but seriously psycho-looking, raptor mask. I was thinking, *Perfecto. A predatory dinosaur.* Suddenly, I saw the genius in Scott's wardrobe selection. Plus, due to my lack of planning, it was this costume or nothing.

"I love you, man."

"OK, Cinderella, let's go scare some kids out of their freaking minds."

I felt ridiculous in that pink dress, but at least no one would know it was me. We waited until after dark, about 9 p.m. By then, all the little kids were tucked away, the middle schoolers were out and about on the streets, and some ticked-off adults were still giving out candy. So we figured we had a good solid hour to scare some middle schoolers out of their minds.

We waited at a busy intersection, where lots of kids were walking back and forth. We were on a steep incline, with the bayou swamp about twelve feet below us. The slope was lightly scattered with bushes, and I was halfway up the incline in a tree whose branches hung over the road. As the street got quieter and quieter, we heard our first victims coming around the south-facing corner. I eyed them: middle school boys. Perfect.

They were headed our way, and I could hear their cocky, pride-filled voices. Middle schoolers always seem to think they own the world, because they have no clue yet what the world is about. These boys, still stuck in kids' bodies, tried to make up for that fact by being complete idiots. It was up to us to show them their rightful place in the food chain.

As they neared, I heard some of what they said: nothing important. As they got ever closer, with their pride-stride thing going, I gave the signal, a low call: "*Whooouuuooo, who, who, who.*"

Scott, who knew the signal, did not call back. We had gone over this a few years earlier. Trust me, he could not, and I mean *not*, mimic the mourning dove song at all. His singing voice sounded like a walrus that just got run over. You'd think that a musical guy would have a better voice. An adequate voice. It had been pitiful to see him in September attempt to sing onstage during *Macbeth*. Man, *Macbeth* seemed as though it were eons ago.

Well, I guess the boys heard me because they turned. The ringleader, in the Dracula outfit, began to say something. "Watch this, you guys," he instructed. He seemed to punch the nearest kid on the shoulder, the playful way, and then he tried to call in mourning dove: *"Yooouuu, who, who, who."*

Wearing my raptor mask, I smiled from up in the tree. I sang again to him and he sang back. I heard one of them say, "Dude, you're an owl whisperer."

The ringleader seemed to get a bang out of that, and he sang to me again: *"Yooouuu, who, who, who?"*

And then I waited, letting the silence speak. It wasn't until I heard their feet shift nervously that I answered: "Me."

Then simultaneously, Scott and I growled a deep, piercing lion's roar. He jumped out of the bushes. He had been standing right there the entire time, camouflaged by his awesome swamp man suit!

Scott, my man. He grabbed Dracula's shoulders, and the kid screamed for all he was worth. I then jumped into the group from above, and that was pure terror. Imagine it: a massive velociraptor princess falling on top of them from nowhere.

I growled an awesome, convincing growl. The boys' machismo had vanished, and their voices were now high-pitched, girlish cries. They took off running as fast as they could, and we gave chase. It was priceless.

But we cut the chase short, for one of the little idiots had dropped his bag of loot. We grabbed it and jumped back into a bush as Scott shone his phone into the bag. We both feasted.

We were cracking up. I ,smiled at Scott as I stuffed my face with a Snickers Bar, and we high-fived each other.

"Yeah, man, that's what I call a scare!"

"No kidding. Someone's having nightmares tonight," I said and laughed.

"That was golden. The bird thing."

I shrugged in the darkness. Smiled and shrugged the kind of shrug that means, *What can I say*.

24

Hey, let's go down to the pier," Scott said. "I heard there's a party going on there." Then I heard the sound of munching. I hoped he wasn't eating all the M&M's; those were my favorite.

I paused, my Snickers Bar halfway in its journey to my mouth. I could not help but remember homecoming and Brook. She was nowhere near accepting me back as a wannabe boyfriend anytime soon. Whatever. It was just so nice not having her breathe down my neck every five seconds.

Part of the fallout from the homecoming thing was that most everyone left me alone, like a punishment or something. No one wanted to talk to Jaden Miller, the attacker. Then that title had been replaced by another: the freak.

That was OK. It was actually rather nice not to have to live up to good-looking jock standards anymore. I'd broken free of those impossible expectations and was free to run around like the madman I was. I didn't care what people thought. When I saw them stare at me, I found that if I just kept my head down and focused on my mission, life was somewhat bearable. The only thing in life that mattered anymore was to discover the identity of the girl with the bloody hands.

Yeah, you're probably thinking I should have a new title: Jaden Miller, the stalker. Man, there is something wrong with me, isn't there? I'm head over heels for a girl every other person on the planet ignores.

25

As Scott led the way to the party, that was what was running through my head, more or less. And then we turned the bend, and there on the pier was a pack of Hampton High kids.

I took a deep breath and entered the scene: music blaring, people shouting, and that nauseating smell of alcohol. My throat burned as Scott dragged me through the crowd. Finally, we reached the epicenter of swaying bodies. As they moved to the music, people shouted to us, "Hey!" and "Here," and then someone handed me a plastic cup of who knows what.

"No, thanks, man," I said. Apparently, no one cared tonight that I was the attacker or the weirdo. Maybe they didn't recognize me in the raptor head, or maybe they had moved on to other teenage concerns.

I continued to shake my head whenever some guy would hand me a beverage, and then finally, after maybe the third time, I took the drink. But I just held it and didn't take one sip. Scott, who was already downing his third glass, gave me a deep smirk.

"Dude! It's Halloween!"

"Yeah, I know. I'm going to go check on something. Be right back."

But he was already shrugging me off, disappearing into the pack of bodies. I sniffed the contents of my plastic cup. Whatever the strange red punch was, I wasn't going to try it. I had heard too many horror stories about punch spiked with drugs or the type of alcohol you can't taste or smell. Trust me, I was not going there. So I set it down safely, out of the way of dancing feet. That was when I saw her name etched into one of the boards of the pier:

Hazel Washington.

Scott's mom.

That made me sad. I got up and saw that the tide had to be high, because most of the pier was above water, not above mud. So I threw my legs over the side of the pier, took off my shoes, and then jumped down below.

It was quite surprising when I dropped down into the knee-high water. The party right above my head suddenly seemed distant. As I walked along the base of the pier toward shore, I heard, and then saw, a few kids making out in the dark recesses of the pier's pillars where it met dry sand. I shook my head, trying to escape that noise of kissing and more. *Get a room, people.*

Well, I walked off. I slogged through the shallow water, and my bare feet sank deep into the muck, getting my pink dress all muddy. *What a shame.* I walked to the edge of the bayou, marked by massive trees dripping with old-man's beard moss. They were the kind of trees you see on *Scooby-Doo*, the monster kind. Finally, the sinking and sucking sounds that I made in the mud ceased as I made it to the forest edge and solid ground. I continued walking along.

I saw it, surrounded by sea-blown grass. If I hadn't been looking for it, I would have walked right on by.

It was the red canoe. Seeing that familiar object made me relax a bit, despite the ominous-seeming area in which I found myself. After a while, I had had enough, so I began making my way back toward the pier and the road home. It was slow going because of the mud and my mood.

I passed the dead-end trail that led to an old wooden structure that was in no better shape than old man Barley's shed and that was sinking into the earth like Madam Marian's Stop-N-Shop. It was an ancient fisherman's shed, filled with nets and ropes and, you know, fisherman's stuff. As I passed the shed, I heard male voices.

I walked up to the shed, toward the voices, which were low and muffled inside the mossy walls. I was trying and failing to be quiet as a mouse. Where did that come from? That idiom, "quiet as a mouse"? Mice, for-your-information, are quite loud when they run behind walls and over roofs. I put my ear to the rough surface of the wood.

"...Old man Barley's shed...He kept slaves there."

"What? Old man Barley! No, you got it all wrong."

"No, for sure! When Connor Ordinal did it. He said he heard two voices inside the shed. Two!"

These kids were deep in an intense conversation about a subject that was commonly discussed by the kids in this town: the tragedies and the mysteries of Duncan.

"That's bull, Jake."

"No! Listen, Connor said he heard two: a man and a young girl, like eight or so. It was several years ago. I swear it!" Jake sounded panicked.

"How do you know it was a slave?"

There was a long pause. Then Jake said, "Because what would a girl be doing in there? Come on, guys, think. A young girl in the middle of the bayou in a creepy old shed with a creepy old man? She must have been a prisoner, a slave."

I could imagine their pinhead brains contemplating that for a moment. I was bored with the story and the night. I began to walk off but tripped over the damn dress and fell into the mud.

As I pulled myself out, I made a sound like I imagine an octopus would make while detaching itself from a rock, that kind of suction sound. As I got to my feet, the four kids in the shed came pouring out.

"Who are you? And what are you wearing?" said the guy at the open door. He had a deep African-American voice that sounded like drums in the night air. That guy, Tyrone, should get a job as a news broadcaster or something.

Jake muttered something, but I couldn't hear it in the background.

"Shut up, Jake! It's Jaden Miller. Let me in, OK?" I called out.

"Jaden? Dude, you scared us half to death!" That had to have been Tyrone speaking.

I shrugged and took off my raptor mask. Now I was embarrassed. I was wearing a really stupid outfit. How had I let Scott talk me into wearing it?

I stepped inside a small, moldy-smelling, dark room. The guys' faces were lit up by their phones, which cast shadows upward, making them look even uglier and freakier than usual. It was Jake, Tyrone, Riley, and Billy, the kid from English.

We sat down in a circle. I had a T-shirt and swim trunks on underneath the pile of pink. I managed to crawl out of the dress but not without ripping some ruffles off. I flung the thing out the window into the bushes. The guys around me were silent. Finally, Tyrone spoke up.

"What were you thinking, Miller?"

"Thinking? About what?" I said cautiously. Tyrone had a good set of muscles on him and he wrestled, so he would have been the wrong guy to mess with.

"You know what I'm saying, Miller. You know." His deep voice sounded eerie in the darkness. I couldn't see his face, only the whites of his eyes.

"Old man Barley's shed?" I finally asked.

"That's it." He said it contentedly. That was good, because I liked Tyrone content. I could see the other guys lean in. I was a living legend because I had been inside the shed and survived. Now I had to tell the tale.

"What was it like inside the shed? Were there bones?"

I thought that was Billy talking, but I couldn't be sure.

"Yes." I breathed shallowly, for the shed stank.

"Gross things?" The voice was timid and awestruck.

"Yes." The shed smelled to high heaven, making me wonder if there was a dead possum in there.

"Slaves?" He was shouting. It must be Jake.

I thought back to the rose and note on the stool. I began to sweat. I was terrified of the rose. Good thing for the darkness, or they might have seen Coward written all over my face.

"No slaves," I said.

What followed was a long period of silence, and then Jake, who had been quiet for a few minutes, finally spoke up.

"Brook Jackson is telling everyone what you said that night." He said it in a dead serious way, as though he would pry the truth from me, no matter what.

"What did I say?" I was confused, honestly forgetting what we had said on that boat. It had been almost two months earlier, that night in the bayou.

"You know."

I could not see where he was, but I could hear the creaking of the floor as he shifted his monumental weight to lean forward. All the others in the room went deathly silent; even their breathing seemed to cease. I turned to Jake again, or at least the area where I thought he might be.

"Honest. I have no idea what you're talking about." My voice was cool but edged with caution. *Where is this going?* And then all at once each one began to say it, tossing the letters back and forth between them:

"D."

"U."

"N."

"C."

I kept turning my head between them as they spelled the name of the unspeakable.

"A."

"N."

"S."

"H."

"I."

"P."

"Y."

"A."

"R."

"D."

I paused for a moment, trying to recall the foggy events of the night with Brook and Scott, and then it dawned on me.

"Now you know," said Jake in a voice that was quiet but brimming with excitement.

"Yes, I know. The Duncan Shipyard." I had said the unspeakable. It was the second time in my lifetime.

Billy Beckham got off his fat ass in the darkness and bolted to what was a wall. With his bulk and his momentum, he crashed right through the wall and rolled out into the night, letting moonlight shine in. He made a beeline to the party, screaming like an idiot.

Tyrone just gave me a *I can't believe you just said that* look, and then he, too took off. He exited through the door, not the wall.

And then it was just Jake and me. Oh yes, and Riley. He sat paralyzed in the corner. I had totally forgotten about that guy.

Jake, the bravest, said something in a low, chopped voice. He sounded shocked and horrified and pretty much amazed at me. "You have guts, Miller, real guts to say that." His voice felt like ice.

"I'm not scared of a fairy tale," I said coolly as well.

"You should be. You damn well should be," he said with honest concern.

"Doesn't matter. I did it. I said the name. Send me to hell for all I care, because frankly, I'm already in it." That was honest, too.

I felt good and powerful suddenly because I had just said two unspeakable things.

"You don't understand, do you?" he said. Trying to break my bravado and get me to admit fear.

"I guess not."

I sounded like a badass.

26

"D.u.n.c.a.n S.h.i.p.y.a.r.d is no legend. It's real. Haven't you heard the story?"

"Of course." I had heard the story so many times I could have recited it forward and backward. In fact, I had used it to scare my cousins on many a sleepover. The tale of the Duncan Shipyard symbolizes our town much better than the old man Barley thing.

But Jake couldn't resist telling it again, and so he began:

"At the beginning of the Civil War, the three Duncan brothers, who were conscripts in the Confederate army, escaped from their regiment and traveled through the swamps for days on end, until they reached the ocean. From there, they traveled along the coast for three nights and four days until they arrived here.

"Two of the Duncan brothers, Marcus and Hampton, were normal. They settled down, building small farms. They cleared the swampy vegetation away, plowed the fields, and harvested their crops. They married and started families.

"More and more people came here to escape the war, and the town came to be called Duncan.

"But there was a third brother, weaker in both brain and body. It is said that while he was being born, his umbilical cord had gotten wrapped around his neck and cut off his oxygen.

"He was jealous of his two prosperous siblings. And whenever he came into town, the people would chase him off. He became socially isolated, and, lore has it, the alligators took him in as one of their own.

"Eventually, after wondering the bayou for months, he found the perfect home: five rusty steamboats, beached and abandoned. The ships formed a perfect circle in the mud, and a colony of plants was beginning to cover them. It is said the names of the ships were *Justice*, *Bounty*, *Devotion*, *Mercy*, and *Courage*. He lived in these abandoned ships and trapped animals, which he would sometimes eat and sometimes just torture.

"As the years went on, he grew more and more crazed, wandering around at night, calling to everyone who walked by."

Jake was enjoying this; his voice was slow and haunted. Though the story was familiar, it raised the hair on the back of my neck. He continued:

"Livestock began to disappear. Pets began to disappear. A pregnant woman was attacked on the road while she was in labor, trying to reach Duncan. She said a wild creature had taken the newborn and run off with it.

"One day, three slaves ran away from a big plantation near New Orleans. These three young men walked along the coast and stumbled upon the D.u.n.c.a.n S.h.i.p.y.a.r.d. They were starving and exhausted and had no other choice but to stay there for the night. And so the men walked into the shipyard and climbed aboard one of the derelict ships.

"When night fell, one of the men asked the others. 'Do you see something moving along the ships over there?' He pointed at the ships on the other side of the inner circle.

"'I see nothing. Shut up and go back to sleep,' said another.

"'It was probably just some animal. No animal in these parts could harm three young, strong men like us,' said the third.

"Anyway, that one worried runaway stayed up. As the night wore on, he thought he saw the moving shadow again, but this time an eerie voice emanated from it: 'Run, run, you'd better run. Hide, hide, you'd better hide.'

"The runaway grabbed whatever he could use as a weapon. He could hear the demon creature coming closer and closer, and without waking the others, the man broke into a run for the edge of the shipyard. He didn't make much progress, however, and his companions woke to the sound of terrified screaming, followed by silence.

"They called and called into the darkness, but their friend did not respond. They searched through the abandoned ships and found blood splattered about, but no man.

"So they immediately regrouped back in their ship. Then they heard what sounded like the cry of a deranged animal echoing off the rusted hulls, but they could not figure out its source.

"'It must be some sort of wild animal,'" said the braver of the two remaining men.

"One of the guys wanted to leave immediately, but the leader, the braver one, made him stay. He believed that staying in the abandoned boat for the night was safer than trying to leave in the darkness. As they desperately needed sleep, his plan was for one to sleep while the other remained on watch.

"He dozed off quickly, while the other, more rattled, slave stood watch. The silence was almost worse than the terrible noises he had heard earlier. He couldn't take it any longer. He knew his sleeping friend would not want to leave until daylight, but he wanted out immediately. So without waking him, he decided to walk as quickly and quietly as he could out of the shipyard. Off the ship and onto the beach he went, but just steps away from escaping the terrible place, he heard a low, menacing voice chanting joyfully in the darkness: 'Run, run, you'd better run. Hide, hide, you'd better hide.'

"Terrified, the man jumped behind a bush and pressed his body against the rusted curved steel of a beached steamboat. A shadow moved in the bushes. Creeping toward him, the creature sang its lullaby: 'Run, run, you'd better run. Hide, hide, you'd better hide.'

"The sleeping man jumped to his feet as he heard his friend holler. It was such a scream that it shook even his sturdy bones.

"He was now alone. Peering through a porthole, the young slave with his first taste of freedom could see only the sky and the silhouettes of the steamboats. The first glow of morning was in the sky, but the deep shadows of the shipyard were as black as ever. Now, even he was terrified. Then he heard it. The sound oozed from every direction at once; it came from every shadow. 'Run, run, you'd better run. Hide, hide, you'd better hide.'

"One horrifying minute later, a scrawny man appeared, a demon. He had crazed blue eyes and yellow, daggerlike teeth. His hair was matted and he had a long gray beard, fit for rodents' nests. He was covered in mud and moss, and he wielded a club embedded with alligator teeth and a rusty dagger.

"The now-not-so-brave slave did not run away or hide but rather froze like a statue in terror. The crazy man took him down with a strength that belied his size and pinned him to the ground. And then the thing raised his dagger and plunged it deep into the young man's stomach."

Jake fell silent as he let me absorb the story. There I was on Halloween night, listening to a creepy story invented by the kids of Duncan to explain the odd steamboats in a circle that were rusting on the edge of the swamp.

I could see little boys and girls tucked away in their sleeping bags listening to the story. Every time I heard the story, the details changed, but I liked Jake's version best. It was universally believed that you would be cursed if you uttered the name of the shipyard out loud.

Jake was about to finish the story, but I did it for him. Like I said, I'd heard the story many, many times.

"And so it is just as it was: the ghost of the crazed third brother lives inside the shipyard, and late at night you can hear the high-pitched wails of the ghosts of the runaway slaves, forever trying to run and hide."

27

Suddenly, I got the chills, the sudden, shaking kind, as if a cold spirit had just walked right through me. Out of nowhere, Riley got up, bolted for the doorway, and ran from the place, as if finally released from a spell. I was right after him, and Jake, after me. I had had enough. That screwball story had crawled into my mind and shoveled out my logic. And now that I could see Jake's face in the moonlight, I could tell that he was equally rattled.

The party was still blazing out on the pier, as if nothing had happened. I turned toward home. My home. Warm blankets, hot chocolate, and a lighthearted movie sounded really good to me right then. I remembered the packet of homework waiting for me on my desk, and that turned my thoughts sour. As Jake turned to look back at me, I yelled, "If you see Scott, tell him I'm going to hit the sack."

"I will, but Jaden, you'd better be careful. You're going to pay someday for speaking the name," he cautioned.

"Maybe. If I believed in ghost stories!" I yelled. But on the inside—never in a million years would I show it—I was shaken. I continued down the dirt road leading to the main road, which would take me to town. Every sound made me jump. It was dark and I was in the swamp by myself. Half an hour into the hike, I heard it.

Distant screams. Human screams? It sounded like a girl or a coyote. Someone screaming as though something were attacking her, ripping her apart. I shook. My heart stopped for a second, and then it was beating a thousand miles an hour. I sprinted home.

28

Life is strange.

You're caught in the river of life. Sometimes it's smooth and slow and boring, and then other times it jostles you around and makes you concentrate hard on just getting through the rapids. But the strangest part is the eddies: those parts that spin you in circles. You get stuck in a circle of confusion, until somehow, by some miracle, you escape and get back into the regular current.

For a few weeks, I had been trapped in an eddy. I was just going round and round and round.

Why?

Not so long before, everything had been on pace: school, sports, and friends. But then I had realized that high school was one big eddy. It was cliché. It was big drama in a small pond. The badass, the jock, the good-looking, and the invisible—we were all swirling around together but going nowhere.

Suddenly, I wasn't sure where I fit in. Was I the ex-jock, the failing student, the freak, or the stalker? I was the only child—lost, pitiful, scared, and lonely—the kid whose dad and mom couldn't even look at each other. The kid who was straddling two worlds and had a long list of unanswered questions.

Not until just after that Halloween night did I break out of the eddy, and then it was free sailing. I decided to let the river take me where it wanted me to go. I was ready for the ride. It could be the mighty Amazon for all I cared. I wasn't going to be any of those people.

Sorry, I get caught up with these things. What I'm trying to spit out is that I decided just to do my own thing. Pave my own path. The advice parents give you but don't ever follow themselves. It takes people decades to figure this out, and by then it's too late; time has eaten up their lives.

But this was where things changed for me.

And this was where things got really weird.

29

The next few weeks were slow and tedious. Everyone was just dying for Thanksgiving break to hurry up and arrive. Somewhere in the middle of that tedium, I, once again, stumbled into English late. Super late, like, twenty minutes that time. You should have seen the death glare Miss Carlson bombed down on me. As I walked in, I said, "The usual" before she could humiliate me with the question. She grumbled as I walked right past her to my desk.

I dropped into my seat, tossing my nearly empty backpack onto the floor. I looked over at Scott, who was a few seats away, under the windows. He had obviously been there a while. No tardy for him; he gave me a shrug, which meant I was going solo to detention. I looked over to my left to see if the girl, the mysterious girl who enchanted and haunted my dreams, had bothered to show up for class.

She was absent. Again. Of course. She was hardly ever there. Like, I mean, ever. Life seemed to just continue on. People living their own little lives, without her. It was as though she didn't exist at all. Then my eyes wandered over to Brook, and of course I caught her staring at me. Her Medusa eyes were turning me to stone in my seat. Talk about petrified wood—I was petrified Jaden.

She had been funny lately. The whole incident of me being labeled a freak had nearly blown over. Brook seemed to be trying to decide whether she should come crawling back to me. As a matter of fact, in flurries of speculating rumors, the whole school seemed to wonder whether she would.

It was funny. Ever since Brook had banned me from the table of cool kids, I'd been a loner. Almost a loner. A few girls, the wannabe, periphery type, had spoken to me. I could see that that still irritated Brook a bit. And Scott? Scott seemed to be onboard with anything I might throw at him. He was loyal that way, I guess.

The banishment thing was pretty tough at first, but once I had nothing to live up to, it was nice that I could focus on getting what I needed most: answers.

That day, as English wore on and on, I stared at the empty seat beside me. Near the end of class was when I saw it: a yellow dandelion, maybe one of the flowers that swarmed the front lawn of the school. Mom loved dandelions, but most students at my school didn't pay any attention to them. This dandelion was clinging by a piece of tape to the bottom of her desktop, and then there was another, on the floor, close to my feet. I dropped my pencil on purpose to pick it up. Then, under my desktop, tucked into the corner and also taped, was another dandelion, hanging there innocently. I picked it up and stared at it. It made no sense whatsoever. But, hey, most everything in my life had stopped making sense.

After school, something weird happened. Well, you know, besides the dandelions; they were weird, too.

I walked into English class, where I would enjoy an hour of detention, and there, stationed at her desk, was Miss Carlson. I walked down my aisle, sat in my usual seat, and slumped down, brooding. I could have been doing ten thousand things more interesting than sitting in that seat. Lacrosse practice, for instance. I just looked back and forth from the clock to the teacher until we had only thirty-five minutes left together.

Miss Carlson got up from her chair, still holding her book, which was open in the middle. She gazed out the window. I looked out the window as well; there was nothing going on inside the classroom, just one big, fat fly buzzing in the void of silence that separated the two of us. She looked down at her book.

"You have a D in every class except creative writing and PE," she announced. She sounded ticked off. It was true; I hated every class except creative writing and PE. I especially hated English. Don't get me wrong: I didn't hate stories. I liked stories as much as I liked New York City, or my cat, Pip, or lacrosse. I liked a story where the reader doesn't know what's going to happen. I liked a story that would answer the questions you might never have thought to ask.

"Yeah," I said flatly. Miss Carlson seemed to be thrown for a loop. She was the kind of teacher who didn't know you had any potential.

"Why is that, Jaden?"

She still had her nose in the book; she couldn't even be bothered to look me in the eye. *Stupid lady.* "I don't know."

"Do you like school, Jaden?"

"I like writing. I'm pretty fast on the keyboard and I like stories." Simple, honest truth.

"Really?" Her eyebrows shot up and she turned a page in her book. "Then why, may I ask, are you sitting here?"

Good question, Miss Carlson. I could ask you the same thing. I eyed her. She was cornered in her own thoughts, and I loved watching her try to escape that corner she had trapped herself in.

"Because you gave me detention." *Duh. Is she stupid?* I glanced at the clock. *Fifteen more minutes and then I'm outta here.*

"No, that's not what I mean. Why are you sitting here and not writing me a story?" Miss Carlson put down her book and looked at me as if considering me for the first time.

I felt the anger pulse through my veins. Was I really going to sit there and take those threats from her? I tasted a dare and I was on it.

"Because. I would have nothing to say in a story written to you." Ouch. But hey, it's the truth. Kind of. I did not want her to learn that I actually had a whole lot to say to her. Right then, I was contemplating whether to write a story about a kid named Bob being eaten by his English teacher. I had little to lose; I already had a D.

She smiled at my insult and said, "Then don't write it to me. Write it to whomever you choose."

Ha, right. For the remaining minutes, I sat in silence, trying and failing to suppress my anger. Coach was going to kill me for missing practice again. As soon as that bell went off, I ran out of the place.

Mom would be making enchiladas for dinner, and her enchiladas were so good I couldn't wait to get home. As I let the door slam behind me, I said over my shoulder to Miss Carlson, "Maybe I'll write a story, maybe not." I waved, more like a flick of the hand in dismissal.

30

Thanksgiving was just days away when something awful happened. It was after school on Wednesday.

I got my enormous bag of lacrosse stuff from the locker room. I unzipped it and pulled out my stick. I tossed the ball up and down as I walked across the field with Luke Twain. The big guy. It doesn't matter if you don't remember. I was forgetting lots of stuff, which was probably why I had mostly D's.

When we reached the other side of the field, we all gathered around the coach and listened to him lecture us on battle strategy and how only a few of us were going to our early morning weightlifting sessions and it showed, blah, blah, blah.

Once he was done hammering us into the turf with his negative pep talk, we started to get ready for our drills. That's when the coach approached me.

"Hey, Coach," I said, strapping my helmet into place.

"Miller, take the helmet off." He wasn't yelling at me. That was a bad sign.

I took the helmet off and looked up at him. *Really?* I was perplexed by the gentleness of his voice.

"Why?"

He sighed and seemed to have a hard time finding words. Then he managed to get it out: "You're being cut from the team." He sounded reluctant to say it.

"What?!" I shouted. How could this be? They would never win a game without me.

"Sorry, Miller, school rules."

"But I'm captain. The team needs me!" I shouted again, irate.

"I know that, Jaden! You're a star player but you're not a star student. You have D's in most of your classes. You have to maintain a C average at Hampton to play sports. Come talk to me when you get your grades up."

He ripped off his hat and rubbed his hand over his bald head as if he were brushing back hair that wasn't there. He slapped the cap back on, dismissing the conversation as though it were an uncomfortable itch. Coach gave me an apologetic smile and walked off, blowing his whistle at the other guys as they lined up for drills.

I tore off my gear, slung it over my shoulder, and walked away. The ground beneath me felt harder than normal.

I grabbed my bike. Naturally, it began to pour. Like, I mean, *pour*. Worse yet, my tire was flat. What luck. So I slung my bag over my bike and began to slowly push it home. I took the shortcut, the dirt road through the swamp, which was now a muddy mess.

As I trudged on, I let just one tear roll down my cheek. I rubbed it off and blinked rapidly. Lacrosse had meant a lot to me. It was the one thing I was good at. Now I didn't have it. Soaking wet from the head down and muddy from the feet up, I made it to the Stop-N-Shop. I stood there looking at it. I was starving. I hadn't had lunch. My hunger raged. It's one thing to be angry on a full stomach. It's way worse when you factor in hunger: sanity goes down the drain.

I tried to read the sign. It was some number washed away by the rain. I was very, very hungry. So I pulled my bike up and leaned it against the side of the building and took a tentative step inside. The dry shack felt wonderful compared with my walk in the rain, punctuated by every swear word known to humanity.

The first thing out of place was the bell on the door; it was no longer there. I then realized that I hadn't been to the Stop-N-Shop since the day before school started. The day that Madam Marian had completely freaked me out.

Soaked to the bone, I shivered. The place was empty of high schoolers or any other customer. Outside, thunder rolled. I shook again. I pulled out a soggy dollar bill. I approached the hot chocolate machine, got a disposable cup, and filled it up. I sipped on my drink. Nice and hot and full of chocolate goodness. I started to warm up a little. Then I went over to the moon pie case and picked out the biggest, fattest moon pie there. I dropped my dollar into the jar on the counter. I snuck a glance at Madam Marian.

There she was, on her stool, reading the paper. She showed no response to my presence at the counter. She either didn't see me or didn't care that I was there. Relieved, I left, got my bike, and trekked home as the thunder boomed. As I walked, I sipped my cooling hot chocolate. When it was gone, I ate the moon pie.

By the time I got home, I had walked two miles in horrible weather. *If I'm lucky, I have hypothermia, which will lead to pneumonia. I wouldn't have to show my face for a whole month. That would be nice. That would also save me the humiliation of people finding out I was cut from the team.*

I went upstairs and took a long, hot shower. I like to take showers during storms. You're all steamy and warm and calm while outside it's cold and dark and violent. Also, showers seem to help me focus. If only I could do my homework in the shower. While I was toweling off, I had a realization.

I raced to my room, with just a towel around my hips. I crouched down and practically jumped out of my skin when thunder exploded right over our house. I still managed to pull it out from under the bed: a boring box. I had just completed it in woodshop. (My next project is a birdhouse for the dove.)

I opened it and looked inside; there was a dandelion flower, the one I had found taped under my desktop. I had saved it. It was dry and preserved and pressed between two pieces of paper. But as I looked closely at it, I noticed that on its stem were tiny splotches of brown. Then the lights flickered and the electricity cut off. I searched around for a flashlight, but instead heard my mom call from downstairs: "Jaden! Dinner!"

So with just the light of my phone, I descended the staircase. It was super dark outside, and the darkness seemed to amplify the sounds of pelting rain and growling thunder. At the dinner table, Mom was lighting a few candles. Some of them smelled like pinecones, reminding me of a camping trip I had gone on in the Appalachians with Dad. I sat down to a heaping plate of ravioli and shrimp. We eat a lot of shrimp in Duncan.

While I devoured my food, Mom talked about how there must be an enormous gopher living in our garden, as her dying plants seemed to disappear overnight, how her friend from work had just had a baby and how the big tornado in Kansas had devastated a whole town and its crop of corn. Blah, blah, blah. Sometimes Mom was silent at meals, so it was nice that she wanted to talk.

While she talked, I pulled the dried dandelion flower from my pocket and held it near a candle to examine it again. Just making sure that the brown prints at its stem were there. They were. Mom leaned over the table. "What do you have there, Jaden?" she asked, her eyes frying my flower.

I looked up at her. Mom and I were alike. When we're trapped indoors, we're desperate for a diversion.

"Dandelion flower," I said cautiously

"Why are you looking at a dandelion?"

Might as well tell her the truth now. "Mom. I found it taped under my desktop at school a few days ago." I carefully placed it on the dinner table and picked up my fork to stab the belly of a ravioli.

"Jaden! Who left it there?" She seemed to emanate an electric charge. A mighty boom sounded over our heads. The lightning couldn't match the electricity coming off my mom.

"Mom!"

"What, a mother can't be curious?" She was leaning way over the table, trying to either read my face or see the flower.

"I know who it was, Mom. A girl who sits next to me in English." I put my finger on the brown fingerprint of dried blood. *Bloody Hands gave this to me.*

"What's her name?" She was so excited that her voice drowned out the sound of the thunderstorm.

I looked up at her. "I don't know."

Mom looked crushed. She had expected more, but that was the full, honest truth. I didn't know anything about Bloody Hands. Nothing.

As I stared at the flower, Mom must have sensed my frustration. She said, "I once read that the symbolism of the dandelion, whose bright yellow color resembles the sun itself, is that it sheds light upon that which would otherwise be hidden."

Mom and her plant parables! Usually, they went in one ear and out the other, but this one interested me. Was Bloody Hands trying to give me answers? Or just make me ask more? When would this sun illuminate my darkness?

That night, I decided to use my free time—no lacrosse—to get answers to my questions. Who was she? And what was her story?

31

Thanksgiving break.

Thank god.

Man, freedom tasted so good. Scott would be gone all week; his grandma had taken him to visit relatives in Mississippi. My dad was busy in New York and then would go to Florida.

So I was home in Duncan for the holiday and kind of dreading the big day. My mom had invited her family to come, and that meant my aunties and their annoying kids, Michael and Henry Peterson.

On Thursday afternoon, they all pulled up in the driveway. I braced myself for the tornado. I should have covered the doors and windows and locked up my valuables.

"Jaden! Why, you're more handsome every time I see you! Get down here and give your auntie some love!"

Reluctantly, I approached her. She wrapped me in her arms, and her large bosom pressed into me embarrassingly. She is a squeezer, that woman.

"You are so handsome! I'll bet every girl in Louisiana has a big crush on you!" she squealed. Abigail is my mom's sister, and she and her wife, Rebecca, have two adopted kids, one Chinese, one Colombian, both plump. Chubby. Very chubby. And, as I said before, annoying. Michael, the one from China, and Henry, the one from Colombia, were born on the same day, so their moms refer to them as "the twins," which is just weird if you ask me.

"Jaden! How tall are you?" Auntie Gail seemed delighted to find that I was taller than her, and then Auntie Becca turned to look me up and down.

"Umm, six feet, I think." I said it really quietly. I wondered how Henry and Michael had survived so long with these two intense women.

"Goodness, no! You're at least six feet two inches!" boomed Becca, slapping my shoulder. I felt the sting of her palm on my shoulder blade. Then my mom approached, arms outstretched to hug her, so I walked quickly to the backyard.

I made it to the glass door and stepped out into the hot air. I could already feel sweat forming on my forehead. Thankful for the extensive garden, which would be a buffer between me and my relatives, I hurried along the trails. Unfortunately, I bumped into Henry and Michael, who were throwing rocks into my mom's lily pond.

"Hey, pretty boy!" Henry called.

"Hey, Henry." I hadn't meant to growl.

Michael spoke up: "Jaden, you have some good junk in your tree house."

I growled on purpose that time. Michael was holding up my journal, which had my latest story from creative writing class. I must have left it up there in the tree house overnight. And the kid had found it. *Yep, I should have locked up the valuables.*

"Hand it over, Michael." I said it firmly and coolly, not a trace of venom on my lips. The pulses in my sweaty palms throbbed.

"No way. This is good stuff." He read it aloud: "*The Fox Trot.* The fox trot?" He was enjoying taunting me.

I smiled slightly. "Spill my words to the whole damn world, you guys! I don't care." I was lying. "The only things listening are the plants," I added. But my psychology was lost on the fat boys.

Michael waved it in my face, the journal. He and his brother chanted, "*Fox Trot, Fox Trot,*" and danced a little jig—the fox trot, I guess.

No one had laid eyes on my story until these little brats had lifted it from my domain and then mocked it. My blood boiled. Henry got out his phone and started taking a video, and Michael continued reading my story in his piercing voice:

*"For some reason or other, I was not alarmed about where I was. I was surprisingly content, as though I had no other place to fill with my presence but my exact location. Into the brisk morning air I made the only bird call I knew: the call of the mourning dove. The low call is, "*Whooouuuooo, who, who, who." *From nowhere, a fox appeared."*

Henry snickered loudly. Michael could barely keep his voice calm as he continued to read and I made lunges at his behemoth body.

"Right below me, with head down, ears forward, and nose to the ground, was a fox. It never looked up, as though it did not expect to encounter a fifteen-year-old boy in a bayou tree, looking down at it. As it walked

beneath me and before it disappeared, I called to it: "Hello." It continued its fox trot into the swamp."

Michael paused for a second, digesting my short story. Thankfully, that was all I had gotten down on paper. As he paused, I snagged the paper from him and ran inside. There, I shoved my paper into an empty flowerpot and walked briskly into the living room.

Trust me, I was glad to see that Thanksgiving dinner was almost ready to be served. I grabbed the silverware and helped my mom set up for the feast. As soon as the last plate was laid, everyone took a seat.

Michael and Henry swarmed the table like sharks at a feeding frenzy. We all loaded up our plates. I took a large slice of the turkey and a spoonful of cranberry sauce, the kind from a jar. Bright-green string beans, mashed potatoes, and a biscuit dipped in honey. Everyone was about to cram food into their mouths when Gail stopped us.

"It's Thanksgiving! I need to hear thanks from everyone at this table!" She pounded the walnut wood table with her fist and then sat down, pleased with herself for remembering what we had all forgotten.

After a fairly painful round of thanks, and after two rounds of turkey, I got up and took my plate to the kitchen.

32

Break slugged on after the family reunion, that is, until *it* happened. I was riding Scott's dirt bike through the bayou just for fun.

I was on a dirt path that had puddle after puddle, and I was going so fast that everything was just one big blur. Even my thoughts were a blur.

I was riding like that, crazy and senseless, down the trail in the middle of nowhere. As I rounded a sharp corner, I saw a duckweed-filled pond. In it was a gator, its giant head resting on the bank. It made a break for water as soon as it saw me, and I also scared a pink spoonbill out of a tree above me.

As I looked up to watch it glide away, I took my eyes off the trail. Just for a split second. Big mistake. For as I rounded that corner, I hit something and sailed into the air. Time stretched and slowed. I glanced back and saw the bike wheels spinning as they rested against an immense tree. A branch of the tree had fallen across the trail. That was what I had hit. I processed all this in a second as I flew through the air.

And then I hit the ground.

Moaning, I moved my hands to push myself up, but gravity won and I fell back to the ground. My face stung. Fire shot up my left hand.

"Ouch!" I yelled into the swamp. I could tell that my arm was broken.

I bent my mud-splattered legs underneath me and then heaved myself up off the ground. Every tendon in my body seemed to cry out. At that moment, I spotted something on the trail.

It was so weird. So strange and out of place

Rose petals.

Really?

I instantly forgot the pain in my arm and just stared at those petals, fresh and lovely, on the ground. Innocent in the mud and blood. The petals were pink and the tips were yellow.

With my good hand, I picked one up and studied it, my jaw dropping in disbelief. Roses don't grow in the bayou, especially that deep in the wilderness. Maybe small, wild ones but definitely not the big, cultivated kind. The kind you buy at the florist for your girlfriend. Real flowers.

I flung the petal back into the mud and drops of blood. Then I gingerly stepped over the annoying branch and pulled the dirt bike away from the tree. The front wheel of the bike was still spinning. I got on and made my way home, one-handed.

Before I could clean the mud off, my mom insisted that we go straight to the emergency room. They immediately took X-rays and then left me alone in a room to ponder my thoughts. I overheard the doctor speaking calmly to my hysterical mother in the next room while he reviewed the X-rays.

"He's fine. It's a simple, clean fracture requiring a cast for six weeks. Then he can take it off and get back out there on the lacrosse field." Ha, that was not going to happen anytime soon. I had not told my mom that I had been cut from the team. I stayed away in the afternoons, and she continued to wash my uniform every day, as usual.

"He's lucky that it wasn't his right arm. He didn't get a scratch on him, and there's no sign of concussion. And not a single drop of blood," continued the doctor. He sounded bored. Another kid with a broken arm.

What?!

I scooted off the examining table and barged into the room next door. "What?" I demanded.

The doctor looked up from his clipboard, surprised. "What's the matter, son?"

"I'm not bleeding?" I asked fiercely. Like a madman.

"No. Should you be?" The doctor raised an eyebrow, half serious and half amused.

I was silent. For the first time, I took inventory of all my parts still covered in mud and couldn't find a trace of blood. Although my skin stung where I had hit the ground, all I could find was dried mud and some grass stains—not a speck of red. *But I know there was blood on the ground. I saw it there with the rose petals.* Then it hit me. It was her: Bloody Hands.

And once again, I was confused. I was getting quite annoyed with being confused. The only answer I had was that I was in love with a shadow of the bayou.

33

Over the next few weeks, I questioned my sanity. Was I in love? How could I be in love with someone who didn't seem to exist? Why did she seem to be going out of her way to avoid me? Was she shy? Or did she just not like me? Had I crossed the line? Was I crazy? A stalker?

School started again in December. At lunch on our first day back, I was sitting with Scott, devouring a peanut butter and jelly sandwich. Scott was talking about something, but I wasn't listening; my eyes were wandering to the faces around me in the cafeteria. I looked at the back corner, and there, all by herself, staring into the crowds, was Bloody Hands.

Her seat in English had been vacant that morning, as it had been for weeks. I was so excited! Seeing her was like spotting an elusive animal.

I grabbed an apple from someone's tray at my table and approached her. Slowly, so she did not know I was closing in on her. Slowly, like the stalker that I am. Then a whole gaggle of girls got up and came over to me, thinking I wanted to talk to them. I managed to weave my way through them, but Bloody Hands was gone. Again.

That afternoon, I had an idea. After school, I headed to the grocery store. I skidded my bike to the side of the building and walked into the dumpy, air-conditioned store. I located the first aid section and grabbed the biggest box of Band-Aids they had. I walked to the register and dumped the box on the counter. The clerk said nothing as he clicked the numbers into his computer. Then he said, "$9.49."

I handed him the money, shoved the package into my backpack, and ran out. I jumped on my bike and raced home.

Finally, the next school day began. I was on campus even before the try-hard kids and the janitor. I waited outside my English classroom, which was not unlocked yet.

When Miss Carlson approached the door, she gave me such a stare, holding her keys; it was priceless. Really, you should have been there.

"Jaden?" The keys were halfway out of her poop-colored purse.

"Yes," I said without emotion.

"Wha—."

"Allow me." I had heard that line in an old movie once. Was it Spencer Tracy? I took her coffee and the keys and unlocked the door for her. She walked in hesitantly.

I put her coffee on the table, and she seemed to regain her composure.

"What are you doing here, Jaden?"

"No reason, really." I said it softly. I even threw in a shrug. That was what the Spencer Tracy character had done: shrugged coolly.

"You're very hard to understand, Jaden." She took a sip from her mug and set down her keys and piles of papers. She placed her purse under the desk.

"So stop trying." I said and turned away. Spencer had said something insolent and stalked off.

I walked to my desk and sat down in the empty classroom. I opened my notebook and stared at a page without seeing it. Finally, I glanced up at Miss Carlson. She was standing in the front of the class, under the whiteboard, eyeing me.

"And why would that be, Jaden? Why don't you want me to understand?" Surprisingly, there was no venom, just curiosity. That was new.

I looked at her for a moment, trying to decide what Spencer would say. "I'm a book you picked up and judged by its cover. Even though you're an English teacher, you're not very good at understanding the story."

Just then, Emily Rider walked in and saved me from the grave I was digging for myself. *Yikes! Maybe Spencer is actually much cooler than I'll ever be.*

As more and more kids filed in, I stole a glance at Miss Carlson. She was taking a sip of her coffee and staring right back at me. I could feel the heat from her fiery glare. And then right before the bell finally rang, *she* walked in.

I couldn't help gawking at her as she walked to her seat and sat down. *My lucky day.* I saw her only on the rare occasions when she came to class, and each time it reassured me that I wasn't crazy, that this angel did exist. Honestly, the rest of the time, I convinced myself that she was merely a figment of my imagination.

But I knew that I could not dream up someone as real and as stunning as that girl. I pulled my eyes away from her. Talk about distractions, man!

Miss Carlson launched into an hour of painful monologue. I pictured invisible cuffs attaching me to my chair, the only thing preventing me from grabbing Bloody Hands and making a break for it.

I glanced around the room. Scott was playing his invisible trumpet, or at least his fingers were fluttering as though he were pressing keys while music swirled in his head.

Brook was combing her hair while peering into a little pink mirror. She caught my reflection in it, staring at her. She turned her head a little, and her gleaming hair spread across her back and shoulders. I expected her to glare and roll her eyes, but she just gave me a flirtatious half smile. Honestly, it made me shiver in repulsion.

I looked over at the girl who had saved my ass, Emily Rider. She was drawing in her binder. A bird. She was watching it through the window. Emily was the artist of the school, the one teachers asked to design everything from T-shirts to posters.

One boy, Alex White, was whispering to a kid named Jeremy Lee, probably discussing the latest design for some microcomputer inserted into your brain. Something wild like that.

As I scanned the kids, I couldn't help but fantasize what each of them would do when he or she finally got the keys to his or her own invisible handcuffs.

34

I fished around in my backpack for the package. Finally, I pulled out the plastic bag. I extended my hand across the space that separated me from the most gorgeous human being on the face of the planet: the prize rose in the king's garden, the angelfish of the sea, the egret of the sky, the tigress of the jungle. How could someone so beautiful ever be in the presence of me, an average Joe?

As I handed it to her, she looked over at me. Her amethyst eyes opened wide. She stared at me. I saw my own reflection in her pupils. She gently extended her hand, and I gave her the bag.

She took out the Band-Aid box and studied it. When she finally lifted her eyes from the present, a miracle happened. First, her eyes lit up. It seemed as though her eyes reflected the sparkle of all the stars in the cosmos. She smiled and then her lips parted, revealing a full, brilliant smile and perfect white teeth. That smile was the best present you could ever have. She was beyond beautiful; she was dazzling. Beyond any word a human could ever come up with. Then as soon as it had happened, she turned and a wave of silken hair blocked my view of her magnificence.

Breathless. I was breathless.

Then I heard someone yapping at me, pulling me away from my brief sojourn in heaven and back to a dull gray classroom.

"Jaden!"

I looked up at Miss Carlson, who was staring down at me like a hawk, ravenous, just waiting to rip the meat from my bones.

"What?"

She slapped my essay down on my desk. I snatched it up. Embarrassed, for on it was an oversized F. I thought I heard someone chuckle.

"Pay attention, Jaden. Life doesn't wait for those who have their heads wrapped up in their own imagination!"

You have no clue, lady.

She walked away, handing out other essay papers. I heard laughter, moans, and yelps of excitement. My essay was covered with red marks; there was more red than there were typed words. I zoomed in on a sentence in the margin; the words were marked with a red star:

One piece of advice, Jaden: If you want people to read your writing, you must first let them in.

What was she talking about? That woman! Shaking, I gripped the table. Then I snapped my pencil in two. That was it. *Get me out of here.*

Then I felt it.

Her hand. Tapping my shoulder.

I had momentarily forgotten about Bloody Hands. I turned to her; she was looking at me, leaning out of her seat, extending her hand to me.

And then an enormous smile lit up her face.

It was a smile that will forever be burned into my heart and soul. It is the image I wake up to, that smile. A stream of overpowering love washed away the fire and anger inside me.

In her hand was a token of thanks: a tiny white daisy, delicate and simple. I gave her a smile and she quickly pulled her hand back. Then the bell rang for the next class. I was slow to move. I just sat there and stared at the graceful flower in my big, bulky hand.

I sighed. I had finally broken through her shell. I already ached to see her again. I longed to hear her voice. I yearned just to be beside her. I wanted to know her, to understand her.

I also wanted to beat the snot out of whoever was hurting her hands.

35

Hey! Dude, wake up? Hello, your human friend Scott here! Finish your trip to Mars. I have a big one on the line!" I could feel his hot garlic breath on my skin. That's what I call close proximity.

I looked over at him; he was leaning back, reeling in a monster fish. His twiglike arms pressed against his chest for more leverage as he wrestled with the beast. I grabbed the net and flung it into the muddy water. But then the line went slack. A bummed-out Scott dropped the fishing pole to the side. I watched it hit the rusty bottom of the boat, and I wiped my forehead. It was hot and I was taking a serious beating from the sun. Not to mention that the damp air made me feel as limp as wet clothes on a clothesline. Scott recast his bait into the water, looking unsatisfied. Then he picked up his shiny yellow trumpet and began to play.

I could tell he was pissed. So I sat there thinking, still draping my sweaty arm across my forehead to block out the relentless sun. I squinted to catch a good look at his face.

"Scott?" I said to my best friend. He blared his trumpet in my face. It nearly deafened me, so I shouted at him. The heat seemed to enhance our anger, not to mention being so freakin' close to each other. Scott had been acting peculiarly all week. I needed to say something.

"Scott, dude, whatever it is, I'm sorry!"

He paused and began to play again, screaming his music at me, and all the while the sun beat down on our backs. There is never any encouragement from the bayou.

I said, "OK, I know I've been lame lately. I've ignored you and I've been running around acting strangely..."

I turned my head to look out over the water and saw a fat gator eyeing me. Scott was playing some high-pitched riff. The water rippled where he swayed back and forth in his seat. I draped my arms over the side of the boat.

"But there's a reason for it, Scott....I think I'm in love."

Scott dropped his trumpet. He stopped swaying. A heron spread its wings and took flight, as if ready to spread the news.

Scott stared at me, his eyes twin daggers. Then he reached for his trumpet and blew a fast-paced tune at me.

"OK! Quit it, Scott! It's the same girl as before." I turned to look at my reflection in the shadow of our boat in the water. I looked the same, yet the person I once knew had vanished.

Scott played his crazy, urgent song behind me.

"The girl with the bloody hands." The words fell from my mouth. "In English class."

The brassy song ended abruptly. "What! Still? Jaden! What's your problem, man? Get some meds. You must have really bumped your head on that log!"

I turned back toward Scott, and he grabbed my shoulders. I glanced at my now completely healed left arm. Leaning in, Scott said, "Listen to me.

There...is...no....girl....with....bloody....hands." He shook me lightly. "Got it?"

I nodded. *Fine, then let me be the keeper of the secret of the bayou. Let me be the only person in the world who knows that there is a girl with bloody hands.*

"Let's go get some oysters and see if we can find freshwater pearls," I muttered. That was what we had done when we were little: hunt up and down the riverbank for oysters. Over the years, we had found a handful of pearls.

He turned to the fishing pole and began to reel in the fishless line. The soft winding left me feeling empty inside.

"Now you're talking!" He slapped my back, got his paddle, and we were off.

36

December came out of nowhere. It kind of crept up on me. I realized three days before Christmas that I had been so caught up in mooning over Bloody Hands that I had not bought presents for my mom, my dad, or even Pip. Laugh if you want, but I got presents for my cat, OK? Scott and I didn't exchange gifts. Guys don't do that.

I walked into woodshop and searched the room for the project I was working on. There it was in the back room. Woodshop was mostly kids who would have had a tough time making a toothpick—and I was one of them. But then there were a few talented students. Emily Rider, for instance. She was building a ten-foot dragon out of chicken wire and wood chips. Duncan's Picasso.

"Hey, Emily!"

She crawled out from the belly of her chicken wire beast, pushed up her welding mask, and looked at me quizzically. Funny, there were a few girls at school who had never drooled over me. Emily Rider was one of them. I kinda liked it, actually.

"Hi!" She looked confused, as though she were trying to recall my name. Or wondering why I had approached her.

"Jaden Miller." I gave her a smile and helped her off the sawdust floor.

"I know who you are. Thanks, Jaden," she said, brushing the sawdust from her jeans. She was pretty cool that way. Most girls would recoil from the sight of their jeans covered in wood dust. Most girls wouldn't wear an ugly welding mask. Emily didn't seem to mind, though: she was down-to-earth. The opposite of Brook Jackson.

"Wow," I said, pointing to her half-completed dragon. "How did you even come up with that?" I was impressed. Trust me, that dragon was cool.

She shrugged, touching it with her gloved hand. "I don't know." She laughed, pointing to her head, and said, "It just kind of comes to me, really."

"Well, then, it probably wouldn't be too hard to come up with a birdhouse, would it?" I gave her my poor drawing. You see what my plan was: sweet talk her into doing me a favor.

She studied it, frowning. I could tell she wanted a challenge. A birdhouse is no challenge.

"Oh, I don't know, Jaden. I'm kind of busy at the moment." She handed it back to me.

"Oh. come on, it's for my mom. She loves this mourning dove in our backyard. She even named it: this is a house for Flower." I gave her my best puppy-dog eyes.

She looked at me and cocked her head to the side, a strand of her brown hair escaping her upraised welding helmet. She seemed to consider it.

"OK, fine." She dragged me to the tables, where she drew a birdhouse in thirty seconds. She explained it but I was lost. Then she dragged me to the wood room, where we grabbed a tawny-colored plank. Then we went to the wall of machines. Each one did a different thing: trimming, cutting, or sanding. Emily welded a mounting bracket on a metal pole for the birdhouse. The whole time, I ran around after her, fetching the items she requested.

"Emily, why are you doing all this for me?" I blurted out. I felt guilty for pulling her away from her own project.

She handed me the birdhouse pieces. All I had to do was glue them together. Smiling, she looked up at me, pulled on her gloves again, and pulled down her welding helmet, hiding her face.

"Because I see what you do," she said calmly. She then crawled back into her dragon. *That must be her favorite place. It's where she's creating her next masterpiece.*

"What?" I felt awkward standing there, holding the wood blocks. For all I knew, I would glue them all upside down. I didn't know what I had gotten myself into.

I heard her sigh from within her nest of wires, and then she yelled over the sound of the machine warming up: "For that girl! You're different from the rest of them!" Then Emily vanished in a spray of fire.

So two miracles occurred that day: First, I got confirmation from another human being that Bloody Hands indeed existed. And second, somehow, against all olds, I managed to glue the pieces of wood together to create a birdhouse. I even managed, with the help of Mr. Crane, to bolt it to my metal pole.

That project complete, I turned to my next. I grabbed a carving knife and a block of soft wood. I carved my dad's name into it and punched some holes into it with a hand drill. Parents love anything you make for them, right? Even a block of wood with a few well-placed pencil holes.

After school, I ran to the grocery store, which also served as Duncan's deli, pharmacy, and pet store. I grabbed a toy mouse. I loved shopping for Pip, because it reminded me that someday I would see him every day. I pictured him, fat and orange, curled up on a windowsill in Dad's apartment. Dad's apartment reminded me of the Sorensen sisters, Amelia and Sophia. The thought of them put a smile on my face, counteracting the depressing, dark, wet December day. Cold? Usually not. This is Louisiana; cold rarely comes to places where gators sleep on warm beaches.

I managed to get home in time for dinner. I ran into the living room, concealing my gifts behind my back. I, of course, was soaking wet from the rains and my shoes squeaked across the hardwood floor.

I went straight to my room and dumped my pile of gifts on my bed. I figured I might as well wrap them right then and there, so I could snail mail Dad and Pip's presents to New York. Maybe they would arrive by Christmas. Somehow.

So I descended the stairs and fetched some wrapping paper. It had green reindeer on it. Cheesy, but hey, they wouldn't care. My wrapping job was lumpy, but whatever. I lugged Mom's gift downstairs and put it under the tree. Our tree was decorated in popcorn and old-fashioned things: handmade ornaments, ribbon, and, of course, sea glass. There were also a half-dozen bird nests my mom had found and repurposed as decorations. Mom hated plastic ornaments; she said they destroyed the Christmas spirit.

When I walked into the kitchen, Mom was bending over the counter, fixing dinner. "Mom!" I shouted, surprised. "I didn't know you were here!"

She held up her wooden cooking spoon and laughed at me. "You didn't look!"

We talked. I said that school should have a longer Christmas break, so I could see Dad in New York. Mom told me what was going on in her garden. That was the main thing she talked about: plants, plants, plants. After years of listening to her, I'll bet I could walk into any garden, anywhere, and identify every plant there. But it's not a very useful skill, if you ask me.

So anyway, I was eating my soup. It was so good. It warmed my stomach and made me happy. And that made me talkative.

"Mom?"

"Hmm?" She looked up from her own steaming bowl and then glanced over at the Christmas tree and my giant present for her underneath it. She smiled and said, "You didn't get me a lacrosse stick, did you?"

I laughed but the word *lacrosse* just made me depressed.

"I was wondering...what you think would be a good gift for a friend?"

"Scott?" Her mouth curved into a smile. "You never get anything for Scott." She slurped soup from her spoon. "Oops. Excuse me."

"No, not Scott. Mom..." My voice trailed off and I stirred my soup. "Not Scott." *Her* face popped into my mind and I smiled.

"Jaden!" Mom leaned closer to me, her smile wide. "Who is it? The same girl you told me about before? What's her name?"

Here we go again. What am I supposed to say, Bloody Hands? "Oh, you don't know her."

Looking frustrated, she drew back. She placed her chin on her fist. "OK, let's see. Flowers?"

I shook my head.

"She likes flowers but there are no good ones in bloom right now."

"What about a record?"

"Mom, no one buys records anymore. Besides, I don't know what kind of music she likes."

"*Hmm*," said Mom.

"I knew it. It's hopeless." My hands dropped to the table, knocking my spoon into my soup. That kind of made me pissed.

"The pearls!" she shouted. "Remember when you and Scott found some a few weeks ago? You could add those to the ones you had already collected and make her a bracelet!" Her face lit up.

"Yes!" Mom was so smart. It was perfect: the freshwater pearls. "Thanks, Mom!" And I ran upstairs, three steps at a time, and crashed into my door. I pulled open my sock drawer and grabbed my tiny treasure chest of pearls. I counted twelve in various colors and shapes. I ran, sprinted really, downstairs and proudly presented my bounty to Mom, who was clearing the dishes from the table.

"Here!" Panting, I put them into her outstretched hand. I guess excitement is contagious. "Can you help me?"

"OK, OK. Hold your horses. I'll make a bracelet; you wash the dishes." She spread a cotton dish towel on the table and placed the pearls, one by one, onto it.

"So how do you feel about this girl, Jaden?" Her back was turned to me, but I could hear the smile in her voice as she inspected each pearl.

I think I blushed with embarrassment. This is an awkward situation with your mom. Guys: I advise you not to do what I did, because if you answer a single question, they'll ask a million more.

"I like her," I mumbled.

"Really?" She was smiling her big smile.

Why are moms *sooo* into this? "Mom!" I said and rolled my eyes.

"OK, OK, fine. Jaden? Forget the dishes. You haven't called your dad in a week. Call him.

I stumbled over to the phone and dialed his number. No answer. Maybe he was working late in his office. I dialed the office number. I looked back at Mom while it rang. She gave me a smile, and I rolled my eyes. Then there was a voice in my ear.

"Hello?" It was a voice that was so rough around the edges it made my throat itch. It wasn't Dad's voice.

"This is Jaden Miller, David Miller's son," I said, confused. My words seemed to drop on the tile floor of the kitchen.

"Oh, Jaden! Your dad is not in at the moment. Would you like to leave a message?" His voice was mechanical.

"Where is he?" I was anxious.

"Out," he said unemotionally.

"Where is he?" I repeated.

"At the doctor's." His words were the thorns on a cactus. It was 7 p.m. in New York. Who went to the doctor's at 7 p.m.? The ER was open all the time. But why would he go there?

"Why?" I demanded. "What's wrong with him?" I wasn't hanging up until I got answers. But he beat me to the punch.

"I'll tell him you called," he said and then hung up. All I was thinking was, *What a jerk that guy is. What's wrong with Dad?*

Last chance: his cell phone. He always picked up for me on his cell. Ringing...ringing...ringing...ringing...voice mail. I hung up.

I looked over at Mom again, and she gave me an outsize smile as she held up her completed masterpiece: a bracelet with pearls hanging from it like teardrops. I faked a smile.

37

On Christmas morning, I woke up late. Call me an old man, but hey, it's a holiday, so I'm sleeping in. But eventually, I awoke to my mom's voice calling me from downstairs.

"Jaden, it's Christmas! Get down here and start the fire while I make breakfast." So I got my butt out of bed. In the living room, the heater was going and the curtains at the windows blocked the view of the monsoon outside. Mom was in the kitchen, preparing breakfast. The house smelled like Christmas: pine needles, candles, and the smoky remains of the night's fire.

First, I brought in wood and tossed it on the black ashes. Soon, the logs spat small flames in the spots where I had coaxed the coals back to life. Then I put our one and only Christmas album on the old record player. It was Harry Connick, Jr. my mom's favorite.

Listening to the music really set the mood. It took me back to those Christmas mornings when Mom, Dad, and I were all together. Once I lit the candles on the mantel, the room was as cheery as could be.

As the fire crackled and "Jingle Bells" filled the air, I sat down in front of the piles of presents. I could always instantly see which presents came from Dad and which came from Mom. Mom's were wrapped in colorful paper, some with jute ribbon. She still did the Santa thing, and I still put out cookies and milk. And carrots for hungry reindeer.

My dad's presents were another story. He always went overboard. His were wrapped in silver and gold paper by a professional gift wrapper. And then there was my one present for Mom. The gargantuan, ugly pole, wrapped terribly.

Mom entered the room.

"Merry Christmas!" I said and smiled. No one could be in a bad mood on Christmas morning. She reached over and kissed me on the forehead, messing up my tousled hair even more.

"Mom. Mooom!" I said happily and reached for her present. "Open this. It's from me." I handed it to her.

"Jaden! You shouldn't have." She kissed me again before I could pull away. Sitting down in a chair, she looked at my bizarre gift and gave me a *What? What is it?* look.

"Woodshop." Only then did I realize I should have painted the thing.

"Ah." She tore away the wrapping and held up her birdhouse. "*Jaden!* No way! This is, *ohh...*" she jumped up again and gave me a suffocating hug. Then she tugged me down the hall and grabbed our raincoats. Pulling up her hood, she jumped into the wall of rain, with me right behind.

"Here!" she shouted over the rain, handing me the birdhouse.

She ran to the shed and came back with a shovel and a bag of cement. She began to dig and finally got a giant, muddy pool. We both stuck the birdhouse in, cramming it into place and pouring the dry cement and rocks around it.

"The rain will mix with the cement and harden it to concrete," she explained. Fifteen soaked minutes later, we had ourselves a birdhouse. My sweats were plastered to my legs, and the rain in my hair dripped into my eyes.

"Call her, Mom!" I said. Holding down my hood, squinting through the rain, I watched and listened as she called and called again. And then, after a brief, especially heavy downpour, Flower answered back. She fluttered over and landed on the new birdhouse. Somehow, she knew what to do and hopped right inside.

We ran back inside and once we pulled off our rain jackets, Mom high-fived me.

"Jaden, she loves it!"

"She does!" Wow, you must think I'm such a lovey-dovey guy. What can I say?

We went into the living room, and I sat next to the roaring fire. As the fire warmed me, Mom fetched her phone and snapped pictures as I ripped open the presents.

I got new boots, boxer shorts, and a pocketknife from Mom. From Dad, I got a watch, a pricey-looking suit, and an underwater camera to use to film gators. It looked like a submarine and was battery powered. Also, Dad gave me a digital camera, a small helicopter camera, and a motion detector camera. With that one, I got a note:

You talk a lot about wildlife in the bayou; it's time you captured it on film.
—*Dad*

38

Even though Dad always got me amazing, extravagant presents, I tried to love all my presents equally. So I pulled on my new boots, slipped the knife into my pocket, and strolled to the kitchen counter, where I stuffed batteries into the cameras.

"Pancakes?" Mom asked.

Tradition is tradition. "You bet."

We had Christmas breakfast together, just me and Mom, and then I got on with my plan. "Thanks, Mom. I'm going out."

"Out where? It's Christmas. And it's pouring out there."

I reached in my pocket and held up a tiny box.

"Oh, I see." She smiled. I dumped my cameras in my backpack, except the digital one, which shouldn't get wet. Then I ran out to the garage, got on my bike, and sailed off down the street.

It was really, really raining. Except for me, there was not a soul on the road.

I pedaled easily through the gray town. I looked into every store window, but all were dark. So I rode on the swamp roads for a while. Then I went to the school and got on the dirt trail, past the Stop-N-Shop. Everything looked dead: silent and unmoving. The only sounds were the patter of the slackening rain drops and the whoosh I made as I rolled through puddles.

After an hour of looking for her, I was getting mad at myself for not giving Bloody Hands her present earlier. Yesterday, for example. Why had I thought that I could just ride around town and find her? .

Unable to fulfill my mission, I finally ended up at the pier. I dropped my bike on the side of the road and let my feet decide where to take me as the gravel crunched below me. I passed the fisherman's shed, with a huge hole in one of its walls. *Billy Beckham.*

Ahead was the pier, disappearing out into the fog. With nothing better to do, I walked out on the pier. Twenty steps later, I looked back and could not see land. The swirling fog had swallowed my bike, the road, the shed—the world.

I kept my head down, reading the names carved into the boards of the pier. The rain was now a light sprinkle, and the temperature was mild. There was not a hint of a breeze, and so the ocean lay motionless except for the plop of raindrops.

I reached the end of the pier and sat down on its edge, letting my legs dangle into the mist. My surroundings looked otherworldly. All I could see were the tops of the pillars nearest me, poking up from the flat, gray water. Behind me, the pier faded away. The air in front of me was so thick I felt as though I could reach out and touch it, feel what another world felt like, let it carry me away. I was standing between earth and another world. Just one step forward would be another world, and one step back would send me back to earth. Which world should I embrace?

Without being able to see the sun for reference, I didn't know how long I sat there: Was it seconds?

Minutes? Hours? As I turned my head to the right, out of the corner of my eye I saw something move.

Startled, I looked back behind me. What was it? I had no idea. But then a surge of fog thinned and an outline appeared, silhouetted against the backdrop of another world. A female shape was heading my way. It moved closer, revealing itself as the fog drifted away from this present of all Christmas presents.

It was *her*.

Bloody Hands sat down right there next to me on the edge of this world. Was it really happening or had I lost my mind? Was I even awake or was this just another one of my crazy dreams? Had I just crashed my bike and died, and was I now at heaven's gate?

Her hair was like a mermaid's. It was long, so long. It must have reached her belly button. It was damp and twirled in dark strands down her back. Those purple-blue eyes seemed to hold the whole universe in them, and her lips were full and very dark from the cold. When she blinked, raindrops flew from her eyelashes.

And then I suddenly realized it: we were alone. Just she and I were there, cloaked from the rest of the world by the fog, the magical fog. It was as if we occupied an entire universe, she and I, with nothing to distract us from each other. *If this is heaven, I'm all in.*

Right around then, I remembered to breathe. "I got you something," I said gingerly.

Her eyes blinked and she looked at the package I had pulled out of my wet pocket. I handed it to her, looking down shyly. She was so pretty that it was hard not to stare, so I looked at my feet in the fog. Her delicate bandaged hand lifted the present from my big awkward one. I lifted my eyes and there she was, holding up the pearls.

Without thinking, I reached over and gently took her hand into my bigger ones. I slipped the bracelet around her wrist and fastened it. I looked up at her angel face and said, "Merry Christmas."

She lifted her eyes from the bracelet to meet mine. Bloody Hands was not wearing any makeup, and her skin seemed translucent. She was so different from all the other girls.

I grasped her hand and felt the pearls, cold and hard, and then I traced her palm, feeling two small Band-Aids. I gently curled her hand into a fist. I could not believe how close she was. There were no desks or gaps between us. Even in the drizzle, I could detect the faint smell of roses.

I looked up and said, "You could tell me your name. That would be enough."

She gazed downward and shook her head. She was going to leave. Before she could pull her hand away from mine, I leaned close to her and gently kissed her cold, bandaged knuckles.

Suddenly, she whipped her head around and looked over her shoulder toward the shore. Then I heard it too: a rustling sound in the bushes. Bloody Hands smiled weakly, pulled her hand away from mine, and slipped over the edge of the dock, disappearing into the mist.

I called to her: "Wait! Don't go. Please come back!"

Perfect moments are rare and never last. I just sat there, staring out at the edge of the earth and looking at the gate to heaven, which was shrouded in a fine vapor.

39

It wasn't until January that Scott and I got our first couple of pictures. It took us some time to master the new cameras and all their features. Time passed quickly while we played with my new toys.

Bloody Hands had not come to class for an entire month; that would have to be the world's record for the longest gap in education. Didn't truant officers, or someone, go around tracking down missing students? Why didn't anyone seem to care about her?

Scott and I had filmed plenty of gators at the bottoms of rivers, streams, lakes, and ponds using the sub cam. It was really cool to see the world underwater. Along with the gators, we got tons of pics of fish, turtles, and snakes, and even a couple of cottonmouth snakes. We put the motion sensor camera inside a beaver lodge and got some amazing photographs.

We would upload the video clips onto YouTube from the library's computer. I got footage of egrets, pelicans, and great blue herons with the digital camera and, of course, lots of Scott and myself doing asinine things. There were also a few of Scott's Tasmanian devil of a dog looking uncharacteristically fat and sleepy.

The weeks seemed to flow slowly downriver, and I kept my mind off *her* by stalking the animals of the bayou with my camera.

One day in mid-February, I was at the library, looking through my photos. I was streaming through some pictures snapped with the motion sensor camera when something caught my eye.

It was a photo of a fox. It was taken at night, and the fox's eyes gleamed as it looked right into the camera. Like, I mean, *right* into the camera. Then it moved off to sniff the closest tree. In the next frame, it was turning to look away from the camera. Then the very last photo was one of its black-tipped tail heading off into the night.

I went back to examine the first photo, the one that made me want to jump out of my seat, the one in which the fox was looking right into the camera. There was something bizarre sticking out of the top of the fox's head. I zoomed in and saw that it was a dove feather, balanced right on top of its head. The feather was wedged into its fur.

I laughed. It was the funniest, weirdest thing I had ever seen. I guess I was laughing too loudly, because the librarian began to make her way toward me.

Right then, the computer crashed. I must have overloaded it. I sat there, staring at the black screen. When the librarian got the computer up and running—after some serious muttering—the files of my photos had disappeared.

40

My birthday.

Sweet sixteen.

Trust me, it was the lamest party the earth has ever seen. I was born on February 1, 1998, at 11:32 p.m. in New Creek Hospital, Louisiana. My parties had always been epic, from the years of pin the tail on the donkey to my fifteenth birthday party, when every cool kid in Duncan and every hot girl in the county had ended up at my house.

The year of my sixteenth birthday should have been the ultimate party of my existence. But it turned out to be nothing more than a few candles on a homemade cake.

This was how it all went down: "Jaden, how many should I expect at your party?" asked Mom. I was headed to my tree house. She was in the garden planting winter bulbs. Mom is an artist: Her canvas is her garden and her paintbrush is her shovel.

"Umm, I don't know if I even want a party this year, Mom." I kept walking, trying to act cool and all, but that got her going like a loose pebble on a steep slope.

"What! You? Jaden Miller not having a party? This should be the biggest party of your life!"

She was on a rampage, flinging dirt all over the place, rambling on about food and gifts and girls. Pretty soon, she was talking about how her garden was ready for once and how she would rebuild her garden after high school students had trampled it and so on and so forth.

"Mom."

She looked up at me, her lips tight.

"Mom, I don't want a party this year." There it was plain, sharp, and decisive.

"Why, Jaden?" Her voice shook a little. "Is something wrong at school? Is this about grades? Lacrosse? Brook? Is this about Brook? What is it? What's the matter?"

I stopped her again. "Mom, it's nothing," I lied.

She peered up at me for a moment, wondering, and then I watched the light bulb go off over her head.

"It's *her*. The girl. The one you like. It's all about her, isn't it? Did she break up with you?" Her eyes got all wide.

"No, Mom, she's done nothing." And that was the very problem, the cause of my antisocial behavior. Ever since she stepped into my life, nothing else seemed that important.

Mom was persistent. "But it is her, isn't it, Jaden? It does have something to do with the girl, doesn't it?"

I didn't respond and turned to climb the ladder to my New York escape, up in the trees over the swamp and gardens. I heard her one last time.

"Sometimes it's best to let go, Jaden."

She was kneeling over a spot of churned earth, her hands covered in soil. Mom squinted against the sun. Her hair, tied into a bun, showed a few gray strands. She wore a hat woven in Africa by women who daubed their bodies with red earth. Her jeans were stained with the dirt she revered. She was where she belonged on this earth, kneeling in her masterpiece. My mom was put on the planet to care for her gardens and to raise me, so I could complete whatever it was that I was meant to do. At least, that's the way it seems to me.

"Let go of what, Mom?" I asked, scared. Suddenly, things seemed to be falling apart. The universe was shattering around me.

"Her." She smiled but her eyes showed sorrow. And her words filled me with rage.

"What! Why would I do that, Mom?!" I stood there, my fists balled at my sides. I was as surprised by my outburst as she probably was.

"Because, Jaden, when you really love something, sometimes you need to let it go. Let it fly free." She stood to look at me, eye to eye.

I couldn't believe it. Tears welled up in my eyes. *A real man wouldn't be so insecure, so...so in love, so heartbroken.* My mom was a wise woman. Maybe, just maybe, she was right. Maybe I should let go of the girl I was desperately in love with. Her absence from class might be a sign that she wanted me to stay away. But why? Almost any other girl in school would have loved to date me, to be with me. Well, at least that had once been true. Before Bloody Hands came along. Nothing made sense.

Mom drew near to me and rested her grimy hand on my shoulder. "It's OK, Jaden, let her go. Let her fly."

I turned away from her. Out of the corner of my eye, I saw the mourning dove, Flower, fly to the top of her birdhouse, singing to the gray clouds: "*Whooouuuooo, who, who, who.*"

"Let her fly," I repeated. My voice was dull. How could I let go of her? I did not want to think about it. I was in love, the kind of love where you feel as though you are actually falling—or flying. I didn't know which one.

So I broke from my Mom's hold and climbed up the ladder. I spent the afternoon there, trying to forget Bloody Hands' face, trying to erase her from my mind.

Mom had secretly prepared a party for me that night. She waited by the door for the entire high school to show up, as always. I sat alone in the living room, staring at the TV screen, watching a show about the monkeys of Japan. I barely registered the words as the hours passed; the decorations hung from the ceiling and walls like a cruel joke. Some of the banners said Sweet Sixteen on them. Cans of soda sat in a cooler of melting ice, bowls of chips and pretzels sat on the coffee table, and a handwritten sign hanging across the staircase said Please Do Not Go Upstairs.

The music on my stereo was blaring the latest and greatest, but it could have been playing the saddest classical stuff for all I cared. My phone beeped and I quickly picked it up.

It was Scott. A message from four hours ago was finally finding its way to my phone:

Happy Birthday! Just got home from lacrosse. We won 8-3! Have to study for AP Euro history tonite so can't come. Enjoy the party.

Obviously, Mom had called him and told him to spread the word. I turned off my phone and slammed it down on the coffee table. Mom came in, looking sad. She looked as though Dad had just left all over again.

She sat down next to me on the couch, and we hung there for a while, listening to the silence, even as the music played. Eventually, I got up and switched off the stereo. The real silence stung.

Mom said, "Jaden, I'm sorry. I thought people would come...."

If only she knew how much of an alien I had made myself at school, how much of a loser I had become.

"Mom, I don't like it here. I don't want to live here. I want to live in New York, can I transfer to a school there?"

"Oh honey, things will get better. You'll see. Finish out this school year."

"Please Mom. At least talk to Dad about it?"

"OK, honey. I will."

41

It was a week later that the real catastrophe struck: the thing I had been dreading and not speaking of for the entire year.

I had ridden home from school, as always, on my bike. Even though I was now sixteen, I hadn't bothered to get my license. What would the point have been? I had nothing to drive. I had nowhere to go. Unless maybe the Stop-N-Shop counted.

But I was partially happy because Bloody Hands was back in school. Yes, she had attended class a few times. However it never amounted to anything, really: she never said a word. But she no longer seemed surprised that I stared at her. And I wasn't surprised to find myself smiling at her more and more.

I kept trying to engage her in conversation. No luck. But sometimes she smiled back. It seemed as though each time I saw her, I fell more deeply in love. But the more I saw her, the more frustrating our situation became and the more questions I had. What was truly weird was how silent she was and how she seemed to constantly elude and even evade me. It wasn't as if she loathed me, but for some reason she wanted to avoid me. It was driving me nuts and starting to break my heart. Why did she do it? I had to find out. But at least she was around again and that was something. At that point, I would take anything. Believe it or not, because of her, I looked forward to English every day.

That day, when I arrived home after school, I was starving. Pining for Bloody Hands and obsessing about her seemed to make me hungrier than ever. I flung the front door open, threw my books down, and ran to the kitchen, where I rummaged in the cabinet for food.

Then I heard it.

A scream.

Followed by gunshots.

I dropped my bag of Cheetos and sprinted for the back door, shouting, "Mom! Mom! *Mom*!"

When I threw open the back door, I saw her. She was running toward me, crying my name: "Jaden!"

"Mom!"

I heard it again. Loud firing from the swamps. Dirt erupted around me in random places. I lunged behind a wheelbarrow lying on its side. I peeked around the edge of the wheelbarrow; across the yard, I saw my mom go down. I yelled and then closed my eyes tightly as I heard a loud clang: a bullet had struck the side of the wheelbarrow.

Sweat poured down my face. I was about to piss my pants. And then—silence. I peered over my protective barrier, and there, emerging from the woods, was a hunting dog. A mangy, mean-looking hound dog, covered in mud. Then out of nowhere, a red fox sprang up out of a hole near the edge of the bayou. Right below my tree house.

It wasn't until that moment that I realized that there was a fox den there. A fox den below my tree house? The fox came out yipping and screaming at the barking dog, and the two, fox and hound, ran off.

After a moment of silence, I looked around me. Mom was gone.

"Mom! Mom, where are you!?" I couldn't help but panic.

"Here, Jaden!" Her voice was equally panic-stricken. I stopped in my tracks and turned. My mom was lying on the ground in between some flower beds.

I ran to her, crouching low and cursing under my breath. She grabbed my shoulders and pulled me down to the earth.

"Are you hurt?" I demanded.

She shook her head.

"Me neither. I think."

We lay there for a few minutes, making sure that the shooter had left the property. Then we stood up.

"Mom, what was that about?"

"I have not the slightest idea." She seemed to be in shock.

Walking back to the house, I noticed something. "Oh no, Mom! Look!" I shouted, pointing to the birdhouse. It had fallen over at a 45-degree angle; a bullet had pierced its metal pole. There at our feet was the saddest sight ever: Flower, the mourning dove. The closest thing I had to a pet. She had been shot. Her feathers blew in the wind, scattering across the grass. I looked at Mom. We both had tears in our eyes.

"I understand now, Jaden," she said, her voice as lifeless as the bird. "It was a hunter and it's dove season. I was singing the song of the dove and then the gunshots started. He must have seen her." She looked down at the small body of the dove on the ground.

Doves were commonly hunted in those parts ,but never so close to someone's house.

I felt sick. "But Mom, you can't shoot near homes. We need to call the police. We could have been killed!" My blood was boiling.

She nodded as we made our way back to the house. "Unfortunately, Jaden, some people don't play by the rules."

42

Mom and I had a funeral for Flower and buried her in a shoebox underneath a rose bush. I kind of wondered what the kids at Hampton High would think of me if they saw me at that moment. But I was too numb to care.

Just before dusk, Sergeant Cultan and two deputies showed up.

"Son, where were you when you first heard the gunshots?"

And so I told him, for the third time, exactly what had happened.

"And here is where I took cover." I pointed to the shelter of the overturned wheelbarrow. He scratched a ballpoint pen across his clipboard and muttered, "mmmm."

"Look at this," interrupted the skinny cop, whose pointy chin looked like an arrowhead. He had been shuffling the dirt with his boot along the perimeter of the scene. He thrust his outstretched hand under the sergeant's nose.

Sergeant Cultan's brow wrinkled and his bushy eyebrows joined together as he peered into the deputy's open palm.

"What? What's this?"

I leaned in, too, to see what he held.

"This...this is a shell casing from the civil war!" He took off his cap and rubbed his forehead.

"Here's another one," shouted the other deputy, the young one who looked about 17. He trotted over and dropped a dome shaped metal slug into the sergeant's wide, rough hand.

"I don't get it," the deputy said. "These are ancient. What hunter would use them?"

"Well, we best take them back to the station and let the guys have a look," said Sergeant Cultan, as he slid them into his pocket.

Yeah, right. He just wants to show them off, or maybe sell them on eBay.

The sergeant turned to me and began to lecture me on the dangers of hunting. *Duh. I was nearly shot and so was my mom.*

"Yes sir," I said, nodding at his monologue. Just then something brushed my leg. I looked down and picked up a tail feather that had fluttered against me.

Once the officer was done talking with me, he turned to my mom, so I decided to investigate for myself. I went over to the waterline, where the land met the swamp, and there I saw the fox den, well concealed in the bushes. I followed the tracks of the dog and the fox into the swamp; fewer than fifty yards away, I found the scene of the crime.

I saw the fox, twenty feet away. Its muzzle was covered in blood, and it was looking at me. At it's feet was a dead dog. I said nothing at first. We just stared at each other for a moment. Then, under my breath, I said, "It wasn't your fault."

The fox turned and trotted off.

I made my way back to the yard, my feet covered in mud up to my ankles. I told Sergeant Cultan that the dog was dead. When he asked me what had killed the dog, I just shrugged and suggested a cottonmouth snake or maybe a bullet.

In a daze, I walked to the front yard, fished my bike from the bushes, mounted it, and rode off. I don't think anyone even noticed.

I rode, still in a dreamy daze, in the direction of school, along the shortcut. As I neared the Stop-N-Shop, I jumped off my bike while it was still moving. It ghost-rode forward until it hit the tree line and toppled over. I dashed into the Stop-N-Shop, not even glancing at the number chalked on the board.

Once inside, I ran to the counter and fished a quarter out of my pocket and clunked it into the jar. The coin made a loud clink that echoed through the vacant store. I laid the feather on the counter and shouted at her: "This! Flower is the one that dies? This is what you mean? Are you joking! Because that's one sick joke!" I screamed at her with such ferocity that my hand trembled.

Madam Marian lowered her newspaper and looked up from her perch on the stool. She did not glance at the jar or the feather or anything else; she just looked at me. I held my breath.

"Jaden. The giver returns." She said it with such control it frightened me. "He has come with a response, along with a feather." She said that last word like the wind might have spoken it, invisible but there.

Then she reached her fat hand into the jar, fished out my quarter, and slid it across the counter.

"But not today." And she sat down and went as still as a statue, whispering one last piece of voodoo advice:

"You know what you know, so that when it is time, you'll know."

"That doesn't make sense! What are you saying?" I pleaded, tossing the feather at her. It fluttered to the floor.

I stormed out of the store and into a Louisiana downpour. I looked at the chalkboard, but its number had been washed away.

43

My mind was spinning and all crazy. But as the storm slowly died, so did my irrationality. I needed alone time. I needed to get away. I needed to reboot. So I launched the canoe and embarked on a solo expedition into the place where I find the most solitude, the swamp.

Time was lost to the rhythm of my paddle sinking into the murky water as I made my way deeper and deeper under the shadows of the haunting trees. I thought back to the lessons Mom had taught me about our state tree when I was a little kid and we went on long walks through the forest.

Taxodium distichum, aka the bald cypress. The quintessential swamp tree. The roots of one of these one-hundred-feet-tall trees fan out at their base, anchoring to the deep mud beneath the tree, and then reemerge above water away from the trunk as what look like knees, some more than ten feet tall. The knees are woody things that look like the termite mounds in Africa I've seen on Discovery Channel. The lore is that these strange knees hold secrets, secrets of the swamp, something no modern computer algorithm or botanist has ever figured out. No one knows why these knees exist. Some think it is for the trees to suck in more oxygen, or to reproduce, or for support. Some even say it is to vent methane, but no one has ever proved *any* of these theories. The knees remain an enigma.

And scientists say that some of these monster-size trees are more than fifteen hundred years old. Think about what they've seen: hundreds of hurricanes, epic floods, countless life dramas of the native animals, and more recently, many life dramas of people, in particular, mine. My drama. Did they care or even notice? What would they tell me in their wisdom of the ages? Just a year ago, an underwater forest of perfectly preserved cypress trees was discovered by divers off the coast. When they cut into these trees, they still smelled of fresh cypress sap. Why was that amazing? Because they were fifty-two thousand years old! What other secrets did these trees harbor? What more could they tell me?

Sorry. Forgive me. I'm rambling again. Sometimes I just can't get my mom's botanical stories out of my mind.

All I could hear was my own breathing and the gentle lapping of water. This is the threshold where the earth and sea mix. Both seem to be struggling to gain the upper hand.

I allowed myself just to be there, in the mix, and soon I realized I was not alone. An alligator, black and scaly, was beached on a grassy bank. A shimmering cottonmouth swam beside my canoe, so close I could have reached out and touched it. Up ahead was a motionless red-eared slider. As I approached, the turtle slipped silently into the water. The sun broke through the canopy and cast a dappled light onto an egret. It burst into flight when it saw me, its wings fluttering gold in the light. Time was lost in this place.

And when time vanishes, the mind clears and memories flood in.

I was thirteen and in the seventh grade. It was springtime and Scott was asleep at the wheel. So I was just letting the slow currents drift us through the swamps. Our fishing poles were baited, waiting for the big one. As a long hour dragged by, we came to a clearing: a small meadow. Our boat came to a slow, steady stop on a shallow mud bar. I didn't know how to get the motor started again, so I turned around to wake up Scott. But as I turned, I saw something out of the corner of my eye.

A girl. In the meadow. A brown-haired girl, covered in dirt. She looked at me with wild eyes. I blinked twice but she was still there. I noticed she had some flowers in her hands, or maybe they were whole plants, roots and all. They looked sickly and dying. Suddenly, she turned and ran away, and in the distance, I could make out the ocean and the circle of rusted ships.

Now I wondered, *Could that have been her? Bloody Hands?* It had been so long ago. If it was her, maybe that actually had been the first time I laid eyes on her—not in the gym, as I had first thought. Had I seen her around town and never noticed? Mixing in with the other invisibles? I couldn't imagine I wouldn't have noticed her. But the day on the boat with Scott stood out; a sixth sense told me that had been the day our eyes first met. It's funny how the mind works. How it can take so much time to fit all the pieces of a puzzle together, even though the pieces are all right in front of you the whole time.

But now, as my canoe glided to the shore, she wasn't there. I saw the shipyard in the distance but no girl. Had that day with Scott really happened? Or had I imagined it? Or if it was real, had I imagined the girl? Had the cypress trees spoken to me? I had come to the swamp to gain clarity. But once again, I had more questions than answers. I sat on shore in my canoe for a minute and then turned around and paddled back to the life I lived on the outskirts of the swamp. Far away from the ring of dead ships.

44

Life was kind of lame for a while, just the same old, same old. You know what I mean? When school gets so repetitive that the days seem to blur together and you can't distinguish one day from the next, not to mention one geometry lesson from another.

Scott and his granny, however, received a surprise.

"Yeah, um, Scott, um what did you get for number 13 on the geometry homework?" Scott and I were in different periods but had the same math teacher, so we often did our homework together – it was much faster that way. I balanced the phone on my shoulder as I shuffled the papers with my two free hands.

"Dude, I haven't even started math yet. I'm stuck on English," he grumbled, and I heard his binder flop onto his desk.

"The essay! Oh man! I forgot about that. It's due Friday, right? I'm in trouble." It was my turn to gripe. Pretty soon, my D would turn into a D–.

"Oh yeah. Hang on a second, Jaden, Tazz just walked in the room."

And then he must have just laid the phone down on the desk, for I could still hear him and it was hilarious. Why did I not record this?!

"Tazz. Tazz! Get out of here. This is *my* room. You hear that? *My* room! Get out!"

Then there were sounds of struggle and snarling and yipping and a sound that I'm not sure came from Scott, but it was like a yip and a whimper.

"You devil dog!" Scott was screaming now. "Get off my bed! Off!"

And then there was more yipping, and there was also whining and snarling and cursing, and then to my surprise I heard the strangest high-pitched wail come out of Scott. Trust me, it was embarrassing.

"Scott?" I was suddenly worried for my friend. Maybe his crazy Pomeranian–pit bull had finally gotten the best of him.

And then I heard it: "You little— *Do not* poop on my bed! *Grandma!*"

"What?" hollered Granny, probably from the kitchen.

"Grandma! Tazz just pooped all over my bed!"

Then came laughter—both Granny's and mine.

"That ain't my problem!" shouted the old lady from downstairs.

I could see her waving her finger at us. "You made your bed. Now you have to lie in it." That was Scott's grandma's favorite saying. You have to love her when you don't feel like strangling the old bag.

There were more sounds of struggle.

And then Scott was back on the line.

"Oh man. Dude, oh no!" he said softly. A horror story seemed to be unfolding in front of him.

"What?" I was surprised to realize that I had been holding my breath. *What the heck is going on in his room?*

"I believe I just figured out Tazz's recent obesity problem. She is now a mama."

It took me a few moments to process the information. "No way, Scott!"

"Yes, way. Right before my eyes. I'm telling you, man..."

By the time I made it to Scott's house on the other side of town, Tazz, or should I say Tazzella, had given birth to five puppies, paternity unknown. Two were black and the others were kind of golden. My first and best idea was to find the boy dog responsible and dump the puppies on the doorstep of his owner. We couldn't deal with the mayhem of five more demons, little ones, running amok.

But when I ran into the house, Scott's granny cornered me.

"Where do you think you're going, young man?" She was pointing a knife at me, for she was chopping up some chicken.

I put my hands up. "Just going to check on Scott!"

"Well, he is mighty fine. He's doing his homework in his room, and he doesn't need you to go get him all distracted, you hear me, Jay-Jay?"

Oh yes, that's right, she calls me Jay-Jay, an embarrassing nickname left over from childhood.

"But—"

"No buts. You best be getting your butt on your bike and cruising home or else—"

"But puppies!" I protested. "Tazz just gave birth!"

She stopped cutting her chicken and stared at me. And then, thankfully, she put down her knife.

"Lord Almighty," she muttered and made the sign of the cross.

Wiping her hands on her apron, she grabbed my left shoulder and marched me up to Scott's room. You'd be surprised at the strength of that old lady.

Before I even reached the top of the stairs, I heard Scott in a panic. Granny and I opened his bedroom door to see that a hurricane had just blown through. Papers, binders, clothes, and boxes were littered everywhere. This was the typical state of Scott's room, who was fond of saying, "Cleanliness is for those with dirty minds." But today the room was beyond dirty; it was bloody and smelled weird. Like death, or birth, maybe.

And in the middle of all of this was Scott, standing on his desk, fighting off Tazz with his trumpet. Apparently, Tazz had claimed the room as the official puppy nursery and wanted Scott *out*. Once Tazz saw Granny and me, she laid down a vicious snarl in our direction. If an animal is dangerous, multiply that danger times 10 if she has babies or, in Tazz's case, times 100.

"Run!" I heard Scott whisper harshly to us from atop the desk.

I would have laughed if I weren't in the line of fire as well.

"What on earth are you doing, Scott?" said Granny, who had armed herself with a broom. She's always prepared. Then, to my amazement, Granny walked right up to Tazz.

"Let me see those mini-yous, darlin'." She smiled as pleasantly as possible—and the strangest thing occurred right there in that room. Granny picked up a puppy from the bed and kissed its fat little head, and Tazz did nothing but gloat. She jumped onto the bed. A noise came out of her, a cross between a chuckle and a whimper. Tazz even wagged her tail, I mean stump. Fearing less for my life, I relaxed a little.

Scott began his descent from the desk. But just as Scott's feet were about to touch the floor, Tazz bounded off the bed and chased Scott and me out of the room, snarling and nipping at our heels. But we would have expected nothing less from that she-devil.

45

Well, after the puppies were born, two things happened. One, Scott began to sleep in the attic, and two, the puppies became a chick magnet. Scott was the most popular kid in town, and I, by association, had reestablished my social standing.

"Puppies? What did you say, Jaden? Puppies?" Jordan was leaning over the lunch table, those dark eyes staring into mine.

"Umm," I said, trying to decide if this was a good idea. "Yeah....Scott's savage dog had puppies." As soon as the word *puppies* fell from my mouth, she jolted out of her seat, her small braids bouncing up and her hair beads hitting her in the face.

"Oh yay! I love puppies! How old? What are their names? What do they look like? Can I see them?"

"Oh no, that would be a terrible idea!"

"What?" She sounded heartbroken. But then the sass returned to her voice. "Why?" She snapped her fingers.

"Because, Jordan, Scott's dog is savage. She would kill you." Hey, it could happen.

"Scott!" she bellowed over to where Scott sat, right beside some girls he was attempting to flirt with. The operative word here is *attempting*.

"What?" He seemed to have been caught off guard. It made me wonder what he was talking about. I hoped that it had nothing to do with me.

"What kind of dog do you have?" Jordan demanded.

Before Scott could answer, Brook sang out, "He has this black Pomeranian. It chased my cat one time." She smiled and gazed at me. "So what's this news about puppies?"

And soon enough, all the other girls cornered Scott and me. So that day after school, we went to Scott's house with, like, eight of the lacrosse girls. Scott and I were terrified that Tazz would bite off their fingers—or worse.

"OK, everyone, the puppies are in this room." Scott pointed to the door behind him, and the girls hugged each other and squealed with excitement.

"*Shh!*" Scott looked pale. "*Shh!* The mom is very, very protective of her babies. We can't wake her up, OK? You all got that? We *cannot* wake her up. I'll just go in and snag a puppy. Wait here."

He gulped and looked over to me, eyes wide. I gave him a nod of encouragement. He was entering the dragon's lair to steal its treasure, but Scott was no knight in shining armor. Somehow the guy managed to screw up his courage, and he disappeared into the room. His room. The room that once was his. Of course, the puppies had taken over his bed.

The girls actually grew quiet and we all listened. I could hear Scott step on a creaky floorboard, and then I heard the bedsprings squeak. I put my ear to the door.

"Hey, Tazz!" Scott said softly. "What cute puppies you have. Mind if I take...one?"

"*Grr,*" replied Tazz. She was not falling for his sugary sweet voice.

I closed my eyes and prayed. This was not going to end well.

"OK, OK, it's all OK! Just go back to sleep. I...need...just...one." Scott's voice shook just a little. I gritted my teeth.

Then I heard something hit the floor and something fall off the desk and growls, yips, and wails. The wails were Scott's.

One of the girls muttered, "He is such a wuss."

I'd like to see you *try.*

All of a sudden, Scott emerged, carrying a puppy. A white one. Its little black eyes and black nose were the only dog parts on it, for the rest of it was just white fluff.

It worked like a charm. The girls swarmed Scott. His shirt was torn and sliced, and he had a bleeding gash on his forearm. Yet he had a dorky grin on his face, as though he had just achieved the impossible and now could enjoy the spoils of his victory: the girls. I couldn't help but smile, too.

"Hey, Scott, you OK?" I asked.

"Now I am," he boasted.

Scott handed the puppy to the girls crowding the hall. They were all wide eyes and big smiles. That was what they lived for: baby animals. Maybe it was just part of their DNA—the maternal gene. Anyway, Scott and I went downstairs for much-deserved Cokes, leaving the girls in the hall with their baby.

We came back up not two minutes later to the horrifying sight of an empty hall. We heard giggling voices. They were coming from the other side of Scott's door. We looked at each other in bewilderment, opened the door, and there was the craziest scene in the world.

The girls were in a circle, with some sitting on the bed. They were passing puppies around. Brook was cuddling Tazz and cooing to her as though Tazz were a baby. *Look who's the real knight in shining armor.* Tazz was licking Brook's cheek while wagging her stump, and her body was wriggling uncontrollably.

Then Tazz stopped and looked up at Scott and me in the doorway. She leaped from Brook's arms and lunged at us. We slammed the door shut and then slid our backs down the door. We could hear Tazz on the other side, snarling, scratching, and biting at the door.

"Dude, what is wrong with us? What are you and I missing that makes Tazz nuts around us?"

"Another X chromosome to replace our Y chromosome," I said with a shrug.

"Chicks..." Scott groused.

46

Later that afternoon, as Scott was talking to one of the girls and I was raiding the kitchen, Scott's granny walked in. She was wearing a vivid yellow blouse. I had just opened a Dr Pepper. I raised it up to my ear to listen to the sounds of carbonation popping inside the can. The bubbles felt cool on my neck and face and sweet .on my tongue.

"Jay-Jay, no matter how much you kiss that soda, it ain't gonna kiss you back."

"Oh darn," I retorted.

"What's that attitude I'm hearing? Jay-Jay, you treat your elders with respect. You hear me, young man?" She made her way over to me.

"Yeah." I took a sip of my soda, ignoring her.

"Hey, you! Darlin', come in here for a moment." She motioned to Brook, who was on the couch in the living room. I had been avoiding Brook as much as possible that day. When she talked to me, I ignored her. When she smiled at me, I pretended I didn't see her. Now, I turned to the refrigerator's ice machine; I caught some of the ice cubes as they fell and hammered them into my soda. Then I turned around and Brook was right there.

"Hey," I said, at a loss for words.

Brook had her hands on her cheeks and was leaning over the kitchen counter, hair spilling around her face like a golden halo. Her tank top, I couldn't help but notice, was too tight and too small to do its one job of covering her chest.

"Jay-Jay?" she said, seeming delighted to have discovered my nickname. I didn't mind so much when Granny called me that, but coming from Brook, it was not good. Even worse than "baby," which once had been her endearment for me.

"Come here, chillen. I have something I want to show you two." Too smart to refuse, we both automatically filed in behind Granny's substantial rear end, and she led us outside. We crossed an ugly lawn, where someone had been working to remove the weeds in patches. Random spots had been cleared of the prettier weeds, violets and dandelions. Strangely, the ugly lawn weeds remained untouched. I asked Granny about it.

"Hey, Granny, who took your weeds?"

She stopped, turned around, and looked at me, puzzled. "Jay-Jay, that's nonsense talk. Ain't nobody taking my weeds. Probably raccoons. But they can have 'em." She shook her finger at me. She turned and we continued our march, and she chuckled at the thought of a weed thief.

Finally, we arrived at our destination.

The old shed.

Three feet up was brick, and above that was wood with terribly chipped white paint. Its roof had been overtaken by vines. She yanked the door open and motioned us inside.

"Go on, check it out. The surprise is in the back. I'll hold the door open to let the light in so you can see it. Keep looking, farther back... a little farther back." As we searched, we heard a slam of the shed door and then the outdoor latch locking. We both whipped around and ran to the door. We heard Granny cackling from the outside.

"You chillen ain't comin' on out until you get your issues figured out." I could see her lemon-colored shirt through the cracks in the door.

"Let us out!" I hollered and banged the door. I've failed to mention so far—because it's never come up until now—that I'm extremely claustrophobic. I hate confined spaces. It didn't help that this shed happened to be a hoarder's dream, stacked tightly on all sides with a bunch of stuff. Hardly space for two breathing bodies.

After fifteen minutes of cursing and punching the door, I gave up. Brook was standing about three feet away, arms crossed. Though I couldn't see well in the dim light, I knew it was mock anger. She was thrilled by her good fortune of being locked up with me.

The tiny shed was filled with dust, which makes the light rays shine in columns. You must have seen this: a beam of light illuminates millions of dancing dust particles? I've always thought it amazing that people breathe this stuff all the time and never notice—unless they're trapped, as we were. Seeing those dust particles and visualizing them entering my lungs was not helping with my claustrophobia. Anyway, I figured the light must be coming from a window, so I jumped up onto a stool and shifted cardboard boxes around until I found the small, cobwebby window. I pushed on the frame as hard as I could; to my despair, it did not budge.

So I climbed down and began to look around for other things. I found a lawn mower, piles of mulch, bags of seed, and old shovels with their wooden handles half rotted off. There were rakes with rotten handles and lots of pots—terra cotta pots—and a whole lot of stacked boxes.

Then I searched the walls and tested them out. One by one, I tapped their sides to see if there were any loose boards. To my frustration, the thing was as solid as a coffin and would not budge, even though from the outside it looked moments away from collapsing in on itself and disappearing into the swamp.

"Jaden?" She said it softly. It was less obnoxious than normal; she almost sounded like a real person and not a Barbie doll. I guess our situation called for desperate measures.

"What?" I barked. I hated being locked up with her. Of all people, why her?

She recoiled. But then she pointed to the ceiling, and there on the roof was a skylight, covered in ivy, which was why I had not seen it before. I grabbed a pick—something to stab the glass with—raced to the stool, and positioned it under the skylight. I stepped up on the stool, stood on tiptoes, and raised the pick up, but the skylight was just out of reach. It was so close! I stretched out fully, stood on tiptoes again, and tried to bridge the tiny gap—but then it happened. I wobbled once, twice, and then I heard a terrible sound. It made me wince.

Crack! It was the sound of the wood splitting. I leaped from the stool, but my feet caught on it, causing me to land on the floor in a face-plant, my rib cage seeming to flatten against the concrete. The dust puffed up around me in a thick cloud. I gasped.

"Ouch." As I pushed myself up, I felt Brook's weak hands try to scoop me up by my armpits.

"I'm OK, Brook. I don't need your help!" I growled at her, and immediately the hands let go. I rolled away from her, got up with the help of the lawn mower, and then coughed terribly. I looked at the broken stool and the window, just out of reach.

"I'm just trying to help, OK? You don't have to get all snippy with me!" She said it as though she had finally found her voice. Trapped somewhere in her lungs, her real voice sounded deeper and kind of gravelly, unlike that fake popular-girl voice I was all too familiar with.

"The only way we can get out of here is if you lift me up on your shoulders and I stab the window open. Then I can crawl out and open the door from the outside. OK?" She stood there, looking straight at me with her arms crossed.

I moaned. I was sore from the tumble to the ground. I was still mad, too.

"No, I'll find another way," I said, not trying very hard to hide my contempt.

"Why?" She sounded pumped up for a fight. A girl fight: one with words. "Are you stupid? Or are you blind? We're not getting out of here unless you lift me up to that window! Why do you have to be so mean, Jaden? Really! I've tried all year long to be nice to you, but you just push me away!" She had walked right up to me and made sure I could not look away when she said that last part.

"I'm not mean; you're the monster here." And to my surprise, I watched real tears flow out of her blue eyes. Her lips were locked and her jaw quivered, as if she were about to lose it. Although she was looking at me, it seemed she was looking through me, at something far off.

Then she abruptly looked down at the floor and did lose it.

"Ahh!" screamed Brook into my ear. Had she broken my eardrum? I looked down and an immense rat was on her foot. It was so big, it must have been part beaver. Brook began to squirm and thrash around. The rat seemed to be running in circles. Finally, Brook found her one safe zone: she hurled herself onto me.

All my anger evaporated as I tried to kill the huge rodent. Brook clung to my neck like a constricting python. Now, not only was I deaf, but I could not breathe. Finally, the rat seemed to become annoyed with our antics and scuttled away.

What followed next was an extremely awkward moment. Brook was hanging on to me. I was holding her by one arm. In my free hand was a rake. She was shaking and looked absolutely terrified. I was about to put her down when all of a sudden she cocooned me in her arms and hugged me really tightly. She began to sob as though there were no tomorrow. And the more I tried to pull away from her, the more she clung to me. Her grief seemed to weigh down her slight body.

"Brook, let go," I demanded, fed up with her drama queen act.

She pulled away from me but just enough to look up at my face. Tears mixed with mascara stained her cheeks, and her hair was messed up. For the first time in a long time, though, she did not seem like an enemy. I felt sorry for her.

And then she reached up, wrapped her arms around my neck, and kissed me, hard and full of purpose. My guard was down and her spell began to work its charm. I just did not want to fight it anymore. Until I came to my senses. I finally peeled her off me, but I have to admit, it took longer than I had hoped.

"No, Brook. I don't like you like that." I said it without anger. I said it with honesty.

"Why? You used to. Don't you remember?" I put her down on the floor; she looked around hesitantly for the rat. "Why do you push me away, Jaden?"

"Because I just don't like you in that way, Brook." I said it almost in a whisper. I wanted to reel in that sentence, but it was too late. It was out in the world.

"You think I'm a conniving popular girl who'll do anything to get her way."

Maybe.

"A monster," she said.

Huh?

When I did not reply, she searched my face for the thing I was not telling her. I could see that she wasn't finding anything. She walked over to the skylight and pointed to it.

I gave in and nodded. So she climbed onto my back and wrapped her legs around my neck. Once again, she was close, so close that I could smell the jasmine perfume on her. I steered my thoughts away from her gorgeous legs around me and instead focused on the task at hand.

I handed her the pick.

"I'm no monster, Jaden. I'm a fallen angel."

I held her knees and heard the drumming at the window. *What are you talking about?* I mused. *What a drama queen!* The tapping on the window stopped. She was making no sense whatsoever. Her voice sounded haunted and so distant. And then I heard it.

"Are you two ready to come out yet? Solved all your differences?" Granny. Finally coming to the rescue.

"Yes, Granny, we're ready to come out!" I shouted. I bent down and Brook unwrapped herself from me. I had dodged Granny's second question. Brook, arms crossed, glared at me as if we had unfinished business.

Then it happened. The door opened, light flooded in, and the dust particles did their magic dance. I escaped the coffin.

"You two were like a couple of alley cats about to have it out! I think any people with a beef should get locked up together until they reach common ground. Think of the wars that could be prevented."

I wasn't at all sure that I agreed with Granny's method, but her lockdown did reveal a bit of humanness in Brook that I had not known she possessed. But of course, I'm in love with someone else. How I wish I could be locked up with her, forever— even if it were in that old shed.

47

Scott, check this out."

I leaned over the railing and spat into the creek below. I was sick of the bayou. Why were we destined to live out our lives in that muddy waste, washed down from the rest of the continent? Nothing good could come from this mucky water world.

Scott slapped me on the back with his notebook and spat a much better loogie into the creek below us. Our bio classes were on a joint excursion to the bayou. He read from the assignment.

"OK, describe something in the creek's ecosystem that requires photosynthesis, and provide an analysis of how it fits into the habitat." Scott looked up from his paper and scanned the area. All he really wanted to see were the girls from my bio class. There was a cluster of them wearing shorts and bending over at the water's edge.

"Plants, Scott. Focus." I slapped his shoulder. Then he nodded and scribbled something down on his work sheet.

"Right, plants. What exactly are we doing again?"

I glanced at Ms. Perkins, our crazy biology teacher, running around trying to get kids to take water samples and to analyze the cellular life in the creek. The lady had to be a hundred years old. She must have fought in the Civil War. I would have bet you anything that her bones were worth as much as a dinosaur's. *This is so boring, so boring. Well, I guess the scenery is better here than in the lab.*

I looked down at my own work sheet. Most of it was filled in with my scribbles. I looked out over the bayou. Bugs were hovering above the water and above the shore. There was no place to stand that was free of bugs. I was being suffocated by bugs, and I started to feel that familiar claustrophobic anxiety overtake me.

"OK. Next question. Go find and label six leaves of different species. Write their scientific names. Additionally, identify a flower and all of its reproductive parts." Scott squinted his eyes at the print. "Please remain within sight of the instructor at all times," he said, imitating Ms. Perkins's ancient, faltering voice. He barely finished his sentence before he was stealing a glance at one of the girls. I looked, too.

Boys were flinging slime at each other. Ms. Perkins was writing them up for disciplinary action, and the girls were squawking and carrying on about the bugs. Scott went over to rescue the girls from their terrifying encounter with wildlife.

I grabbed my work sheet and began to walk toward the swamp. It was impossible to find a damn flower and keep my Converses mud-free. As I trudged on, scanning the ground, I could tell the classes before me had cleared the area of flowers. So that meant I had to delve farther into the swamp. Before long, I had walked to the point where I could not even hear the class behind me, let alone be within sight of Ms. Perkins.

That was when I saw my first and only flower: a swamp rose. Just a single, out-of-season flower on a large bush. I'd seen this plant around the swamp before, but usually they didn't have flowers on them until June. Lucky me. It was growing on the edge of a pond. No, bad description. "Pond" doesn't fit. "Mud hole with water in it" is better. Native swamp roses were a far cry from the large-petaled fragrant garden varieties, but at least it would suffice for the assignment.

Anyway, as I made my way to the swamp rose, I realized something: I had somehow stopped thinking about her. She had just slipped from my consciousness. Just like all those years ago in seventh grade, when I had first laid eyes on her: once I forgot she was there, she was never there, erased from the world.

As I reached out for the small rose, I felt a sudden, sharp pain at my ankle. Something was underneath my pant leg. My ankle burned at first, and then it turned to fire.

"What was that?!" I looked down and there before me was a dead-eyed cottonmouth snake, its tongue flicking. I saw two angry-looking fang marks right at my ankle. I'm pretty sure all the blood drained from my face. My heart began to race. The thumps ran away in my chest like a freight train that has lost its brakes and is gaining speed down a mountain. Faster, faster, ever faster.

I blinked.

The world spun.

I saw the snake uncoil and slither away. I tried to get up to move my foot from beneath me, but the pain was unbearable. As soon as I put weight on the foot, the fire turned into an inferno. I shrieked but the sound was stuck in my throat. Snared by my lungs. I coughed; then I vomited.

Feeling that I was losing my wits, I looked around. The treetops seemed way too far away. My hands looked too big. Had they inflated or had they grown? I wasn't positive which. The pain. Trust me, the pain was immense. No other pain I had experienced compared to the enraged fire pulsing in my leg and spreading with unbelievable speed up my thigh. It was engulfing my body, setting my nerves on fire, and trying to snuff out my heart.

That was when I felt the hands wrap around me. Holding me. I felt the tug. But I did not move; the ground was still there beside my ear. The world bounced and the fire...it began to itch. I shook like mad. As though I were getting electrocuted. I felt either blood or foam drip from my gaping mouth.

The world blurred green, a haze of green. I rolled my head to the side, trying to find something else but green, something to focus on to take my mind off the fire raging inside me, and there I saw it.

Her face. I blinked, trying so hard to look into her eyes. I peered deeply into that world that was her eyes, and then I closed my eyes and could not open them again.

I heard Scott's voice, but it was underwater or very distant. I felt my grip on consciousness weakening; a swooshing sound was taking over my reasoning abilities. I tried to hang on, but the fire was too great. I let the darkness consume me. The fire drifted away, along with the light.

48

Beep. Beep. Beep.
Shut up!
Beep.
What is that?
Beep.
Why is it not shutting up?
Beep.

Exasperated with whatever it was, I opened my eyes, and then closed them shut again. It was way too bright. The place was way too bright. I tried again: flood of light. I groaned. Too bright. I couldn't figure it out. I waited for a few moments, and I let my eyes flutter open once more.

This time, I let the harsh white world come into focus. I saw the ceiling tiles and flickering fluorescent lights. I blinked and scanned the room without moving my head. It smelled of cleanser and blood and rot.

But then I smelled flowers, too. Roses, trumpet lilies, and carnations. I saw several vases of flowers on the table next to the wall. Orange bird-of-paradise, bottlebrush, and that African flower. *What is it called? I always forget the name of it, but it's Mom's favorite. Protea. That's it.*

I found the source of the beeping. It was a heart monitor or something. I watched the green line zigzag across the screen, wondering whose heart it belonged to, until I realized it was mine.

There were all sorts of tubes and things, and they were all hooked up to me. I felt greasy and disgusting, as though I hadn't taken a shower since the Ice Age.

I saw Mom sitting in a chair under an ugly pink-framed painting. She was trying to read a book.

"Mom?" I was surprised by how coarse and thick my voice sounded.

"Jaden?" She looked up at me, startled. She flashed a big smile, and the book fell to the floor. She ran over, crouched by my bed, and ruffled my hair.

"How do you feel?" she said with such concern that I wondered if I had gotten hurt, but my body was numb and my mind was a blur.

I ignored her question. "Mom, where am I?" I knew the answer but I wanted it confirmed.

"The hospital, sweetie. You were bitten by a cottonmouth." Her voice sounded hollow and exhausted.

"What?" I croaked.

"Jaden, you were out with your class, and you were bitten and had a terrible reaction to the bite." I remembered that. The snake with dead eyes and a flicking, forked tongue.

"Who—"

But she finished my sentence. "A girl found you and somehow got you back to the class, and in the chaos she disappeared. No one seems to know who she was." She sounded regretful.

"But hey, look at what your fans left for you." She motioned to the countless flowers, balloons, and notes. I guessed that some fifty people had showed up.

"Smells like a flower shop."

"Your dad was here, too. He didn't leave this room for days. And your aunties and cousins. All your friends have come by."

"Where is he now?"

"Your father?"

"Yes."

"Well, he had to get back to New York. Your vitals were stable, so he had to go."

"Oh." We were silent for a moment. Then I asked, "What day is it?"

"It's Tuesday. All the kids are in class; otherwise, they would be here. I think Scott ate everything in the vending machine yesterday. Cleaned it out." She chuckled.

I smiled, too, but it strained my face and it hurt my brain. As the fog was clearing, the hurt was seeping back in.

"How long was I out?" I was horrified to think that time had swum by, leaving me trapped in the past.

"You were in a coma for nearly a week. You had a terrible reaction to the bite. Apparently, you have a rare genetic makeup and your system is particularly susceptible to this type of bite. The antivenom they administered to you had almost no effect. For a time, we weren't sure if you would make it. And if it weren't for that girl, we certainly wouldn't be talking right now, sweetie." She sighed and I noticed the rings under her eyes. She must not have left the room that entire time. I thought about the books that probably went unread in her hands as she sat in that chair, unable to process the meaning on the pages. I felt terrible for putting her under that strain.

"Mom." But I squeezed the sentence back. I wanted to tell her to go home and get some rest. I wanted to say I was fine. But the pain came back, not at the same level of intensity as that day in the swamp, but it still burned.

She saw me grimace and called for the nurse. She appeared out of nowhere, as though she lived in the walls or something. She pulled out some tube and attached a bag of clear liquid to it, and I immediately felt the world slipping away.

Mom said, "I'm staying right here, Jaden." She smiled and stroked my hair.

"That should do it," said the nurse in the background.

But before I checked out completely, I looked at the table next to me. Five vases stood on the tabletop, along with one small dried flower resting on the surface.

It was a swamp rose.

49

In and out, in and out, in and out.

That's what it was, life: pain and freedom. In and out of the world. Conscious of being conscious. Aware and then unaware. Strange dreams. Time warped. Don't ask for how long. It seemed to be hours, but it might have been days. I had no measuring stick.

"Jaden, Jaden!" somebody whispered in my ear. Hissing in my ear was more like it. And it sounded like a girl, kind of like Brook or the other girl—Jordan or Ally?

Well, anyway, I tried to open my eyes, but somehow they could not open. It was just too much work, so I just lay there and listened.

"Jaden, I love you and always will. I will always be there for you, baby."

Hmm. It could only be Brook. Man, I despised her, but then I had to remind myself that underneath that beauty queen persona was a person—corrupt and rude, maybe, but a person. Maybe she was, as she had said that day in the shed, a fallen angel. Maybe she was just trying to do the best she could in this world.

OK, also Scott played his trumpet below my hospital room window. I did not have the strength to open my eyes or talk or do anything, so I just listened to him and it was great. I'm sure he would have come into the room to play if he could have snuck that trumpet past security. I'd be surprised if he didn't try.

And I had another conversation with Mom. Talked mostly about her work. Did I tell you she was a bank person? She worked as a teller at the bank in Duncan. Yeah, so we talked about that.

Talked to Dad on the phone, too. It felt good to hear his voice, and it reminded me of New York.

At one point, I woke up in the dark of night. But a nice nurse was there to talk to. "Hi. You OK?" I opened my eyes and she was bending over me. I was surprised to find the world as dark as the one I had just stepped out of.

"Fine." I smiled and she nodded. She straightened and was about to walk away when I realized I did not want to be left there alone. I had finally gotten my mom to go home to sleep. The nice nurse sat on the edge of the bed, telling me her life story until I dozed off.

It started in New York. I was in Grand Central Station. I was standing right in the middle of it and I was still. Time spun around me as people bustled all around me, walking rapidly, glancing at their watches, and talking on their cells. Their eyes did not meet mine. They were dead to the world, dead to me.

I yelled at them, for some reason thinking I had to get them to look at me. It meant everything to me. I was desperate to get their attention, to tell them that their lives were flying by. That they were not really living them.

Trapped. I felt trapped and the harder I tried to warn people, the faster they walked, until everyone turned into a blur of color. Speeding by at impossible speeds. I was dizzy.

Panicked, I screamed at them to stop. Just to wait, just for a moment. But then the blurs of colors blended, and they got lighter and lighter until everything went white. White as though the world were empty. White like a big blank canvas. White like a paper without any words, without any story.

I was still in Grand Central Station, but everything was polished a blinding white. And then I saw someone. Her back was to me, and I called out, "Hello?"

She paused and turned to look at me. She was in her old, tattered jeans and orange T-shirt, her hair wild. Gorgeous, even in my dreams. Her hands were not bandaged, and I could see several open gashes. The blood dripped onto the white marble floor. Then she turned and ran away.

And I had never run so fast. All that could be heard was the sound of our footsteps bouncing off the polished white walls. The place was entirely empty.

We made it to the train platform, which was also vacant. The train doors slid open and she disappeared inside. I ran faster but all I could hear was the train starting up and the hydraulic swoosh of the closing doors!

I was so close, right there, a few feet away. Inches away...and I dove inside and fell to the floor.

I looked up as the train rolled down the tracks. It was still white outside. But she was not in the compartment. The only thing there was a single rose lying on the floor. A red rose. The kind you see in movies, the kind in a king's garden, the kind at the White House, the kind you give to your love. Except that this one was in a pool of blood. And then I heard the doors open.

Outside was a beach. The type of beach you would find in Duncan. So I walked out. This world had color, lots of it. Mostly swampy greens and ocean blues. I walked along, sinking into the hot sand. As I did, I felt chills spread through me, and then I rounded a corner. There before me was the Duncan Shipyard.

I was caught off guard by how close I was. Closer than I had ever been. I froze, sure that I had already signed my own death certificate. There, emanating from those old rusted steamboats, I heard them. The cries of the slaves: the wails, the air-stabbing screams of pain.

50

And then I woke up. I was home in my own bed. Everything looked normal. It was just a bad dream.

Then the dull, throbbing pain reminded me about my leg. Curious, I lifted the sheets to see what my leg looked like. It had a jagged line of black stitches. The whole thing was swollen and purple. It made me want to vomit right there. I would have a nasty scar, but at least I would have two legs. And my life.

My phone was on my bedside table. I looked at the date. Two weeks had vanished to the coma, drugs, and deep sleep. I had thirty-seven messages. Later, I would read them. Right now, I just wanted to get out of my smelly hospital gown. My greasy hair was unbearable; I immediately got up to take a shower.

I shuffled to the bathroom, my leg seemingly unawake. I dragged it behind me like deadweight. As soon as I got to the bathroom, I looked at the image in the mirror. My eyes were bloodshot, my lips were blue, my body was thinner, and my brown hair looked darker than usual and was matted in various places. And I was so pale I looked like the son of a zombie.

I took a shower and afterward I felt better. Much, much better. So when I looked into the mirror again, I was pleased to see I had human-colored skin again, no longer ghostly. I got some clothes on and hobbled downstairs, and there at the table reading a book was Mom.

She looked like a zombie, an exhausted, frenzied mama bear. It made me feel guilty.

"Hey, Mom!" I said cheerfully. I was happy to be up and about for once instead of a bed sloth.

"Jaden!" She sounded ecstatic. "You're up!"

"Finally." I found some leftovers in the fridge, dumped a pile onto my plate, and shoved it into the microwave. I sat down and began to devour the food. It had never tasted so good, food.

I looked up at Mom, who was watching me eat. "Mom, what are you doing with my baby book?" The book she held was a scrapbook your parents put your pictures in as you grow up.

"What pictures are you adding?" I leaned in, my mouth full of pasta, and pointed to the picture she was gluing into the book.

She just went quiet and looked up at me. I was still staring at the photo. Out of the corner of my eye, I saw her wipe away a tear.

"Mom, what's wrong?"

"Nothing, Jaden. Nothing." She began to close the book, but I snagged it from her. I flipped to the last page, and there in the tenth grade section were three pictures: one was me at the airport terminal, arriving from New York with all my junk. I looked so depressed in that photo. The second was of me, still looking depressed, in my suit, about to go to homecoming without the girl of my dreams.

The one Mom had added just then was a picture of me in the hospital bed, my leg an impossible black color. I looked dead. My head lolled to one side, and I had a tube in my mouth. I was attached by pipes and tubes to three outsize machines behind the bed. I don't know what looked more disturbing, the machines or me. The handwritten caption read "Jaden at the Duncan Hospital getting treated for cottonmouth bite. His heart stopped for more than a minute."

I shivered and looked up at Mom. "Is that true?"

"When we got you to the hospital, they gave you the antivenom. You seemed to be doing better but then took a turn for the worse. That night, your heart stopped. They had no choice but to administer another dose of antivenom. They said it was a miracle you didn't die, Jaden." She was looking at the linoleum floor and had her arms crossed in front of her as if she were trying to hold herself together. "You really scared me, Jaden."

"Mom, it's OK. I didn't die. I'm right here." My voice was weak.

"But you almost did, Jaden! That's what I'm trying to say. Seeing you there on the brink of death for so long...it was a painful thing to realize that you are my world. Not my garden or this town. You. And I almost lost you forever..." Her voice trailed off and more tears spilled down her cheeks.

I got up and hugged her. I had forgotten how small she was. *Poor Mom.*

"I'm alive, Mom." I whispered it and looked out the window. The first flowers of spring were popping up. Blankets of yellow and orange and purple filled the view from where I stood.

"Let's leave here, Jaden. I forgot how precious life is. How delicate it is. How life needs to be lived." She stared out the window. Then she said, "Let's move to New York this summer. Permanently."

"What?!" I let go, staring at her. "Mom, you love it here! The plants, the weather, the swamp, the smallness of the town! New York would be a living hell for you!" I was blown away.

"Yes, and Duncan is a living hell for you, Jaden. And besides, it turns out, as the doctors explained to me, you are highly susceptible to snakebite venom. Had I known that, I would have moved you far away from anywhere that had venomous snakes. New York fits the bill. I don't know what my life would be like if I didn't have you. I'll get an apartment with lots of windows so I can have some flower boxes. Can you make me some in woodshop?"

"Mom, I don't know if I have enough time. Only April, May, and a little bit of June are left of the school year." I paused, processing how I would go about constructing a windowsill box. "Mom, are you positive about this? Really? I don't think you should move because of me." I was still in shock.

"Yes, I certainly am. Remember how you said you wanted to go to school in New York? Well, that means you would not come back to Duncan anyway. I want to go where you go, Jaden. You were in the hospital for a long time. Over there is all the homework you have to make up." She pointed and I gawked at the piles of missed assignments. I walked over to where seven piles, one per class, were neatly stacked. Some piles were high, such as geometry, and others were low, such as woodshop.

However, biology was unusually low. Surprisingly low: just five papers. I think Ms. Perkins was feeling kind of guilty about what had gone down on her watch. I turned to look at my mom. She was rubbing her chin, the way people do when they're thinking, and I could tell she was thinking hard because her eyebrows were knitted.

"Mom?"

But she did not respond. She grabbed some sticky notes and a pen and dragged me outside as fast as my lame leg could go. She began to march down the path that wove through the plants. We dodged the yucca. I have avoided the pointed-tip yucca ever since I fell into one, butt first, when I was six.

She looked lovingly at her plants. It was hard imagining my mom cooped up in an apartment in New York, squeezing all her love into a couple of planter boxes. The thought made me depressed. She belonged in her garden.

Then I realized I would be taking finals soon. After that, I would pack my bags to move to the city of my dreams. And I would never have to live another blasted hour in that armpit.

51

Man, the first day back at school sucked. Completely.

I rolled out of bed and was driven to school by Mom. I thought about the piles of assignments getting ever so dusty on the kitchen counter. I was late and my mom seemed too happy to care. She was just glad that I had recovered.

As we pulled into the parking lot, I looked at my leg, bare below my shorts, and for the first time became self-conscious about it. Embarrassed by my feebleness.

I hobbled to English. As I neared the door, I stopped for no particular reason, other than to pause for a second to collect my courage. I looked into the little window and saw Miss Carlson armed with a meter stick and a stack of essays. I began to wonder how much time I could just stand there before I had to go in. But I took a deep breath and reached for the door handle. Just then I heard my name...coming from the empty hallway.

The source was so far away, the sound echoed. I wasn't sure if I had actually heard it, but then I looked down the hall and I saw her. Her back was to me, and she was looking out into the courtyard. Looking at some spring flowers. Her hair was like silk waves. I stepped into the center of the hallway. She turned at the sound of my footsteps and gazed at me. I gawked at her beauty, stunned again by her eyes and just everything about her. She smiled a real smile. But then I heard my name for sure, and it came from the English room.

"Jaden!" It was Brook's diva voice. I turned; she was leaning out of the classroom door. I looked back down the hallway, but Bloody Hands was gone. Again. I expected it now. But still every time she slipped away, my fascination grew.

"Jaden!" Brook was hissing at me again. "What are you *doing*?" I heard a rumble of voices inside the room, and Miss Carlson's dry, scratchy voice growl at them. I walked into class and Brook engulfed me in her arms.

"Yay, Jaden's back!" she announced proudly to the class.

She then moved to her seat, and I stood at the door like an idiot and realized that everyone was staring at my leg, my permanently disfigured leg. I felt very self-conscious. I should have worn long pants.

"Welcome back to class, Jaden Miller; we were so sorry to hear of your mishap."

Mishap? I wanted to walk over there and choke her, that stupid woman. "Thanks," I croaked and then took my seat and stared at the Shakespeare posters. I had stared at those uninspiring posters who knows how many times.

Miss Carlson continued to lecture about the use of the magical semicolon. As soon as the bell rang, people swarmed me as I tried to hobble my way through the crowd.

"What did it feel like?"

"Were you scared?"

"Does it hurt now? How big was the snake?"

"Jaden, I heard you almost died. Is that true?"

I tried to plow through the kids and make my escape, but for a cripple that did not work so well. and I was the last one out. Well, I almost made it out. Then I heard a voice I had learned to despise.

"Jaden, I need to speak to you for a moment." I turned and Miss Carlson was eyeing me from her desk. I should have pretended not to hear her and kept walking to freedom, but instead I limped back to her desk.

She gave me a halfhearted smile and put down the novel she was reading. She inhaled loudly and then got right down to business. She pulled out a paper and slid it over to me. It said this:

To Jaden Miller,

"There is nothing to writing. All you do is sit down at a typewriter and bleed."
-Ernest Hemingway

I looked at the words, rereading them several times, and then finally looked at Miss Carlson. Her head was bent over her book again. The first kid in her next period ambled in.

Suddenly, Miss Carlson looked up. "OK, so I know you are probably dreading the stacks of makeup work you need to complete by finals."

"Well, yeah."

"So I will give you a choice, Mr. Miller. You say you like creative writing? Write me a story. Any story. Or you can spend the rest of the year after school with me, reading the things you missed." She smirked and I heard the bell ring. I didn't respond; with difficulty, I made my way out the door.

As I stumped down the empty hallway, I stopped and looked out the windows to the courtyard. Of course, she was nowhere to be seen. Something caught my eye, though, and I looked down at the row of flowers. One was gone. The entire plant had just vanished. Just then, a janitor walked by, and he didn't seem to notice the hole in the ground in the midst of a row of brilliance.

52

I spent the rest of the day trying to adjust to being differently abled at school. By the time I got home, I was feeling ornery, so I threw my backpack on the floor and began to climb the stairs. I stopped when I heard Mom.

"Jaden! Jaden, I need your help. Hurry!" She sounded panicked.

"Coming!" I said halfheartedly. That was how I felt. But I dragged myself into the backyard, and there my mom was trying to push a huge Canary Island date palm into place. I ran as fast as I could and took her place at the heavy part of the trunk. I managed to push it up and secure it in place. I backed up, admiring its beauty. It looked happy, finally in the earth instead of a pot. I looked over at Mom, who was smiling broadly. Nothing made her happier than a new addition to her family of plants. Funny how she continued to improve her garden despite the fact that she intended to abandon that place and move to New York. I guessed that she just couldn't help herself.

I turned to go back into the house when Mom shouted from behind me.

"Jaden!" she called happily. "Jaden, I still need some muscle out here!"

So I headed back to the garden. Mom was wearing her favorite sun hat, the one from Africa. She led me through the garden to a wheelbarrow full of our homemade compost.

"So...what's the plan?" I asked tentatively. I was glad not to be doing my homework, yet dreading the fact that I still had to do it.

"OK," she said and pointed to the wheelbarrow. "I found an empty patch in the garden that we'll fill with this compost. Then we can bring in the lilies that I got from my friend Martha. Ms. Millbury." She sounded quite satisfied when she showed me her new lilies. They weren't in bloom but were just beginning to open their flower pods. I thought that they would be white ones.

I followed behind Mom as she led me along the paths to the empty spot. She also talked about her day at the bank and her plans and ideas for the apartment in New York. Such as turning her shower into a greenhouse and blah, blah, blah. As usual, I just trudged behind her like a good soldier.

"Why is there an empty spot?" Several small areas of torn-up dirt were surrounded by various shades of green.

"Oh, I don't know. Some critter must have dug up the plants." Her breathing was labored as she moved the dirt with a shovel.

"So what were they?"

"Hibiscus." She added in a mutter, "They weren't doing too well. It seems that as soon as a plant begins to decline around here, it disappears." She planted the lily in the old hibiscus spot, wiped sweat from her forehead, and turned to look at me. She smiled broadly.

She put me to work in the garden, and I listened to Mom's chitchat and the sound of chickadees socializing in the garden; both Mom and the birds sounded delighted just to be there. I was the alien.

My mind wandered to the piles of work collecting dust on the kitchen counter, which I had to shove into my brain. All I really wanted was to do mundane work, such as chucking banana-smelling compost under flowers that had yet to bloom. But cruel homework awaited me.

So I said, "Mom, I have an assignment to write a story for English, and I was hoping to get some ideas. Do you have any ideas that might make for a cool story?"

She leaned on her shovel. "Is there a prompt? A title? An idea to work from?" She wanted something to work with. I wanted that as well. I didn't see much of a story in everyday things.

"Nope." My voice was flat. I tried again. "I'm just supposed to pull a story out of the world and write."

"Anything then?" Mom sounded excited by the challenge. She looked around her garden, as if she might find a story there. Pluck a brilliant idea from the air or the earth. That's how my mom rolls.

"*Hmm*, you know what? Have you ever read a story that had a surprising point of view? A voice you wouldn't expect?"

I was lost.

"OK, look. You see this lily?" She pointed to the plant.

"Yeah?" I was very lost.

"Well, I want you to think of this lily describing something entirely differently than you would. Think of it as a person."

Still lost.

"This lily is a person. A girl perhaps, very beautiful, very well balanced, but still has not opened herself up to her greatest potential. Now she has just been placed in a new environment."

She got up and motioned to a giant coral tree, "And here is another person. Let's say he is a survivor because he was the first one planted in the garden. So he has had a great chance to expand his new horizons." She opened her arms to replicate its canopy of branches.

"And here's a golden barrel cactus. He's a grumpy, fat old man; no one wants to go near him. But every once in a while he produces a flower more gorgeous than the rose or the lily. It's his loving heart overcoming the fact that he is just a grouchy old cactus." She smiled, pleased with herself.

"OK, Jaden, now you. What are you?"

I shrugged.

"You're a houseplant, Jaden, a golden pothos. It is one of the most popular houseplants in the world. So common you could probably find thousands in New York City alone. However, there is one special thing about it. When you take it to where it belongs, it does something completely amazing. It grows immensely from the tiny little houseplant into a magnificent plant that can dwarf entire trees. Its leaves grow from the size of a dog's ear to the size of an elephant's ear." She stopped and imagined that. She looked into my eyes. "It flourishes."

I was still standing there, lost.

And then in that alien universe, I got an idea that was out of this world.

53

I made my way to my room as quickly as I could, where I looked for an old paper lost in the piles of trash on my clothes-strewn floor. After what felt like a thirty-minute CIA search, I found what I was looking for.

It was the piece that Henry and Michael, my two cousins, had tormented me with on Thanksgiving. All I had written down was this:

Jaden Miller
Creative Writing
Period 4

The Fox Trot

For some reason or other, I was not alarmed about where I was. I was surprisingly content, as though I had no other place to fill with my presence but my exact location. Into the brisk morning air I made the only bird call I knew: the call of the mourning dove. The low call is, "Whooouuuooo, who, who, who." From nowhere, a fox appeared.

Right below me, with head down, ears forward, and nose to the ground, was a fox. It never looked up, as though it did not expect to encounter a fifteen-year-old boy in a bayou tree, looking down at it. As it walked beneath me and before it disappeared, I called to it: "Hello?" It continued its fox trot into the swamp.

I had never turned in the story or even finished the rough draft because I had thought it was pointless, but now I saw that the story had possibilities. So I grabbed some scratch paper and began to write.

54

I watched Brook break into a cloud of bubbles and swim toward me in slow motion. She was transformed. Her blonde hair was suspended gold as it flowed around her face. Her eyes were closed, her face at peace.

She came alive and clawed herself up along with the bubbles to the world above. My lungs strained and I, too, peeled myself away from the underwater world. I sucked in oxygen and then was assaulted by the noise of splashing teenagers. I opened my eyes and gazed at the heads and arms around me, all breaking the surface of the water and bobbing there.

"Jaden!" I turned and there was Scott, doing a perfect backflip off the diving board.

"Nice!" I shouted in response.

We were in PE. It was Friday and we were swimming. No one was paying the slightest attention to our PE teacher, a bored man who sat in a corner of the pool deck on a little stool, sleeping, or at least everyone thought he was, for he was wearing sunglasses. I guess thirty years of teaching proper swimming technique to high school students had never worked, and he had surrendered, letting us do whatever we wanted. As I rode Scott's waves to the diving board again, Brook cut me off.

"Jaden!" She sounded frantic. "Don't look. My top fell off!" She crossed her arms over her chest, and as soon as those words were uttered, every guy within a radius of fifty feet looked over at her, eyes bulging. I was no exception.

"Ha! Gotcha! You looked!" She smiled and splashed me and swam over to the ladder. I just groaned. I should have expected as much.

Scott surfaced, crying out, "Woo-hoo! Full gainer! Did you see that one, Jaden?" He swam over to me, and I turned to the ladder to watch Brook climb out. Swimming was the most exciting unit in PE—well, for the boys, anyway. Spending weeks on end seeing the girls in their bathing suits was great, and for the girls, or at least the cute ones, it was a blast. They got lots of attention, especially good ol' Brook. She, of course, reveled in that environment. For the not-so-fit ones, it seemed to be a nightmare. They ran around in full-body-length towels, taking them off only when they were about to slip into the water. And it seemed all the girls would complain about having wet hair for the rest of the day. Also, if a girl happened to be on her period, well, everyone knew it, as she would sit out class. I could tell this was a bit embarrassing to the girls. Of course, no one ever asked why they weren't swimming. No way.

Brook was hogging the ladder, so I couldn't leave the pool. I waited below and to her left for her to move, but she just stood there, looking off into the distance. She was blocking the sun with her head, and honestly, she looked like an angel: her blonde hair now in loose strands falling down around her shoulders, her skin golden. She belonged on a beach in California, not in a high school swimming pool in Louisiana.

It was her eyes. The way they were glazed over. Caught in the past or a dream or a haunted thought.

"Brook!" I shouted at her. She looked down at me, frazzled, but then regained her composure.

"Sorry, Jaden, baby!" She gave me a half smile and took the last steps up the ladder. She made it to the pool deck and just stood there, hugging herself, lost again.

Just then, the bell rang, and students—masses of nearly nude girls and boys—swarmed toward the locker rooms, grabbing their towels off the bleachers. I took one last look at Brook. She wore a dazed expression, as if she were in a far-off place and not a good one. I almost felt a tinge of sorrow for her, and I made a wish. I wished for her to regain her wings and fly back to the golden world from which she had fallen.

I rushed to the guys' locker room and took an extra-long shower. I did not have to worry that I would be the last one out. I was not going to another class. Along with Scott and a few others, I was headed to New Orleans.

55

As I exited the double doors of the locker room and looked up at the sun, it warmed my face. I felt refreshed and ready to tackle this adventure.

Scott ran right up next to me, smiling widely. He pulled out his trumpet. As he filled the sunlit air with the sounds of jazz, it warmed my bones to the marrow. We strolled out to the parking lot, where some other kids had gathered. We all climbed into a cool old Volkswagen van. Eight of us. Five guys, along with Brook, Ally, and Jordan. Our designated driver, Bryce, fired up his dad's vintage hippie van. It sputtered to life, not quite sure of itself as we rolled forward, but then, as if on cue, as we pulled out of the Hampton High parking lot, the engine roared to life. We barreled down the road, eating asphalt faster than we could look at it.

The drive took about three hours. That meant three hours of nonstop rock 'n' roll, jazz, and hip-hop. Also, miles full of gossip, mostly orchestrated by Brook Jackson. I gazed out the window. Lost mostly in my mind, trying to suck the noise from the atmosphere and delve back into the quiet and calm of an underwater world. I had no luck and soon I fell under the spell of music and voices.

"Jaden! Jaden!" I knew what was coming. Everyone did; the girls in particular had been talking about the Mardi Gras dance all year long. There was a going-away party at the end of school every year. That was the Mardi Gras dance.

Trust me, you can forget about homecoming and prom, because the Hampton High Mardi Gras dance was the biggest and most important event of the year. It was on the very last day of school. That was actually why were going to New Orleans: to buy costumes and dresses for the Mardi Gras dance.

"What?" I shouted, mimicking the high-pitched level of enthusiasm in Ally's voice. Some of the guys laughed. The kid behind me gave me a slap on the back. The girls were leaning out of their seats, their hair still a bit wet. Nothing ever dries completely in this humidity.

"Who are you taking to the Mardi Gras dance?" Ally smiled and gazed up at me. She was holding one of the puppies. One of Tazz's puppies. Scott's grandma had fallen in love with one of the puppies, the one who took after its mother. Its name was Buckaroo. Tazz and Buckaroo: double trouble. But the other four puppies needed to get new homes, and there was no better solution than to hand them over on the streets of New Orleans and get some cash to boot. I mean, who could resist Pomeranian puppies (even ones with a little psycho pit bull in them)? So Scott had packed up the little fluff balls in a big cardboard box, and we planned to sell them to the suckers of New Orleans.

Ally's question: that was a big one.

"Don't know," I muttered.

"Oh, we know you know, so tell us!" begged Jordan.

Ally handed a puppy to Tony, the guy next to me. Some of us were sitting on the floor of the van because there weren't enough seats.

"Lying!" cried Ally. "He's lying!"

"Nah, I don't know." But they would not drop their questioning until they got a definitive answer out of me. That's what girls do. It's bro code to keep quiet.

But I didn't know who to take or whether I would even go. But I had to for my dad's sake; he had sent me that suit for Christmas.

"I'll probably just go with the guys," I said.

I gazed out the window as they continued their attempt to pry the truth from my lips. Fortunately, a road sign saved me.

"Look! We're in New Orleans!" And that broke the spell. The girls fell from the subject like moths from a light that had just been turned off. They went straight to their new topic and began squealing and hugging each other and wriggling in their seats. Even the puppies felt the vibe, got hyper, and started to yip. Girls. Man, understanding them is like trying to map a maze.

Fifteen minutes later, the city of New Orleans rose into the sky in front of us. Its mighty buildings gave me a charge. We headed to the French Quarter; that's where you go in New Orleans for action. We ditched the car. Then Scott and I rounded up the puppies, and we strolled down the street. All eight of us. What a gang we were.

Down by the river levy, we watched as a supersize freighter passed by above us. It was surreal to stand on a dry street and see a ship float by *above* you. The freighter was floating on water held back by a pile of dirt. But that's what happens here, the impossible: a city below sea level right next to the Mississippi River, the greatest river on the continent. Of course, during

Katrina, that didn't work out so well. But that was in the past, and it was time for us to embrace all that the place had to offer. We continued to walk and sold one puppy before we even set up base camp.

We got settled and the girls were given two hours to shop to their hearts' delight. They took off, dragging Tony along, much to his dismay. Or so he said. Scott got his trumpet out of its case, and one of the other guys, Mike, pulled out a set of bongos. In a few moments, we were rocking the pavement of Bourbon Street.

Crowds swarmed past us, and Scott and Mike made $100, mainly in ones. While they were working the crowd with their music, I was working the crowd—particularly the ladies—with the three remaining puppies.

In the midst of this street party, a group of guys strutted up to us. They had tattoos, swagger, and a load of instruments. They had been planning to spend the day rocking the street, and we, apparently, had stolen their spot.

"Y'all come see this! We got some dopes stealing our plot!"

I turned around. There were about eight kids, and the one in front,—a short, stocky guy—looked none too happy to see our clan. The stocky one focused on me in particular.

"Chum, what y'all think you're doin'?"

He looked as though he were about to fire off, but I held my ground. I could feel the other guys start to gather behind me, and as they did, the tension skyrocketed. There were just the four of us: Scott, Bryce, Mike, and me. We were outnumbered.

"Slim it, dude. Nice and cool." I tried to stay serene and motioned to him to calm down. My other hand was cradling a sleeping black fluff ball.

The stocky kid just stared at me. "Where are you from, chum?"

But before I could answer, the one and only Scott walked up and stepped between us, like Mercutio, stealing the show and disarming the Montagues and the Capulets.

"Why fight"—he raised his eyebrows, smiled, and motioned to the stocky kid's trumpet—"when we can party?" And he set off. That golden trumpet roared across the town. His eyes were closed, his cheeks were puffed, and his fingers were dancing wildly across the keys.

The guy, the stocky kid, stood there staring at Scott. Suddenly, a tiny boy bailed out of their pack. The kid must have been, like, nine. He jumped out of the crowd and let it rip on his tuba. It was the funniest thing I had ever seen: Scott rocking with a tiny tuba player. But it was brilliant.

Clyde, the stocky kid, actually turned out to be awesome, and so did his band. I can't explain the magic that happened between us all as the sky grew dark and the stars came out. We were swarmed with all walks of life, every nationality, and every age. Singing and laughing erupted and mixed with our music as the street came alive in its own kind of way. Everyone was drunk on the New Orleans vibe and Creole food, not to mention lots of booze.

The girls came back with a surplus of Mardi Gras loot, and soon we were decked out in masks and beads.

Purple and green were everywhere. Those who could not play an instrument danced. That is, except for this one guy called Frypan. He cooked up gumbo for everyone right on the sidewalk, and it was the best sludge I had ever had.

It's funny when I think of it now, how possessed I was. Under the spell of the warm air and the brassy jazz. The tourists were psyched to be in that magical place. I was, too. Truth be told, I was one of them, the tourists. I was in the heart of a city so unlike the one I had just come from. I was stoked.

Oh, and if you were wondering, I brokered three more sales, and the rest of the puppies were sent off to torment other unsuspecting souls. So it was a good night, that is, until I did something boneheaded. Ha! Boneheaded is my best friend, and it follows me around as if it were my own shadow.

I was so swept away by the blaring sounds and crazy sights, I was dancing wildly with a masked blonde girl and we were singing. My eyes focused on everything and nothing at the same time. I was caught up in the moment.

I tried hard and the masked girl slowly transformed into *her*. And then it all came crashing down as a burly man, grotesque in a yellowed and sweaty tank top, reached out for *her,* snagging the girl at the waist. It all happened so fast. He pulled *her* away from me, and the girl punched him in the gut. He yelled at the girl and didn't let go. She screamed. That was when I became the fox.

I lunged at the brute, smacking him off his feet. It felt good. I kicked him in the shins. I punched him in the jaw, and it was like hitting a beehive because it released a frenzy of anger from him. That was not good, for the guy got up and barreled into me, and I was knocked to the ground. However, before he could smack me, I rolled to the side and his fist hit the asphalt. He bellowed again and I got to my feet. Before he could get up, I plucked an empty beer bottle from the street and sent one nice smack to his head with it. The bottle smashed into pieces.

What had I done? Some folks stared at me as if I had just committed murder. Others kept dancing without a care in the world. I straightened my mask and turned to *her*. She was shaking with sobs. I took the girl into my arms. She was tiny and vulnerable and precious.

And then the brute turned his bloody face to look up at me. If he got up off the ground, he would kill me for sure. So I grabbed the girl's hand, and we hauled ass.

We ran for a while. I'm not sure how long we ran, because time seemed to suspend us in our flight. And I didn't know where we were. We had taken a series of side streets off of the main one. The only thing I felt sure of was the small hand in my hand. Finally, we stopped when the crowds had dispersed and the street was empty. It was quite late, dark, and it began to rain.

I turned and looked at the girl. She was standing there underneath a streetlight. I looked around. Where could we go to stay dry? And then I saw it. Across the street, there was a shop with a warm glow coming through the windows. A haven in the darkness. As I pulled her hand, we sprinted across the vacant road toward it.

"This way!" I yelled, even though there was no need to shout. The girl tugged on my hand and followed. We jumped inside the building and shook the water from our bodies the best we could. I laughed. "Man what a night, huh?"

She laughed, too. "Yeah, totally blows."

I smiled and looked around the shop. Trust me, the place was weird: skulls with candles coming out of them, Mardi Gras sculptures, wooden masks painted in neon colors, and glowing amulets. Candles were everywhere; there was not a single light bulb.

I soon felt the girl at my side, her shallow, sweet breath at my shoulder.

"Let's get out of here. This place is creepy," she muttered.

"Right there with ya." We slowly retraced our steps to the exit. We were about a foot from the door when it slammed on us. I pushed it. It was locked!

That was when the fear sank in. Sank deep. I was shaking. And then, as if we both weren't spooked enough, we heard a voice.

"Welcome, welcome to Madam Mabel's House of Hoodoo Voodoo."

The girl beside me pressed closer to me and looked up. She, too, was trembling with fear. "What the hell is going on?" she asked me.

Before I could answer, a voice came booming from all corners and angles of the hoodoo-voodoo place. "Don't speak of hell. And don't utter the devil's name, child, or he will find you and make you his."

Then a hand grabbed each of our shoulders.

We spun around and screamed. But no one was there. Then, right before our eyes, as if materializing out of thin air, a large woman in African tribal garb appeared. Uncannily, she looked exactly like Madam Marian at the Stop-N-Shop. This woman could have been her or maybe her identical twin.

"Come, come sit at the table of fate." She grabbed hold of both of us and dragged us deeper into the store. Soon we came upon a carpeted area with thick red and purple velvet drapes. A low table stood in the center, and it was covered with nails and bones and wax and candles and carvings. Things dangled from it, including a bizarre chandelier.

We were rammed onto the table platform. Our chairs were pulled out, and we fell into them. My knees bumped into the dangling objects under the table. Beads of sweat formed on my forehead. I gazed across the table at the masked girl. I now knew she was Brook. Then Madam Marian's weird sister sank her talons into Brook's shoulders, trapping Brook in her seat.

I kept blinking my eyes, trying to make sense of the situation. Then the madwoman began to sing: "Welcome, children, welcome. / Let me prick your thumbs." She reached for my hand and jabbed it with a knife until my thumb had a nice slit in it that produced a steady flow of blood. It looked like a little burst volcano, its lava flowing down my finger. I held my bloody finger across the table as it dripped steadily into a burning candle, swirling around with the orange wax and causing the smoke to turn black.

She grabbed Brook's thumb and did the same. A cry escaped Brook's lips, and she struggled in her chair, but it was no use. Invisible ropes tied us both down. Madam Mabel stirred a giant black pot of some type of liquid. The pot was suspended from the ceiling by three metal cables, and I wouldn't have been surprised if it contained eye of newt and toe of frog and a lizard's leg and whatever else crazy witch sisters cook up.

"Let us walk, let us walk, all the way into a sleep walk." She then grabbed a handful of Brook's hair and tilted her head back. She scooped her ladle into the pot of bubbling brew and poured the thick golden liquid onto Brook's forehead. It trickled down her face, and I nearly choked when I saw her.

Brook's face was shimmering as though tiny diamonds were embedded in her skin. Her hair looked to be made of golden spun silk. Her eyes were tightly closed. She looked dead to the world. I, too, closed my eyes, and as I did, I heard Madam Mabel chant, "I sense that you were once harassed. Time to take a step back, back into your past. We must all join hands. Close your eyes and walk with me to your days gone by."

Everything was quiet, unnaturally silent, and the colors seemed to go in and out of focus like a swirl of watercolor paint. It was as though we were molecules of paint on an artist's canvas. Suddenly, it all changed and the colors seemed to gather and form into shapes, and soon the murky colors morphed into a room, the artist roughing out an image.

I could tell it was a trailer. For some reason, my vantage point was down low, as if I were on all fours or as if I were a dog. Then a man walked into the room from outside. He was shirtless and unshaven and wrinkled. His eyes were sunk deep into their sockets, and his nose protruded, along with his belly.

And then a younger Brook stumbled in. I was witnessing a scene from Brook's childhood. She seemed to be trying to escape the heat. She was younger but very much the same, and when I forced my eyes open and peaked across the table, there was the very real person, Brook. Her hair was gold and her skin shining, but her eyes were vacant. Standing beside her was the madwoman, Madam Mabel. I closed my eyes again. We were all watching the same trailer park scene play out.

The shirtless man's eyes followed the younger version of Brook as she walked into the room.

"Girl, get over here." He downed the rest of his beer.

He crinkled his can and tossed it on the floor then motioned for younger Brook. He began walking toward her. He walked right through me and kept walking. I was floored. What was going on? And then Little Brook followed the man, but from Brook's horrified look, I could tell she knew that something bad was about to happen.

"What is it?" Little Brook asked, looking around nervously.

"No!" the Real Brook was crying. She was terrified, "Take me away from here!" She was screaming now at the top of her lungs, but Madam Mabel just looked on.

"What is done cannot be undone," said Madam Mabel.

"It's on the table." The man motioned to the small kitchen table, littered with plates of moldy food. Then Little Brook stepped closer to take a look. And then it all happened very fast, and I didn't know who was louder:

Real Brook or Little Brook. Both seemed to be living in the horror of the moment. I was powerless and paralyzed in this scene. I looked away and closed my eyes. I couldn't watch this.

Suddenly, they both stopped screaming. Actually, all the noise stopped. I looked up again and witnessed something that time could never erase from my memory. Little Brook was standing in the kitchen. She held a knife in her hands, and it was dripping with blood. Below her was the large man, with a long gash across his neck. Blood gurgled out in spurts and then slowed to a trickle. His eyes were fixed wide open.

Slowly, the nightmare began to swirl away and Little Brook disappeared.

I immediately turned to look across the table at the real Brook. Her eyes were glazed and troubled. Just as she had been earlier today at the pool, she was lost in thought or a bad memory. Finally, her eyes found mine and a tear fell down her cheek, which she quickly brushed away.

56

"Jaden, it is time we see your destiny. Let us learn from the fox."

Madam Mabel grabbed a fistful of my hair, tilted my head back, and trickled the wet substance all over my face. All I saw was the shock in Brook's eyes as I fell back into the world of washed-out colors.

Soon those swirling colors transformed into a new scene. I saw a guy in a suit. It was me. I was walking and then I realized where I was. For there behind me was the silhouette of the Duncan Shipyard, and I was walking away from it.

I was wearing torn, blood-streaked clothes, very nice clothes—the suit my dad had given me. My hands were covered in fresh blood. I was crying.

The me in this scene looked back at the shipyard, and he looked so sad, so pained. He was feeling something I could not grasp. I could not delve into his mind, for it was not my own head. The other me suddenly stopped and gazed up into a tree. He smiled and then seemed to talk to the tree. I could not hear what he said, but it seemed his whole mood suddenly changed. Although he still cried, the tears changed from those of sorrow to those of joy. He advanced on me, coming so close, and then he stopped. He looked down at me. Unlike the way it was in Brook's adventure, he seemed to be able to see me. He smiled a real smile, and his red, teary eyes filled with a new sense of hope.

"Hey there, Jaden. The fox trot is over," he said to me. Then I began to lose him as the swirling colors turned black.

57

My eyes flew open and I was standing on the street. Behind me was a sign on a door that said Madam Mabel's House of Hoodoo Voodoo. It was no longer raining. It wasn't even dark, for the first light of dawn filled the air. It was still too early for people to be out and about. The cooing of pigeons and the lone bark of a dog, however, told me that the world was alive and well. Then I felt something else, a small hand in my hand. I looked over and Brook was standing there smiling at me.

"Of course, silly! Of course I'll go to the Mardi Gras dance with you."

Brook wouldn't shut up about the dance, and I was completely taken prisoner in the Land of Confusion. So by the time we got to the motel where the rest of our gang were cooped up, I was honestly just brain dead. What had just happened?

We walked down the hallway, and I knocked on the door to room 201. That was our room. At least, I thought it was. That was when Brook cried, "Jaden, what's wrong with you? You look possessed!" She sounded kind of pissed. Her hands were on her hips and her brow was furrowed.

"You really don't remember?"

"What? Saying good-bye to the puppies?"

"No." I knocked on the door again.

"What? That guy who hit on me? Thanks for beating him up, by the way."

"No, that's not..." I pondered telling her about the House of Hoodoo Voodoo but instead I just said, "No, nothing. I mean, I'm just tired. It's, like, 5 a.m."

"No, it's officially 6:30 in the morning, Jaden," announced Scott as he opened the hotel room door.

"Where have you been, Brook?" said Ally, as she opened the door across the hall.

Brook laughed and hugged me. "Good night, baby," she whispered as she broke away and disappeared into the girls' room.

I followed Scott inside the guys' room, which smelled like farts, socks, and sweat all at once. The guys were asleep and lying on or in everything: bed, floor, and bathtub. Scott flopped down on the bed and put the pillow over his head.

58

After spring break, Bloody Hands rarely came to class. She seemed to be going out of her way to avoid me, and I began to take it personally. I was making an effort to actually do well, so I studied and went to the library every day. I only had one more semester to go – if I didn't get decent grades I would not be accepted to the school in New York. I could not let myself be distracted by gorgeous girls and hoodoo voodoo.

We had test after test, and of course every girl was bouncing with excitement about the Mardi Gras dance, which seemed to be looming ahead of me like the iceberg that sank the *Titanic*. Brook, especially, could not seem to contain her excitement. The days seemed to progress rapidly as we rode the roller coaster of anticipation and distraction until, finally, it was the day.

The sunlight filtered in through my window. It, along with my alarm clock and the cries of my mom, pulled me into the world.

"Jaden Miller! It's the last day of school!" she shouted from downstairs. I threw back the covers and nearly tripped over my suitcase. My room was dismantled: bare except for some boxes and my suitcase, all ready to go.

I was forever leaving the mud pit of the bayou. I felt that my life was just beginning. I pulled on some shorts and a shirt I had left unpacked so that I could wear them this very last day.

I grabbed my backpack from where it was slumped against the floor; there was nothing in it except for one last thing that needed to be put to rest.

My mom hugged me until it got awkward. She was bubbling with joy and nervous energy. This was it: our last day. I felt guilty about that, I really did. I wanted her to stay in Duncan with her garden and her life, but she insisted on coming with me. But then as I looked up at the clock, I realized something.

"Mom! I'm going to be late for English!" She just laughed and shoved a lunch bag at me. I stuffed a granola bar into my mouth and was out the door before I knew it. I ran to my bike and raced off down the street. I had known for what seemed to be forever every turn and pebble on that road. It seemed strange that soon, very soon, I would never ride the road again.

As I wove around potholes and curbs, I avoided houses with dogs like Tazz. I took a shortcut through the woods for old time's sake, and I saw a muskrat and a gator in the swamps. I looked but saw neither a fox nor a dove.

It seemed as though I could not pedal fast enough, and I leaned into my handlebars to increase my speed. As I swung around the final corner, I saw something in the middle of the dirt road right in front of me: a huge silhouette.

I slammed on my brakes, dug my heels into the ground, and skidded to a stop. After a few seconds, I realized that I had been closing my eyes tightly, awaiting the impact that never came. I opened them and there, inches from where I sat on my bike, still gripping the handlebars, panting and sweating, stood

Madam Marian. Her hands were on her hips, and she stared blankly at me.

I sat stock still, as though I were gazing at a lion ready to eat me alive. "Hey!" I blurted out.

But her only response was to turn her head to the side. I followed her gaze, and there, hanging on the side of her tiny shop, which was sinking into the mud of the bayou, was the chalkboard I had forgotten all about. Scribbled upon it was the number 1. I shivered and began to back my bike away from her. I took off and sailed between the trees dripping in moss. I turned my head over my shoulder to look at her again; she was unmoving in the middle of the road, her legs planted like thick tree trunks in the ground, still staring at me. It seemed I could not get far enough away from her to escape the gravitational pull of that stare. That ominous stare.

I soon came to the school parking lot, where all the familiar cars were parked in their familiar spots. There was a parking hierarchy at Hampton High: cool seniors in the front stalls, juniors with cool cars next, and lastly, the uncool kids with the embarrassing cars. My bike didn't even make the cut, so I rolled it into the bushes, the way I always did.

I grabbed an apple from my bag and took an enormous bite. I ran up the steps to the school and raced through the front doors. Once inside, I took another bite, and as quickly and as quietly as I could, I raced down the halls, the sounds of my footsteps echoing off the walls. As I turned a corner, I slammed into a janitor.

"Sorry, man!" I shouted. He bent over to pick up his mop.

"Get to class!" he hissed and I obliged. I took off again and then tried to sneak into English class. The kids didn't need to look up to know it was me, but they did, because what else is there to do in English?

Miss Carlson, who was leaning over her desk, looked up at me. This was the last straw and I knew it. She slammed her fist against the desk. The startled kids in the front row jumped and then went back to taking their English final.

Her eyes were bloodshot and her face red. She marched over to me and I backed up, stepping into the hallway.

"Be right back, class," she cooed and then shut the door. Alone in the hallway with Miss Carlson, I somehow found my courage—or my stupidity—and stared her down. She didn't speak a word and motioned for me to follow her. We retraced my steps to the front of the school. She had a grip on my wrist and was pulling me to my certain doom. We passed the janitor, who smirked at me. He knew what I was in for and that I deserved it.

The stomping of my shoes and the clicking of her heels accompanied us to Mr. Alamo's office. I froze at the door and she, being a foot shorter and fifty pounds lighter than me, could not pull me. This caught Miss Carlson off guard. She looked up at me, but before she could say anything, I handed her the only thing that was inside my backpack.

Her eyes went wide. She looked at what I held in my hands.

"It's story time, Miss Carlson." I smiled my best smile as she ripped the pages from me.

She flipped through them, wincing at every spelling mistake and grammar infraction. She read the entire thing in less than two minutes, and as soon as she finished, she said, "What is this garbage?"

"A story," I said.

"This is a terrible story!" She was really upset. "No plot, no theme, no anything: it's just, it's just…" She was at a loss for words.

"Miss Carlson," I said, keeping my cool, "it's a story I haven't finished writing." I paused. "No, actually, it's a story still in the making."

She frowned, trying to grasp the concept that a story could be unfolding in front of us. Then she opened the door and tried to push me into Mr. Alamo's office.

"No, I insist, Miss Carlson," I said and smiled. "Ladies first." So she stepped in and I followed, and there was Mr. Alamo, the principal of Hampton High.

He looked tired as he exchanged a few hushed words with Miss Carlson, and then she finally left the room to go back to her class. I hoped she took a long vacation after that, as she seemed to need one desperately. So there I was, standing in the room with the principal on the last day of school.

"Sit, Jaden," he demanded. He sighed as he sat down in his large leather swivel chair. I could tell he was burned out. He took off his glasses and rubbed his face with his giant hand.

He slid my English final across the desk to me. I set to work on it in silence. I finished half an hour later, way too early. I didn't proofread it, and I knew it was full of incomplete sentences and probably a bunch of run-on sentences. But I didn't care. When I put the pencil down, Mr. Alamo looked up at me.

"Why did you choose not to come back to Hampton High?" He knew I was transferring to some other school in New York.

"Because I don't belong here, Mr. Alamo."

Hmph, he said. He cocked his head. "You have bayou in your blood, son. As my dad used to tell me, you can fall from the apple tree, but at some point that fallen apple will grow into an apple tree, too." He smiled at me.

Huh?

I waited for the bell to ring, and finally, after what seemed to be decades, it did. As I got up out of my seat, Mr. Alamo said, "Sorry to say good-bye, Jaden." He did seem sorry, too. I nodded and turned and walked out.

59

The next final I had to complete was woodshop, and that was a joke, a complete joke. I just sat at the table with some of the other woodshop idiots, and we signed our yearbooks as girls flocked to our table. In each yearbook, I just signed my name. The girls, however, took up entire pages with their big, swoopy handwriting.

The remainder of the classes passed like a slow-moving cargo ship making its way across the horizon, seemingly not moving at all but then suddenly gone. Finally, we counted down the seconds to the last bell, and then it rang and the kids rushed out of the room. I was the last one out, and before I made it through the door, I heard a voice: ."Jaden, uh, could you help me with this?"

I turned to see Emily Rider, the artist girl. She was carrying a sculpture of an eagle and wanted to load it into the back of her pickup truck. I dropped my things and ran to her. Out in the parking lot, I pushed the massive metal sculpture into place on the truck bed.

I turned to Emily, who breathed a sigh of relief. She looked really happy that school was out. I had forgotten to thank her for her help with the window planters for my mom, and she beat me to it.

"Thanks, Jaden." She gasped a little and wiped her brow of sweat. I did the same. The heat of summer was already beating down on us. I hopped up onto the truck and looked at the eagle.

"Wow, this is a badass eagle." Trust me, it was.

"Thanks." She sighed and looked back at the school. "I'm going to miss this place."

"You leaving, too?"

She smiled up at me, using one hand to shield her eyes from the sun.

"Yeah, I'm going to California. I got a scholarship there in a 3-D art program." I was shocked and then remembered that she was older than me, even though we were in the same English class.

"So cool."

"Well, you have fun in New York."

I jumped off the truck as she climbed inside and revved up the engine. As she backed up, I called to her, "Have fun in California!" She turned and gave me an unforced smile. I guess I wasn't the guy she had thought I was after all.

"Make sure you say good-bye to that girl in English. She seemed sad that you weren't there this morning." And then the truck rumbled out of the parking lot, and I just stood there, frozen to the asphalt.

60

I set off on my bike to the pizza place, where I was going to meet up with the gang. As I sailed through town, I felt strangely uplifted. I felt light and almost free. Everything seemed to be coming to a close for me there in Duncan.

I walked into the restaurant, and there in the corner booth was everyone I knew. We just messed around, doing harebrained things and talking for hours.

Do you know what I will remember the most? Everyone was smiling and having a good time. I mean, no one was complaining about this or that class or homework or job. No one was complaining about what this guy had said or that girl had done. Everyone was just relaxed and having a good time. Well, that is, everyone except for me.

The lacrosse boys were talking about the final league game, in which Nathan made that awesome goal with two minutes left. The girls were talking about their Mardi Gras dresses and what shoes would match them.

I realized I wasn't really a part of any of it anymore. I wasn't a star player on the lacrosse team; I wasn't even on the team. I wasn't the guy with a swagger that every girl wanted. Plus, I was leaving and they knew it. I was as good as gone. To be honest, I was a nobody.

I stuffed a large piece of pizza into my mouth just as Brook drew near to me. She put her hand on my shoulder, and I looked up, my cheeks stuffed. She seemed less than charmed with the picture.

"Jaden, pick me up at 5:00." She then gave me a half smile, grabbed her purse, and strutted out on her long legs as though she owned the earth. Yes, she was queen and we all knew it.

I finished chewing, swallowed, and stayed put. I didn't feel like getting up. So I just sat there for a few minutes, thinking about nothing in particular.

Scott got me up and off my lazy ass. We walked out of the cool restaurant into the relentless inferno steam bath. I immediately began to sweat. I turned to Scott, who was looking at some girl off in the distance.

"Scott?" I yanked my bike from where I had left it. He did the same with his dirt bike.

"Yeah?" He squinted up at me. For a moment, he looked like his father. But I didn't want to think about that evil man, so I shook off the thought.

"Scott, man, would you like to come over?" It sounded like pleading. And it was, too. I was really dreading having to say good-bye to him. It wasn't until that moment in the blazing sun of the parking lot that I realized Scott was one of the few things worth a damn in Duncan.

"Sorry, man. Can't. I have to jam. Granny needs me to do some chores." He sighed, bracing himself for the manual labor he would have to do in that oven.

"Been there. Just make sure she doesn't lock you up in a shed." We laughed and I slapped him on the back.

I took off before my tires melted, but I had forgotten about my cottonmouth injury. It ached on hot days, and I groaned a little as I set off.

"Yeah, see ya, man. Oh, hey!"

I turned on my bike to look back at him, wobbling a bit.

"Tonight will be the best night of our lives." He gave a grin and began his journey in the opposite direction.

I smiled, too; I couldn't help it. The anticipation of that night was like that feeling you get in the pit of your stomach right before the roller coaster starts its descent.

61

When I got home, I had to help Mom pack up the kitchen and haul boxes on to the front porch. Finally, I was able to jump in the shower and rinse off a day's worth of sweat and dirt. I brushed my teeth and got dressed in that suit Dad had given me for Christmas.

I looked in the mirror and barely recognized myself. I was badass. I needed to remember to thank my dad again for that suit. I walked downstairs and there was my mom, standing at the foot of the stairs.

"Jaden!" She clasped her hands to her chin, smiled, and got all teary eyed.

"Mom!" I said and groaned.

"Look at you!" She made me stand in various poses as she snapped photos with my camera. The only one I had left; I had given the others to Scott, so that he could continue to photograph the creatures of the swamp.

"You're growing up too fast. Stop!" She smiled but it seemed to break her heart. She was living every mother's nightmare; her baby bird would soon leave the nest.

"Mom!" I groaned again.

"OK, OK, sorry." She stepped aside and watched me walk out the front door. But before I could get past the porch, she called me back. "Jaden, wait!"

"What!?" I bellowed. I was a nervous wreck, and now I was going to be late.

"You forgot something, honey!" She handed me my mask. *The* mask. The one I had worn in New Orleans when all the crazy stuff happened. Wow. New Orleans: that seemed as though it were a lifetime ago. Once again, Mom yelled, "Wait!" She handed me a bouquet of lilies she had picked. "For Brook," she said.

"Thanks," I grumbled, and I pulled out the keys to Mom's car. I got in and laid the flowers on the passenger seat. I gunned the engine and it roared to life. As I drove by our house, I glanced at it. I saw the window that was my room; all around it was a wall of green. The tangle of greenery was trying to engulf our house, and after we left, it would. I gave it five years before the bayou swallowed it.

It took less than ten minutes to get to Brook's house. I parked the car and stepped out into the heat. I walked up the small brick walkway to the front door. Nut grass was popping out of the cracks in the brick, and the lawn fought for space with the weeds.

I paused on the porch in the shade. I sensed that someone was looking at me, but when I turned, no one was there. So I knocked. I waited, listening for footsteps, but instead I heard shouting. There was a deep male voice and a young female voice. That had to be Brook.

"Shut up, Dad!"

"Watch yourself, young lady!"

"I don't care! Please just leave me alone!" She started to cry. "Let me live my life!"

"Your date's here."

A few seconds passed and then I heard footsteps and the click of the door opening. Brook gave me her best smile, but her eyes were red.

"Damn, you look good." And she did, too. She was wearing a pale-blue dress, super tight and so short that I dared not look. There was nowhere safe to rest my eyes, so I just stared at her face. It was made up elaborately. Her silky hair was straight and shone like gold.

"Come in, Jaden." Her voice was hollow. I stepped in and felt the cool fan. I had been in Brook's house before, and as I scanned the downstairs, I saw familiar sights: the living room, the dining room, and the stairs.

Out of the hallway came Brook's dad. A tall, balding man with a sour look, as if he had just sucked a mouthful of lemon. Then Brook's mom, an older version of Brook, came in. She smelled so strongly of perfume, I held my breath. She wore a blonde wig and a short skirt.

"Welcome, Jaden!" She squealed and hugged me. More perfume: *ugh*. It was a cloud that you could not escape from. Meanwhile, Brook's dad looked as though he desperately wanted to cut my throat and pour out all my dirty truths.

"These are for you, Brook." I held out the lilies.

"Thanks."

"This way," said Mrs. Jackson. I followed Brook's parents to the living room, where they proceeded to swarm us like paparazzi. We had to smile and pose, change positions, and smile some more.

The whole time, Mrs. Jackson talked about when she had gone to the Mardi Gras dance. She seemed to be one of those women who had peaked in high school, many years earlier. She blabbed on and on about how lovely the flowers were and how was my lovely mother? And so on and so forth. I thought of my mom at home in her torn jeans, with her graying hair and her genuine smile.

"Gosh, oh no! We're going to be late!" said Brook. I felt her hand on my shoulder, and Brook gave me a "Let's get out of here right now" look. I nodded.

Finally, we were released. I escorted Brook to the passenger side of the car and opened the door for her. Just then I heard, "*Whooouuuooo, who, who, who.*" It came from somewhere in Brook's yard. A mourning dove was singing its last song before nightfall. I paused and scanned the area and there on a telephone wire, all by itself, was the silhouette of a mourning dove. It seemed that I was in mourning, maybe because I was leaving forever.

"Jaden, let's go!"

I turned and waved to Mr. and Mrs. Jackson at the door. I slid into my seat, turned on the engine, and pulled away from the Jacksons' house.

62

Mardi Gras night at Hampton High was always a wild night, a night that the town braced itself for. The dance was open to not only to Hampton High kids, but also all the other high school kids from surrounding parishes. The dance seemed to get bigger every year as word spread about how cool it was. The only kids not welcome were freshman boys. Scott had tried sneaking in the year before and had been immediately canned by a bunch of seniors. He had left after just five minutes, tail between his legs.

The people who didn't attend the dance would hunker down at home with earplugs. Others would leave in their boats and spend the night at sea. The Duncan police—what few there were—would be out in force. As a kid, I had fantasized about being old enough to go to the Mardi Gras dance and partake in all the wildness afterward. It was all a bit mysterious. I remembered those nights as a kid, listening to the music, the sporadic amateur fireworks, and the screech of trucks skidding on pavement. I recalled the smell of chaos in the summer air. Legendary stuff happened on that night.

So I pulled away from the curb, and off we went in dead silence, except for the sound of the engine and the tires chewing asphalt.

The drive to school seemed longer than usual. I was feeling the excitement of Mardi Gras and the melancholy of my last night in Duncan, but I was also feeling fear as Brook and I drove past Madam Marian's shop. The number on the chalkboard read 1. Would it change to 0 at midnight? Or maybe 364?

As we neared the school, we heard the first sounds of the night: shouts, cries, and booming electronic music. We saw the lights and the cars and the dressed-up people. Girls were in sexy getups, their hair done to perfection. Guys were in suits and ties. And, of course, everything was purple and green and gold, the colors of Mardi Gras. Everyone wore a mask, whether plastic, feathered, velvet, or whatever. Guests were not supposed to know who was who.

And so it began. I helped Brook out of the car, bowed, and took her hand. Her hand fit right into mine, and together we ascended the red velvet steps that led into the gym, which seemed too small to contain the event that night.

I stepped in and we both stopped. Brook let go of me and shouted when she saw some of her friends. She ran off to talk to them. I felt a tap on my shoulder. I turned and there were a bunch of masked guys. They shouted to me over the darkness and deafening roar of the music: "Let's go!" I thought that I knew who they were, but I couldn't be sure. But I followed them, and we stood for half an hour at the edge of the mass of moving people, watching. The costumes, the colors, the dancing, and the hot girls: it was wild.

Then one slight kid standing next to me was handed a concoction in a cup, and that was the beginning of the end. I could see the kid's brown eyes and the way his pupils dilated and the way a smile crept across his face.

He leaned his head back, raised his hands in the air, and yelped: "*Aaaeeeiii!*" Welcome to crazy town.

Man, the gym was getting hot. So many bodies. I was so thirsty. Then another guy handed me a drink, and I threw it down my throat. I didn't care; it was my last night in Duncan. It was all like a dream, a bizarre dream. In one moment, I would be jumping and running though the masses of writhing youth. In the next, I would be slow dancing with some masked girl. I didn't care who it was—who could tell! And at one point, I think I felt hands underneath me carrying me, floating me across the crowds.

63

The wolves, the wolves. Run!" I muttered to myself. I was on the pier. At some point, the party had moved to the pier. I looked at the stars; they seemed blurry to me, and my forehead throbbed from the blaring music. A full moon turned the heavens a strange purple-blue.

"Wolves..." I blinked and everything shook, as though the world were trying to rock me to sleep. How late it was, god only knew. I saw someone standing near the edge of the pier. He removed his mask and rubbed his eyes. The guy raised a trumpet to his lips and began to play.

"Hey, Scott." I smiled, blinking and squinting from my headache. I was trying to resurface from the chaos.

"Jaden Miller!" he shouted. He blared his trumpet in my face, and then he pointed it at the moon and blared to it as well. My eardrums rang and my head felt a thousand times worse.

"Dude..." He seemed to search in the mush that was his brain for something. "Tell me."

"Wolves. The wolves." I shook my head. We were both drunk, beyond reason or help.

"Wolves." He looked at me, confused, and I nodded.

"Dude...what...what did Madam Marian tell you?" He peered into my eyes, totally lucid for a second.

"Death." I whispered.

"What?" he yelled, trying to hear me over the music. He cupped his ear with his hand.

"Death, Scott! Someone's going to die!" I cried. His golden trumpet suddenly fell from his hands. I looked down as it landed on the boards of the pier, on the names of the lost souls carved in the wood. I shivered and looked up at him. He had changed.

"The wolves, Scott, they're coming. I have to leave. You might die if you're near me." I looked at the moon and back at the face of my friend, who had gone pale. My best friend, staring at me.

"Good-bye, Scott. You were always my best friend, man." I clapped his shoulder and pulled him in for a man hug. He nodded.

"Bye, man. Promise me...me..." Intoxication seemed to interfere with his ability to get words out.

"What?" I felt a wave of dizziness.

"Promise me you'll dance your jam, man! Dance your life!" He smiled his crazy Scott smile, picked up his trumpet, and began to play. A wave of noisy revelers drew near. In the next moment, Scott was gone, engulfed by the partiers.

I took a step back toward the edge of the dock as four immense brutes, looking like a wall of soldiers, advanced on me,

"Wolves?" I hissed.

Their faces were covered by creepy-looking white plastic masks. Their voices were deep. "Jaden Miller," growled the tall guy in the center.

"Say it, say its name! Say it out loud! I dare you!" said the guy flanking him.

"You touched old man Barley's shed!" The tall guy grabbed my lapels and lifted me a foot off the pier. "You think you're some kind of badass? Prove it! Truth or dare," the tall guy demanded.

"Dare." I had no choice.

"I dare you to prove yourself!"

"*Fine!*" I responded.

"Go into the Duncan Shipyard tonight!" he bellowed. Then he tossed me off the dock.

64

Everything slowed down. Everything. I saw the hands that pushed me, the lights, and the colors. And then I saw the darkness. Above it all, bearing witness, was the moon.

I saw my hands rise up, trying to grasp it, the moon. But I fell away from it and sank. The sea warmed my body, caught it, and consumed me in its underworld.

As I sank, I felt the bubbles gurgle through my hair on their escape to the world above. I was stung by the silence and the pounding in my ears. Loud, yet muffled and strangely peaceful. I relaxed when I heard a different sound, quite subtle but right there inside me. It was my heart thumping. I smiled as I sank deeper until I felt the soft, muddy bottom of the ocean. It must have been six feet deep. I lay there, looking up at the top of the water. I thought of all the things that made me who I am, the things that made my heart continue to thump.

And then it all ended. My lungs caught fire and I pushed myself up to the world above. The world where I was supposed to live my life. I felt sober, awake, my five senses coming back from their zombie state as I broke the surface of the salty sea.

I was under the pier. I looked around but my mask was nowhere to be found. Then I saw something that sent chills down my spine, spreading to my fingers and toes, making my hair stand on end. I looked beyond the pillar inscribed with a boy's name in my own handwriting. It was Brook.

I swam the breaststroke as I made my way to her. I didn't want to put my head underwater for fear of losing sight of her. She was down the beach, among the ropes that kept the boats from drifting to freedom in the Gulf of Mexico.

When I got to the point where I could feel my shoes sinking into the soft mud, I worked my way to shore. I almost lost my shoes to the sucking mud, but I finally made it. I stood next to her. She was staring straight ahead, out to sea, I knew that stare and where it took her.

"Your uncle hurt you, Brook." My bluntness surprised even me.

Her trance was broken. She turned her head to look at me. "What? How—"

"I was there. I saw it all. I saw what he did to you, Brook, how he hurt you. It's something you'll never forget."

"No, I'll never forget." A tear rolled down her cheek. It dripped off her chin and fell into an ocean of salty tears.

"Then don't forget, Brook." I took her shoulders. "Don't ever. But do this."

"What?" Her eyes were terrified.

"Remember who you are. Brook, you are an angel. You'll grow your wings back, and then you can fly your way to heaven or to wherever you want to go."

She smiled slowly. The real deal, a true smile. I felt that I was finally meeting Brook.

We walked back to the party, hand in hand. She rejoined the living. Brook gave me a kiss on the cheek before I headed back to the pier. Ally, Jordan, and her group of girlfriends surrounded her, and she was all smiles.

65

As I got near to the pier, I heard it before I saw it: a girl screaming and a pack of wolves howling. I ran so fast I don't think my feet touched the earth.

In the shadows under the pier of the lost souls were five figures; only one was female. Four guys were slowly circling their prey. Wolves. Each was laughing and taunting her. I didn't recognize them, but I did recognize their prey: a girl with long, thick, dark hair falling in waves down her back. She wore a pink evening dress, and her mask was made of feathers from the birds of the bayou. She was the mystery girl of the bayou, the girl with the bloody hands.

I approached silently and swiftly. The first guy didn't even see me coming, so I smacked him hard between the shoulders. He reeled to face me and I kneed his thighs, kicking him to the ground, where I gave him one last punch to the stomach.

"Die, wolf, die!" were the words that came out of my mouth.

He lay on the ground, spitting and moaning. Instantly, the other three were upon me.

"Who are you?" one shouted as he lunged at me. I ducked, stepped to the side, and tripped him. He fell into the mud. But his friend was fast, too, and he slammed his fist into my jaw. I fell back against a pillar, banging my scalp against its rough, barnacled surface.

"Die, wolves!" I bellowed at them, spit and blood spurting from my mouth.

"*You* die!" one roared as he came at me. I ducked behind the pillar. Then I grabbed his mask and in one precise movement, pulled it over his eyes, blinding him. He wailed as I bashed my fist against his abdomen.

Another guy was already on his feet. The first one I had knocked down had rolled over and was looking up at me with a death glare. I looked for Bloody Hands, but she wasn't there. And then I saw her; she was running.

I picked up my feet and ran quickly. My bad leg burned; it screamed for me to stop. But I kept running.

Her pink dress fluttered behind her like silk in the wind, as did her hair. And she ran quickly! Man, it was as though she were running on asphalt and not deep grass and mud, the way I was. I heard the pack behind me. I heard them over the loud music and the sounds of people dancing and conversing.

I flashed on a scene from the PBS show *Nature*: the cold Yellowstone field of white snow and the wolves running, baring their teeth, a mix of gray and black fur, chasing their prey. I was a fox and I was their prey. An innocent moon, on the ceiling of the earth, was watching.

I blinked and they became four guys in tuxes and Mardi Gras masks sprinting over the soft mud flats with a blaring masquerade ball behind them.

The girl had vanished into the tree line of the swamp. I ran, my funky leg holding me back. I spotted the red canoe under a screen of bushes, hidden and stowed away for just such a purpose.

I ran to it and yanked it out of the tangle of vines. It was heavy but adrenaline was coursing through my body, so I heaved the red beast out of the bushes and dragged it to a large section of the swamp.

"You're dead!" one guy shrieked behind me. I pushed the canoe into the water, where it bobbed, waiting for me. I heard their heavy breathing as I leaped into my boat. It wobbled, water spilling into it, but against all odds, it stayed upright. I braced myself with the paddle and pushed away to where the water turned deep.

Safe. I looked back at the wolves lining the edge of the swamp.

"Die, you wolves!" I shouted one last time as they hurled their drunken insults. I began to paddle into the swamp, following the sounds of footsteps somewhere deep in the bayou.

66

I remember bits and pieces after that. The sounds of a creature moving through the brush. Water lapping against my boat. An alligator's eyes peering at me in the shadows. Floating, paddling. The swamp looked haunted, its trees dripping in silver moss and lit by a ghostly moonlight. I was doing the insane. The impossible. The suicidal. The thing no one had done in two centuries. But by now, I think you know what I am: a madman.

Minutes or maybe hours went by. I blinked my eyes to focus on the dim, swampy surroundings. I don't know what felt more strange: where I was or how I had come to be there. I was in the swamp, lying in a red canoe in a soggy suit in the wee hours of the morning. I felt the cool breath of the ocean drifting through the cypress trees, their old-man's beard moss swaying.

The moon had already set, and the sky was dotted with stars, fading stars, that is. If you looked closely, you could tell that the sun was on its way; the horizon was a dark purple slowly overtaking the surrounding blackness. I shifted my weight, sat up in my canoe, and watched the ripples form and fade into the swamp. It was strangely peaceful out there. I moved to the end of the canoe and crawled up the bank into the thick grass. I established my footing and looked around.

I was near the ocean. I could tell that from the mangrove trees and the breeze. The air was filled with the last of the night's noises—nocturnal animals finishing their business. I left the canoe behind and walked toward the salty breeze, trying to piece together how, exactly, I had gotten there. I remembered the dare, the masked faces, and the wolves—everything and nothing. My mind screamed and searched to understand.

I stepped out of the bayou and emerged on the beach. I looked out at the dark sea reflecting the surviving stars, and I felt a presence. Yet I did not run or hide. I simply looked over my shoulder, and there it was: an ominous circle of rusty ships, lurking in the darkness.

The Duncan Shipyard was less than fifty feet from where I stood. I could smell the rusted metal. I was so close. As far as I knew, I was the closest anyone had ever been to the Duncan Shipyard since those slaves had met their terrible fate.

The dare was really just a final excuse to go there. I had always had a fascination with the ships, always felt a gravitational pull to the place, and I had resisted it for as long as I could remember. Until now. I feel a deep calm, as if my fate, my destiny, lay within those rusted hulls, and it was the job of my body to walk right in, so my destiny could be revealed.

And so I did what I had been dared to do. I stepped forward and walked toward it. The only thing that could be heard was my feet on the sand and the sea wind in my hair telling me to turn and run, but my body would not, could not yield to such a command.

I felt completely alive as I walked into the unknown. I was not scared. I was not courageous. I was just...me.

And that was all I needed to be. I saw a gap between two of the old steamboats. The rusty alleyway was deep in shadow, and it was hard to see, so I felt my way through it. I felt cobwebs and barnacles.

Then I emerged and my eyes were flooded with color...green. I was standing before an immense green wall. I blinked, not trusting my eyes. In front of me was a jungle paradise.

I saw fern trees, magnolias, heliconias, and mandevillas. You name the plant and I saw it there. The garden was bountiful, more than beautiful, and otherworldly. I stepped under a looming ginger plant, its flowers scented with the sweetest fragrance on earth. I couldn't believe my eyes.

Colors were everywhere: red, purple, blue, and orange. That was when I noticed something else. I knew these plants. I had seen them all my life. They were the ones Mom had planted in her garden, hoping they would flourish. They were the ones that had been trampled and neglected on the school grounds. They were the ones that grew wild in the bayou. That was when it all made sense. They were the plants that had been dying. Or they had been hopeless. Or they had been overlooked. They were the ones that had been saved by the weed thief.

My eyes were drawn to the very center of the garden, to the jewels of that jungle: the roses. They bloomed hugely and brightly. Mom's lovingly tended roses paled in comparison.

I took a few steps around a mighty magnolia tree, and that was when I saw her: Bloody Hands. There she was: the weed thief, the eyes of the bayou, the invisible.

She seemed at home in a world run by the laws of nature and not the laws of people. I stood frozen. I could not have looked away, even if the world were in flames.

She was crouching, an elbow resting on a knee, her body framed by her long, dark hair. And the dress. The pink dress. She was wearing my discarded Halloween costume. I had worn it as a joke; she, for pure beauty. Although the dress was torn, she looked elegant in it. Her hair was loose and wild, spilling around her face and down her back.

She clipped a rose, a brilliant red rose. She traced her fingers along the petals. She held it close and pressed her face into the flower, inhaling its fragrance. I was mesmerized. She did not seem to know I was there.

Then she gazed into a small, dark pond filled with water lilies. She was staring at her own reflection, completely at peace. A gentle smile graced her face, and I smiled to see it. Abruptly, the smile changed to a look of wide-eyed surprise. I looked into the pond, too, to see what moved her. And then I saw it. Her reflection, her eyes, looking at mine.

Our eyes met in the dark waters of the pond. We raised our heads at the same time. And then the earth gasped because the impossible happened. The girl with the bloody hands spoke.

"Jaden!" she said, astonished.

Hearing my dream girl speak my name out loud was music to my ears. *She's real. Bloody Hands is real.* We both existed, right there, right then. Just the two of us. In paradise.

But immediately, the expression in her eyes transformed from surprised affection to terror. She dropped her pruning shears on to the path below. She shook her head slightly, still staring at me. I was stung. "What are you doing here?" Her velvet voice contained the same terror that I saw in her eyes. She was on the verge of tears, and her small body shook.

What did I do?

"You can't be here!" The panic was consuming her. It pained me to see her like that.

"Why?" I asked desperately.

She approached me, glancing over her shoulder. She turned to me, eyes almost as wild as her hair.

"Jaden, trust me..." It came out in a sweet whisper. Her voice was lovely. "Leave. Run. Go!" She put her small, bandaged hand against my chest and pushed me away. Her eyes darted around urgently. I took her tiny hands in mine and pulled her close to me.

"I'm not leaving you. I love you."

"Please, Jaden, you *must* leave, now!" she begged. A tear fell to her cheek, and I wiped it away.

"Why do you want me to go away? What did I do?" The hurt rang in my voice.

"Run, run, you'd better run! Hide, hide, you'd better hide!" a man screamed in a hideous voice. I looked at him. So did Bloody Hands. On the other side of the garden was the grossest man I had ever seen. He had uncombed hair and a grizzly beard. Half of his face was burned; one of his ears was gone. His eyes were two big black holes oozing with insanity.

I could feel Bloody Hands tremble in my arms, and the man knew it. He smiled and tears welled up in

Bloody Hands' eyes. There before me was the real madman.

The dam broke and all the answers I had been seeking suddenly flooded over me. I understood everything then, but the answers were not the answers I wanted. Nor could I have dreamed them up in my worst nightmare. I gulped. *The legend is true.*

"Please, Jaden. Run!" I heard her whisper at my shoulder.

My body went rigid, my muscles tensed, and I stepped in front of the girl, protecting her from the approaching beast. I held my ground. "I'm not going anywhere. I'm not leaving you."

"Have you come to take her away?"

And that was when I noticed the gun in a holster sticking out of a belt that could not contain his belly, the belly of a bloated alcoholic. He grinned madly and drew the rusty old firearm. The thing looked as though it came right out of the Civil War. He pointed it at me. He was almost upon us.

"You can't have her. No one can!" Then he fired.

Bam!

She screamed. It was a high-pitched, ear-splitting cry, and I recognized it. Anyone in Duncan would. It was the scream of the slave ghosts.

The round just grazed my shoulder. It burned and oozed red. Enraged, I barreled toward the guy. *The devil. The demon. The legend. Whatever he is.*

I smacked the handgun from his grip, and it arced through the air, landing somewhere in the jungle. I landed a punch on his jaw. A yellow tooth flew from his mouth, along with saliva and blood. He punched me in the nose. I fell, clawing at his shirt and pulling him down with me.

He wrapped his python arm around my neck, robbing me of air. I glanced over and saw the unthinkable: Bloody Hands, lying face down, blood pooling around her. She was struggling to stand up. I realized the cruel truth. She had been hit by the shot intended for me.

"Stay there!" I yelled with all my might.

I coughed and sputtered, kicked and scratched, and tugged at his arm around my throat. No good. My eyes bulged as I struggled to suck in oxygen. I couldn't break his grip. I was losing the fight. His horrendous breath and broadening sadistic smile inches above me: Would that be how it would all end? Would that be the last thing I saw in this world? The last thing I smelled? No!

Dizzy. Going dark. Surrendering. Limp...

67

Then it happened. His eyes suddenly bulged and his jaw clenched. Then his muscles went slack. He made a gurgling sound, and a trickle of blood funneled between his teeth and dripped onto my face. His grip released and he collapsed over me. I got air. Oh, sweet air. I heaved myself out from under the dead man's weight. And then I saw it. The pruning shears deep in his back, her hands still clenching them. Then I saw her: slumped over him, breathless, and pale.

"Jaden?" It was a whisper.

"Oh no, oh no!" What had I done? I was in a panic. I crawled to her and pulled her away from the shears *and him*. I gathered her into my arms. Her eyes were wide and full of understanding. I cradled her. I felt her heart beating against mine.

"Hold on, hold on, you're going to be fine. I'm right here. I'm never going to leave you." I felt my voice crack. "I love you."

She smiled as I brushed her hair from her face. I could now see her flawless face clearly. So clearly now. I held her hand in mine and kissed its scarred knuckles. Her eyes locked on mine. She loved me.

"Jaden?" she gasped.

I felt my heart whimper, felt it cry.

"Did you know that roses, beautiful roses, have thorns?" She looked serene. Peaceful.

I nodded. I understood. I understood it all. I understood her story. And then before she was gone to me forever, I leaned in and kissed her. My first real kiss. I felt her kissing me back. It could have lasted seconds or years; I would never know.

But then I felt her heart stop beating against my chest. I held her until her skin grew cold. I couldn't let go.

Madam Marian was right. Someone I loved had died: the only girl I would ever love. I felt the tears coming, I couldn't stop them. I buried my face in her soft hair and sobbed. I held her for so long. I held her in her garden filled with the plants she had rescued.

Finally, the light was starting to fill the sky, and I knew I had to go. I lifted her body and took her to the edge of the pond, where I gently washed the blood from her face. I then carried her to a soft, grassy area, laid her down, and placed the red rose in her hands, her cut, bloody hands, her lovely hands. Then I closed the universe of her beautiful eyes for the last time.

I turned numbly and walked out of the garden. Along the path, a metallic glimmer caught my eye. I bent over to pick it up. A shell casing. From the civil war. I put it in my coat pocket.

I looked back at the first rays of sunlight peeking over the ships behind me. Such an exquisite scene for such a horrific truth. I heard the last calls of an owl and the first verses of the waking songbirds. But they could not stop my stream of tears as I walked away.

"*Whooouuuooo, who, who, who.*"

I stopped and searched the coral tree above me until I found it: a mourning dove. But I didn't think it was mourning, it was simply announcing the morning. I smiled and my sorrow disappeared, replaced by a profound happiness—it was *her*. I gazed at the bird and called back.

"*Whooouuuooo, who, who, who.*"

"Who is you." Time stood still, it seemed, as she silently returned my gaze. I saw love. I saw understanding. I saw eternity in those eyes. Our universe was perfect for a moment. Then she flew off into the morning and disappeared into the fire of the sun. The sunrise illuminated the sky and ocean, and the full moon was now a memory. Then, without looking back, I walked out of the jungle, the Garden of Eden.

But as beach turned to grass beneath my feet, he stopped me cold in my tracks. I felt his presence. I looked down and saw him. A fox, a red fox. He was staring at me. I was so close to him. He cocked his head to the right, trying to see something that wasn't there. Trying to figure out what I was thinking, feeling. Trying to understand what had happened.

"Hey there, Jaden. The fox trot is over," I said to him. I saw his blue eyes looking at me. Foxes don't have blue eyes. I turned to look one last time at the garden and the ships and the truth. When I turned back around, Jaden the fox was gone. I reached into my pocket, pulled out the bullet and hurled it into the ocean.

68

I paddled the red canoe to the nearest trail. Then I beached it and ran. And oh man, how I ran. I could have been on the cross-country team. I made it to school where I retrieved my mom's car and raced home.

As I neared our lane, I cut the engine and rolled into our driveway. I ran into the backyard and looked at the old hickory tree, judging the distance of the jump to my open window, and decided it was my best bet.

I wrapped myself around its trunk and scrambled up it to the largest branch. I scooted along it until I could make the jump into my window. I leaped and cleared it, falling onto the hard carpet of my bedroom floor. It absorbed the sound of my fall, however, so that was good. I scrambled up and looked at the clock; I still had time. I ran to the shower and got in, fully dressed. I scrubbed furiously and watched the blood, hers and mine, flow down the drain until all traces of it had been washed away. The suit, of course, was now ruined. Dry clean only. I'd have to make up some story or other about what had happened.

I jumped out, dried off, and threw on fresh, dry clothes.

"Mom! Mom! Mom!" I yelled and banged on her door. She was smiling when she opened it.

"Gosh, Jaden! You're excited!" She rubbed her eyes.

"I know!" I yelled. "Hurry up, Mom. I'm going to New York!" She was right: I was almost dizzy with panic and tension. In the span of hours my life had been irrevocably changed. Now, before anyone stopped me, I was leaving behind a world I had grown to hate. A world that had stolen my life.

"*We're* going to New York," she corrected me. And she went to change while I started loading things into the car. I looked at my empty house; it was kind of sad, but today was the start of a new life. Mom and I ran around like mad for half an hour, packing and loading things into the car. We were about to leave when Mom called to me.

"Jaden, look!" She pointed to the black-and-white police car pulling into our driveway. I looked surprised for her sake, but deep down I wasn't. I watched, frozen, as the cop pulled up to our house. He got out. It was Sergeant Cultan. He had dark circles under his eyes from chasing teens all night.

"Can I help you, Sergeant?" Mom called to him.

"I just need to have a chat with Jaden." He looked at me and drew near to us. "Son." He nodded to me. I nodded back.

"Officer." I raised my eyebrows. "What's going on?" I asked.

"We got a call this morning from Jed Barley, the old fisherman who lives out in the swamp. He said he heard a gunshot from the shipyard early this morning." He looked as though he could use some coffee.

"What!" I squawked, perhaps too loudly.

"Yes, it was from the old shipyard. Mr. Barley was out fishing nearby. Said he heard a gunshot and thought it was hunters. He decided to call it in anyway, as it's not hunting season. We sent a few deputies out there to take a look, and we found two bodies, a teenage girl and an older man." He seemed perplexed. All he had signed up for was chasing drunken kids and rescuing the occasional cat stuck in a tree. Not this.

"Oh no!" I cried, "*No! What happened?* Who died?" I hoped that I was a good actor, given my state of mind.

He sighed. "Well, the deputies have been asking around, and no one seems to know who they were." Then he turned to my mom and continued, "It appears, ma'am, that your son took a dare to go into the shipyard last night. Four boys confirmed it this morning. We have to take him in for questioning."

My mom stepped in. "Oh no, he can't! We have to catch a plane. We're leaving. Moving to New York today. This morning!"

"Son, did you go into the shipyard last night?" He raised an eyebrow.

"Actually, if you want to know the truth..." I looked down. "I was at the pier with a bunch of people during the dance. And the guys dared me to go into the shipyard. I told them I was going, so I took the canoe out into the bayou, but I...I...well, I chickened out and came home." I shook my head. "But please, Sergeant, don't tell the guys I'm a wimp. Please?"

Then Mom spoke up. "Sergeant, look, I know he was home and in bed early last night because he was up, ready to go, first thing this morning. I'm absolutely sure my son had nothing to do with this. Interview us by phone from New York. We have to go. I'm sorry—so sorry—about the girl and the man. You have no idea who they were?"

"Neither this parish nor any of the surrounding parishes have a missing person report matching either of them. We think they were homeless drifters who were squatting out in the ships. If you think about it, it's the perfect place to shack up. Nobody ever goes out there."

I felt a lump in my throat but kept my composure. "Yeah, I've always been terrified of those ships. Never been there. I don't know anyone who has."

"OK. Sorry, son, I know you had nothing to do with this. I won't bother having you come into the station. I believe your story. I don't know anyone crazy enough to go out to that creepy place. Truthfully, it looks as though there was a struggle and they killed each other." He sighed.

"If I have any further questions, I'll just call you in New York. Sorry to have bothered you, and have a safe trip." The sergeant wrote down Mom's cell phone number and email address. He shook my hand, I thanked him, and before I knew it, I was standing there watching the taillights of a squad car slowly disappearing down the gravel road.

I breathed a sigh of relief and turned to my mom, but she wasn't there.

"Mom?"

"Here." She had walked into the backyard. I walked back there and saw her standing next to the pond in the center of her garden. I approached her.

"What a tragedy. What has our world come to?" she said softly. I checked my watch as she looked over her green masterpiece.

"Mom?" My voice broke. "I'm sad to leave that girl, you know, the one I told you about."

"Oh, honey, I'm so sorry!" She tried to comfort me. "Jaden, everyone you have ever known will always be with you, whether they are physically present or not. They live on in your life through you and your thoughts. Besides, you can always come back down here and visit her occasionally."

If only she knew. My eyes were dry. There was nothing left in them, and so I just stared at the garden around me, knowing I could never unload the burden weighing on my mind, not on her, not on anyone, ever.

She smiled at me and then turned to look at her plants one last time, each one representing something that only she knew.

"I'll never forget her," I said softly, more to myself than Mom.

And then I thought of the dove.

69

And so our flight was delayed. I sat down and began to type and didn't stop until we reached New York. My fingers were flying; I was typing like a speed demon.

When we finally touched down, we exited our gate.

"Dad?" I smiled, dropped my things, and ran to him. "Jaden!" he yelled, and I leaped into his arms. I didn't care how dorky I looked; I felt as though I were a little kid again.

Dad staggered back. "Son! How tall are you?"

"Six feet three," I said and smiled broadly. I unwound myself from him. "Dad? You're OK? You're not sick?"

"Of course, I'm fine." But he was looking beyond me at Mom, and I realized this was the first time they had seen each other in years.

"Gabriela?" He gasped.

"Dave?" She squinted.

I stood back and watched them stammer their hellos, and I felt something, a spark, between them. It was as though I were watching the sea and the earth look at each other. So different yet so close.

We had to wait for a while to collect our luggage, so while my parents chatted, I continued to type.

"Hey, Jay?"

"Yeah?" I turned to Dad.

"What are you writing, son?"

"A story."

"About what?"

"A dove, a fox, and a hound."

The weathered old man was the caretaker of the park, the most beautiful park in the great state of Louisiana. The park was nestled between the blue plane of ocean and the green wall of jungle and was protected by a ring of rusted ships. The ships were named for the virtues of a king: *Justice*, *Bounty*, *Mercy*, *Devotion*, and *Courage*. They were practically swallowed by creeping vines and a canopy of mighty trees. Flowers bloomed from their portholes. A riot of calla lilies and bougainvilleas covered the area. A section in the center was dedicated to roses, and that was why the locals called the place the Duncan Rose Garden.

Many stories surrounded the mystery of the rose garden, where the most stunning, award-winning roses of the South were grown. They were famous for their color and fragrance. The rosebushes were known for their bounty. Aside from shrimp, the roses were the town of Duncan's main crop and export.

The old man stood up and reached into his pocket. He pulled out an oddity for the time: paper—and rarer yet, paper with handwritten words on it. Silently, he read the letter once more:

Dear Jaden Miller:

I did indeed receive the email you sent me with the story titled "The Fox Trot." I have just finished reading the entire narrative. It is a compelling story that deserves publication. But I understand why it can never be published. I am glad to say that I had you in my class, Jaden, and that this story is one of the best I have ever had the pleasure of reading. Forget all this year's troubles, Jaden. I'm sorry that I never had the chance to meet you while you were here. But I'm grateful now to be able to say that I know you.

Sincerely,
Miss Sarah Carlson

The man folded the letter and stuffed it into his pocket. He knelt down and gingerly began to dig until he had made a hole large enough for the plant with the purple flowers. His mind wandered back to the small girl to whom, long ago, he had given one of the flowers. He wondered about her life. He packed the plant into the hole and meticulously sealed the earth around it. Then he poured some water on it from a tin pail. The purple flowers seemed happy already.

He took a step back and smiled. Then he heard a voice behind him.

"Isn't it something?"

He turned around and there was a middle-aged woman holding a bunch of lilies. He noticed the star-shaped tattoo on the back of her neck.

"It's so strange! A garden in a swamp? My little boy is in third grade and just finished writing a story about it. An assignment for class. They had to create a story about how they thought the rose garden got here." She smiled.

Jaden wondered why children still had to attend school. At ten, they were implanted with a microchip and became like everyone else.

"Sir, your hands—they're bleeding!"

He looked down at them. Sure enough, blood oozed from scratches on his palms.

Looking up at her, he smiled and asked, "Did you know that roses, beautiful roses, have thorns?"

The woman just stared at him, then said, "Of course, sir, everyone knows that."

The End

◊◊◊◊

The Fox Trot

ABOUT THE AUTHOR

The Fox Trot is Raea Gragg's first book. She wrote it during the summer between her freshman and sophomore years. She lives with her family in Northern California where she runs track and is a cartoonist for her high school newspaper.